CALL ME ADAM

JO MCCARTY

Call Me Adam

Editing by The Pro Book Editor
Interior and Cover Design by IAPS.rocks

eBook ISBN: 978-1-941175-00-2
Paperback ISBN: 978-1-941175-01-9
Hardcover ISBN: 978-1-941175-02-6

      1. Main category—FICTION / Dystopian
      2. Other categories—FICTION / Fantasy / Dark Fantasy

First Edition

For Noel

CONTENT ADVISORY

This book contains adult themes and explores the darker nature of the human condition. Readers will be exposed to content they may find upsetting, controversial, or offensive, including fictional portrayal of self-harm, suicide, and suicidal thinking.

If you are considering suicide, call or text the National Suicide Prevention Lifeline at 9-8-8, or text HOME to 741741 to reach a trained Crisis Counselor through the Crisis Text Line, a global not-for-profit organization. It is free, 24/7, and confidential.

If you've lost a friend or family member to suicide, SAVE (Suicide Awareness Voices of Education) offers free grief support. Visit save.org.

PROLOGUE

WHEN SUE HANDED THE CASH from her drawer over to the thief, all she could think was, *What a dumb way to die.* She had barely graduated from high school fifteen years ago, but she knew a lot of things right then. The thief was Louie, whom she'd known since the first grade and would recognize anywhere even if he'd bothered with a disguise. The gun in his hand was fake, and he was certainly there to get himself killed. Oh, and her next prevailing thought was, *What a* dumb *way for him to do it.*

It wasn't her own death she was thinking about, though that would've been normal during a bank robbery, just like it would have been normal to be worrying about picking up her three-year-old son from daycare in twenty minutes or whether the gun wavering in the thief's hand would go off. It was hard to think of anything *but* death, because she knew that's exactly what the thief wanted. It just wasn't her life at stake.

She watched his panicked eyes dart from the sweaty cash in his hand to hers calmly placed on the counter.

"Well?" he said. "Are you going to do it?"

"Do what?" Sue asked, a bit miffed if she was honest with herself, because there was no way she'd get to daycare on time now and that mattered to her more than Louie. She blinked her wide eyes at him, a move that would have turned him bright red back in high school.

Louie did blush now, but Sue suspected it was about more than her looks this time. True, she was still just as cute as she had been back then, and he surely couldn't see her ill-fitting skirt or swollen ankles behind the counter. It was also the second week of a heat wave, and it was hot as hell in the bank, even this late in the afternoon when it was empty of customers, because the manager was too cheap to run the air all day. No, Sue thought Louie's excited color was mostly from humiliation. He was trying hard, and failing, to look like a bad guy. He held the gun like she had held her first cigarette in the girls' bathroom in middle school, as if it would burn her if she got too comfortable.

He poked the gun at the space under the glass. "The button," he hissed at her. "You have to hit the button."

"I know my training, dummy."

"Well, did you do it?"

"Of course I did!"

"OK, well, I didn't see it," Louie said.

"I did it quick like, just how they taught us," Sue replied.

They stood staring at each other for a moment longer, and then she sighed. "This is a terrible way, Louie. So dumb."

As she spoke, the sheriff and his deputy eased through the front door of the bank, their shiny shoes quiet on the orange carpet. They slid past the counter lined with pens on chains, their hands resting on their holsters.

Louie saw their reflections in the glass and stiffened. "You don't have to watch when they gun me down," he said.

He probably thought this a rather brave statement, but Sue rolled her eyes. "I don't mind," she said.

"I'm so sorry you have to see this."

She shrugged.

Louie squared his shoulders, and before he swung around to meet the sheriff, he said, "So long, Sue."

"Yeah, whatever." Sue eased away from the counter and grabbed her purse. It was past time to get her son. "See you tomorrow, Louie."

CHAPTER ONE

One week later

L OUIE STARED AT THE TV screen for too long before he reached for the remote. A commercial came on before his fingers found it—a harsh, colorful blast interrupting the dim light of the old sitcom he was barely watching. The man in the commercial shouted at Louie to buy an all-purpose cleaner that would literally change his life. The product was brightly labeled and prominent in the man's hand. The man's bold blue shirt clashed with the stark white background. But what struck Louie most was the idea the commercial gave him.

Louie reached for a small flip pad of paper and a pencil on the coffee table and flicked through the pad. He found a clean page and scratched "Poison" at the top. He tossed the pad on the table and fell back with a satisfied sigh, the act of writing this one word itself a relief.

The commercial cut to another one. No longer interested in TV, Louie's eyes drifted back to the pad. The used pages were fanning themselves back to their original position. He could see words and phrases floating, page over page. Once written with such hope, now crossed out in thick strokes. Words like shoot, suffocate, cut, choke, and overdose mocked him silently.

He glanced to the living room coat closet, its accordion-style door ajar. Just inside, he could see the curled edge of a red cape. On the floor, a mask lay where it had dropped after the tie had come unwound from the hanger above. His costume—abandoned but not forgotten. His one big idea. His chance to apply his odd *gift* of survival to something good. Whether he saved someone or died in the process, it would be a success.

Superhero was written on his death list too, but Louie had made a pathetic caped crusader. Bullets and knives couldn't kill him, but he possessed no extraordinary strength, no sixth sense for danger, no catlike reflexes, no charisma. He was in his early thirties and fit, yet his physique didn't scream hero. (Though with a little hair gel and styling, he thought he looked handsome in his tights.)

The greatest barrier to being a superhero was that Louie lived in a rural Michigan town. The last census poll had counted a population of 1,786, and if one of the survey questions had asked about his reputation, every single one of those people would have answered that Louie was a loser. He was a loser back in school and now an out-of-work mechanic for whom life hadn't gotten better. That survey question would have come as a surprise because few people had ever bothered to think about Louie at all before this summer. The handful who knew him a little might have expanded on their answers. They would have called him odd, a guy who said strange things at the wrong time, used big words others didn't understand when irritated, and still slept in his childhood bedroom. Not quite bad enough to be the town outcast, weirdo, or screwup, Louie was the town *nothing*. Thus, the few people he'd found to rescue actually fought his help. They were unimpressed, appalled even, by his heroics.

Louie had abandoned the superhero idea just as he'd abandoned many other methods of killing himself. After the bank incident, he'd nixed the option of being a villain too. Though villains in movies usually had money, infamy, and women, he simply couldn't see himself as the evil type. When he'd tried to get killed committing a crime, Louie had hated how it felt. All he'd ever wanted was to be a hero, and playing the bad guy felt just like wearing that awful suit from the resale shop to his mother's funeral. He wasn't a hero, but the other didn't fit either. Which meant that, even being indestructible, he was still nothing. The cops at the bank had thought so too. Instead of gunning him down, they'd only shaken their heads, taken his weapon, and shooed him home. They'd heard the rumors, of course. No threat here. It's only Louie. The guy who doesn't die.

After dozens of efforts, he was certain now that he *couldn't* die, but still, Louie had mortal fears. What little confidence that came with that knowledge failed to comfort when he was faced with a steep ravine or raging fire. These particular dangers were so frightening that, despite his compulsion to end his life, Louie couldn't bear to write "jump" or "burn" on his list. Germs, things he couldn't see, were also a worry that had increased since the Covid pandemic several years earlier. But the thing that scared Louie most was that he would live forever, never understanding why he couldn't die. Why he had been chosen. Immortality was a gift he didn't want.

Louie rose from the couch and clicked off the TV. He hitched his pants and grabbed his car keys, shaking off some of his self-pity now that he had a new plan.

Outside, huge maple trees lined the street, lifeless in the intense heat. He could see the summer sun shimmering like oil over the cement. Louie opened his car door, and feeling the hot air escape, closed it. Too hot to drive today, he decided. The car was twenty years old and had been poorly maintained since he lost his job. It was bound to overheat.

As he crossed the dead grass of his front yard, he made a mental note to add heat to his list. Burning was out of the question, of course, but maybe he could take advantage of this epic heat wave and work too long outside. For that matter, why not freezing? Another good one for the list. He could shovel everyone's snow in the winter until he froze to death or had a heart attack.

The three good ideas he'd had today added a little pep to Louie's step.

The bell chimed overhead when Louie entered the corner store. He paused to eye a rack of Hostess cupcakes near the door but moved on when he noticed Chet, the elderly clerk and owner, watching from the counter. Louie went to the aisle of cleaning products. The one from the television commercial wasn't there, but he wasn't picky. He grabbed two jugs of all-purpose drain cleaner and approached the register.

Setting them down in front of Chet, he avoided eye contact. Chet had one hand on the register. The other was out of view. He made Louie wait a long moment before saying, "I heard about what happened over at the bank last week."

Of course he did, Louie thought. *Everyone knows everything around here.* It was no wonder that Chet, who'd known

Louie his whole life, eyed him like a stranger. "I'm not here to rob you, Chet, if that's what you think."

Chet shrugged but withdrew his hand from under the counter. He lifted one of the jugs to check the price on it. "Well, how should I know?" he grumbled. "You've damn near lost your mind this summer."

It was embarrassing that the whole town seemed to know what he'd done, even if that wasn't so many people, and even if no one had gotten hurt or lost any of their money. Not only had he failed to get shot as intended, but the teller hadn't even taken him seriously. She'd taken one look at his gun and laughed. "Oh, please, Louie," Sue had said when he'd first walked up. "At least try to *look* like you could shoot me."

"It's a wonder you aren't locked up," Chet continued, though it was no wonder at all. He was just Louie, after all. Suicidal but harmless. The sheriffs had never even pulled their guns.

Chet's hand still rested on the jug. Louie willed him to continue ringing up the purchase, but the old man seemed to be warming to his topic.

Louie sighed. "It wasn't a real gun, you know."

"I know that. It was a water pistol you bought right here that you painted black, with paint you bought here too. You're lucky it was Sue at the window and that everyone knows you're…" Chet hesitated, "…special. If not for that, you'd be sitting in jail, mark my words." The man finally seemed to notice that he was supposed to be ringing up the purchase. "Got a problem with your plumbing?" he asked with a sarcastic smile.

"I haven't tried this yet," Louie said, looking down at the floor. No point in trying to hide the drain cleaner's purpose.

"Louie," Chet said sharply. "You don't *have* to try anything."

"Something will work eventually."

Chet shook his head. "Look, you're a nice guy," he said. "A good-looking kid. You just need to get out of here and meet a girl. A nice girl who'll appreciate having someone around who can't ever, you know, leave her. And a good job, like washing windows on skyscrapers in Chicago or something. Something everyone else would be scared to do. Maybe you should try to think more positive."

Louie shrugged. It was a pretty speech and nice that Chet cared to make it. He only wished he could make every-one understand. After dozens of deaths, Louie was his own personal unsolved mystery. He couldn't stay dead. If he was hurt, he didn't stay hurt. How could anyone let that go and start cleaning skyscrapers? He might not even have let it go if he were a happy man, which he was not.

Chet was right though. He had been acting crazy this summer. The heat, the everlasting heat wave that was baking his insides, seemed to have escalated his desperation in direct proportion to the rising temperatures. Either it was the weather itself actually driving him nuts, or he was running out of good ideas and all that remained were the bad ones.

Chet had made similar overtures toward Louie before, and as usual, Louie didn't know how to respond. Chet ex-pelled a long-suffering sigh and rang up the bottles of drain cleaner. "You want any of those?" Chet jerked a thumb toward the rack of Hostess cupcakes.

Louie had been loading up on sweets for months. In the beginning he'd thought maybe high cholesterol could accomplish what other methods had not. Later, he just liked the idea of eating all the calories he wanted. He'd gained weight, as evidenced by the small, round belly just starting to bulge over his belt, but his blood tests remained normal.

"Not today," Louie said and patted his stomach. "Not if I want to meet that nice girl." It was a small gesture, a way to say thank you to Chet for his kind words. He laid a ten-dollar bill on the counter. "Keep the change."

Chet started to smile, but his mouth dropped as he glanced at the jugs of drain cleaner he was handing to Louie.

"Thanks, Chet. Be seeing you." Louie hoisted them under his arms.

"I bet I will," Chet said. "That there won't do nothing but give you the runs for a solid week. It'll fix your plumbing all right, mark my words."

"Sure thing," Louie said, and shouldered his way out the door as Chet turned the volume of the radio back up a little. *Mark my words.* Chet's favorite phrase. Louie almost regretted that this might be the last time he heard it. Almost.

"Hey, Louie," Chet called, just before the door swung shut. Louie stopped it with a hip and poked his head back through the doorway.

"I've got one for your list, by the way."

Louie brightened. "Yeah?"

"This damn flu."

"What damn flu?"

"The one they're talking about on the news here." Chet turned up the radio broadcast but raised his voice over it. "You ever hear of a flu that starts in summer? NPR says this one is killing people faster than Rona. Maybe worse, 'cause they think it's on surfaces longer, like on packing boxes. I'm going to have to start wiping down the shelves again, I guess. Anyhow, they say a lady died over at County. Went in just a day ago, and she was young like you. Didn't have anything wrong with her but the flu. So maybe you'll get lucky and be thanking the Chinese! I'm sure they made this one too."

"Good tip, Chet, thanks." Louie let the door close behind him. Conversations with Chet eventually turned to something racist, sexist, or manly if you hung around long enough, and none of those things interested him. He considered the flu as he walked home in the heat with the drain cleaner in his fists. That wouldn't be one for his list, despite Chet's helpful suggestion. The mere idea of trying to get sick actually made him shudder. The flu was germs, and Louie had issues with germs. Besides, he'd been very close to the first and worst strain of Covid-19 without getting it.

That evening, after tidying up his kitchen and living room, Louie chased two boiled hot dogs and a TV dinner with half a jug of drain cleaner. It was sickeningly thick and tasted like hot, metallic plastic, but it didn't feel life-threatening at first. He took his drink into the living room and pretended it was chocolate milk, sipping it throughout the late-night talk shows, feeling a small thrill when fire began to spread down his throat and blossom in his stomach. By the time he went to bed, he felt the cleaner eating through his insides as if they were a clump of hair in a drain. Both jugs stood empty on the kitchen counter, and as Louie closed his eyes, he felt hopeful that tonight was the night.

CHAPTER TWO

Three weeks later – New York

KATHERINE TURNED THE STREET CORNER and watched Sharon approach from the opposite direction. Like her, the other woman wore a mask, but Katherine recognized her easily, even with her face disguised and her body hidden by a sweatshirt and track pants. Though Sharon's usual bohemian style was absent and she looked like she was on her way to the gym rather than the office, Katherine couldn't mistake Sharon's neat afro or bouncing gait.

Katherine stopped about six feet away and gave her friend an awkward wave, tugging on the blue surgical mask that made her lip sweat.

"Hey," Sharon said from behind a piece of cloth dotted with butterflies. Barely forty, her hobbies and personal style made her seem older to Katherine.

"Nice mask," Katherine said, knowing Sharon had probably sewn it herself to match her bright shoelaces. "I don't remember that one." Having recently turned thirty, she had never seen a sewing machine in real life.

"It's new. Reusing Covid masks is so 2021," Sharon said, flipping her wrist like a sophisticate.

Katherine smiled beneath her mask. Her friend was good for a joke whenever one was needed. It made the work-day go faster, even now when there was no work to be done. "How did your Zoom go this morning?"

The two moved into step together and continued down the street. "Well, it actually happened, so that was a shocker. But otherwise, it was a disaster."

They passed a darkened restaurant that used to be Katherine's favorite lunchtime spot. A sign on the door read *closed for flu.* "No salads and Pinot today," she said. "Disaster how?"

"This definitely would have been a drinks-for-lunch kind of day," Sharon said. "Basically, Mark didn't back me up at all. I think it's nuts that they expect everything to be business as usual, even meeting quarterly goals at a time like this. And besides that, I know I looked totally unprepared. Which, let's be honest, I was. Renee is usually the face on this stuff. And it's not like I had any help when my entire team is sick."

As they walked toward their office building, they continued to point out businesses they were surprised to see closed. At one point, Katherine said, "No lines at the deli. No crowds, nobody slamming into me. It's kind of peaceful. If I'd known New York would ever be like this again, I never would have, you know…" She tossed imaginary pills into her mouth.

"Katherine!"

"Well, it's not like it's a secret," Katherine replied.

Sharon shook her head. "You say it like it's no big deal."

"I guess the end of the world is making me kind of punchy."

Sharon stopped walking. "You're being flippant about it."

Katherine halted next to her. "It's a weird time."

"Since you brought it up…"

"God, I know you've been dying to ask me. Go ahead."

"There's a terrible choice of words," Sharon said. Katherine could see her frown above her mask.

"Why did I do it? That's what you want to know?"

"Yeah."

Katherine started walking again. "Nothing makes a difference. Come to work. Go home. Work again the next day. And the next. I started to question the point of doing it all."

"We all question why we bother, at one time or another. But questioning it and doing something about it are different things," Sharon said.

"I wanted to do something about the way I was feeling. I needed something drastic."

"Suicide is about as drastic as you can get. Look, I've been wanting to say this for a while. For what it's worth, I'm glad that you're still here. You know I can't survive this hellhole without you, right?"

Katherine resisted the urge to link arms with her like the old days, when masks and social distancing weren't part of every interaction. "You either. You better not get sick on me."

"We got through Covid times, we'll get through this. We're in this together, sister."

They reached the main door of the office building, and Katherine checked her watch. "We still have a few minutes."

Sharon shrugged. "Let's try anyway. I don't like being here on the street." She looked up and down the corridor, which was nearly empty but for a man shuffling a block down with a grocery bag crushed under one arm. "Forget salads and Pinot. This would have been a beer and mac-and-cheese day. I need comfort food."

Katherine pressed the intercom button and waited. The building receptionist, working remotely like everyone else these days, replied after a moment, asking them to show their work badges to the security camera. "What time is your appointment?" she asked, her voice tinny through the speaker.

Sharon replied, and they were promptly buzzed in. For two days, building management had been scheduling tenants and their employees to retrieve personal items or essential work equipment, limiting the number of people in the building at any one time. Sharon was right. It didn't matter that they were a bit early. There was no one here.

"You know, I get that we're essential. People still need the news. But Mark has to get that productivity isn't going to be the same. Did we learn nothing from Covid?" Sharon said, and Katherine realized her friend was back to worrying about her boss again. "And it's kind of bullshit that all the 'we can do this' spirit went out the window after a week. It's like 2020, only worse. I don't even feel like we're on the same team anymore."

"Maybe Mark needs to get the flu," Katherine said as they walked through the lobby. "He obviously doesn't get that things have changed."

Sharon punched the button for the elevator and then reached for the small bottle of hand sanitizer in her purse pocket. The door opened instantly. They exchanged glances. "When's the last time that happened?"

"In this building? Never." Katherine entered the elevator after Sharon. "I know they're only letting maybe a few hundred people in at a time, but still."

"No shit," Sharon agreed. She pressed the button for the thirty-fifth floor. "If we get all the way to our floor without getting stopped, you owe me lunch."

"If I can find a place still open for carryout, you buy lunch," Katherine rejoined.

The elevator didn't stop. They walked through the deserted foyer, Katherine's heels echoing on the hardwood floor, Sharon slapping sanitizer on her hands and pinching her slipping mask into place. Katherine pushed open the door to the press floor.

"Wow," she said, taking in the workspace. Papers in messy stacks on desks, coffee cups that read "World's Greatest…," the occasional ergonomic keyboard or lumbar back support pillow—all signs of a busy office where employees had put in long hours. But the workstations seemed abandoned. Across the open desk space and beyond the more private cubicles, Katherine could see that the executive offices were all dark.

She flipped one of a dozen switches on the wall, and a bank of light appeared at the far end of the office. She toggled a few others, searching for ones that would light the way through the dim space.

"Why am I here?" Sharon asked. She rubbed her arms even though it was warm and stuffy.

Katherine laughed. "'Cause you have a work ethic?"

"This is creepy."

"When we're the last two people in the city and newspapers are blowing in the street like tumbleweeds, then it'll really be creepy. For now, it's just kind of sad." The office had the feel of when employees were coming in on a holiday, or staying late to get a few things done, except there wasn't even the head of a custodian bobbing through the halls.

"Let's just get our things and get the hell out of here," Sharon replied.

Katherine smoothed her dark ponytail and flicked her hands over her skirt, a habit any of her coworkers would have described as her "let's get down to business" ritual. She headed to her cubicle with Sharon following and, finding everything as she'd left it last Friday when she'd only thought she was going home for the weekend, hit a key on her keyboard to dispel her screen saver.

Sharon watched for a moment, then moved to her own desk. Seconds later, she called through the partition. "Are you taking everything?"

"I guess," Katherine answered. "We might be out a while this time. I already have my laptop at home."

"Same."

Katherine's computer had been sleeping, but now she shut it down. She dialed into her voicemail to change her settings to forward calls to her extension to her cell phone. She stood, grabbed her favorite water bottle and Sharper Image world clock, a gift from an ex-boyfriend (and certainly the best thing to come out of that relationship), and went to Sharon's cubicle. Sharon was piling picture frames and other miscellaneous clutter into a box. Her screen saver, unlike Katherine's default image of lines twisting around themselves, was personalized, showing a slideshow of her cats. Shutting down her computer apparently didn't take priority over gathering bobblehead dolls.

Sharon stopped. "Is that all you have?" she demanded.

Katherine shrugged. "Well, yeah."

"Typical. Unlike *some* people, I prefer to surround myself with crap." Sharon took a framed picture of her ex-girlfriend from the top drawer, considered it for a second, then stuffed it back inside. "That way, when I get fired, someone has to stand there while I take my time packing up my stuff, before I have to take the walk of shame."

"Kind of like now," Katherine said, feeling impatient.

"Without the shame part. Don't worry, I've done this drill a hundred times in my head. I've always been ready to leave at a moment's notice." She inventoried her desk, almost giddily. "This kind of feels like Christmas, doesn't it?"

"Christmas?"

"I don't know. Exciting. But kind of scary exciting. Maybe more like Halloween. Or a tornado warning."

Katherine watched Sharon pilfer her stapler, weighted tape dispenser, and stacks of sticky notes from her desk and drop them into her box of personal items. Sharon glanced up at her and, as if reading her mind, said, "I don't have a home office."

Through the partition, Katherine heard her desk phone bleep. The odd ring signaled that it was an outside call not directed to her personal extension, which would have been redirected to her cell anyway.

"You going to bother with that?" Sharon asked after the phone had bleeped several times. She was rummaging through her file cabinet.

"My calls are forwarding. That's the main line," Katherine replied. "Not mine."

Sharon stopped tabbing through folders to arch an eyebrow at her. "Miss Management letting a call go to the general mailbox? This is it. Armageddon! It's one of the signs!"

Sharon was still teasing as Katherine slinked back to her side of the partition. She set her things down, but her hand hesitated over the receiver.

"Fire and brimstone. Floods and locusts!"

The office was officially closed now, should she even bother?

"And Katherine Coburn letting a phone ring."

Ignoring Sharon, and the impulse to hit the Do Not Disturb button, Katherine pulled her mask down around her chin and answered with the beleaguered tone she typically reserved for discouraging long conversations with her boss.

"I'm not sure who I should be trying to talk to," said the man on the line, "but I thought maybe you might be interested in a story on me?"

"I'm sorry, sir, but we're actually closed at the moment," Katherine replied. *That was dumb*, she thought to herself. *If we were closed, I wouldn't have answered.* She tried again, "I mean, we're technically open, but everyone is out sick. There's no one here for you to talk to at the moment."

"Oh." The man sounded so disappointed that Katherine had to bite her lip to keep herself from offering suggestions that would only result in more work for her.

The prolonged silence compelled her to fill it. "I'm actually in finance," she said. "I don't take the news tips." When there was no response, she added, "But I suppose I could take down your information, and pass it along…"

"I didn't think newspapers closed," the man said.

"Well, like I said, we're not really. But our physical offices are closing because of the flu. Actually, yesterday's print was the last one for now, until this is over. We'll continue online publication, though, remotely."

"That's what I'm calling about. The flu."

Katherine tucked the receiver between her chin and shoulder and reluctantly sank onto her chair, reaching for a pad of sticky notes. "I can take down your information, and someone will get back to you." She thumbed through the stack of notes, waiting impatiently.

Now that the offices were officially closed, the magnitude of the situation had amplified. The man was right. Newspapers don't close their doors, not even ones with online publications like theirs. They hadn't even physically closed during Covid. Most people had worked from home during New York's mandated shutdown, but even then, there were people who worked in the office, Katherine included. It had never been emptied like this.

With effort, she turned her focus back to the conversation. "I'm sorry, what was that?"

"My name is Louie," the man repeated. "And I live in Michigan. Northern Michigan."

"OK," Katherine said slowly, writing his name in her neat cursive. "Louie from Michigan."

"Northern Michigan."

"Right."

"And I thought someone might want to do a story on me," Louie continued.

"You said this has something to do with the flu?"

"Yeah, it's about my town. I don't know about the metro area, but up here, everybody is gone."

Katherine stopped writing. "I'm sorry, I don't understand. Gone?"

"Well, we were pretty small anyway, less than 2,000 people, I guess. But as of yesterday, yeah, everyone's dead. I'm the only person left alive in my town. Which is kind of crazy, because we hadn't even heard of the flu three weeks ago." The man's matter-of-fact tone didn't dampen the impact of his words. Katherine dropped her pen and pressed her fingers to her mouth. She could tell this man was telling the truth.

Sharon appeared with her box of personal items. "Ready?" Her eyes flicked around the space nervously, as if the concept of walking through the suite to the elevators without Katherine was as unsettling as the idea of remaining there with her for a moment longer. The gravity of the situation had apparently hit her too. When they'd gotten their assigned time to pick up their things, neither of them had thought they'd be the only ones doing so.

Katherine shook her head. For Sharon's benefit, she said into the phone, "I'm sorry, did you say that you're the only one left alive in your town?"

She reached to hit the speaker button. Louie's faraway voice filled the air. "Everyone up and died. And it happened just like that. A few weeks ago, only a few people were sick. The flu was still mostly a rumor. We were just talking about how it was getting bad downstate. And now everyone is gone. I thought that maybe I better try calling someone while I could. I have Internet and my phone line for now, but no cell connection, and I imagine my power's going to go soon. I've got a generator, but still, that's going to suck."

Now that Louie had started to speak, it was as if he couldn't stop. Katherine and Sharon sat in stunned silence.

"So I tried calling the *Free Press* first. That's the *Detroit Free Press*," he said, enunciating the name as though Katherine were actually taking notes. "A couple of papers, local ones. But I guess the newspapers down there are closed too. Either that or…" He let the thought hang unfinished. "Anyway, I saw your article posted just this morning, about all the people in California and them running out of beds and all the overflow in the parking lot. I figured everyone already being dead here is a bigger story than one about people just getting around to dying out there."

Sharon had set her box on a file cabinet to listen. Now she reached for it. Her voice trembled. "I'm so sorry, Katherine," she whispered, "but I've got to get going. I've got to call my mom. And our time is almost up before the next appointments are supposed to come."

"Wait," Katherine said, rising. "Mister…uh, Louie? Just wait a second, OK?"

"Sure," she heard Louie respond. She reached for Sharon. "Are you going to be all right? You don't want to wait just a minute?"

"No, I'm going. Katherine, promise me you won't stay here. You have to get home too."

"Of course. Right behind you, I promise."

"This is so wrong," Sharon said as she pulled away. "We're the freaking news. How didn't we know that whole towns are gone? Why didn't anyone tell us? How could we not be ready for this?" And then Sharon was gone, half running down the empty aisle in her track suit and athletic shoes, box bouncing under one arm.

Katherine watched until Sharon turned into the shadows. She was hit by the awful thought that she'd never see her again, so fierce it was like a premonition, like Sharon was already dead and gone. She was suddenly shaking all over.

"Are you still there?" she heard Louie say.

She came back to the phone. "I'm still here," she managed. But all she could think about was what Sharon had said. *Why didn't anyone tell us?*

Why *hadn't* anyone told them? Why were they just now shutting down in New York when apparently whole towns had been wiped out in the Midwest? It was like the opposite of what had happened with the coronavirus, when metro areas were hit hard first, and the rural states followed later.

"Well, anyway…" Louie fumbled. "I guess if you're not the person who does news stories."

Katherine snapped to. "Yeah, I'm sorry. But give me your number. And maybe you should give me your address and any other contact information. I'm sure someone will want to call you back."

He recited his information and she wrote it down.

"Thanks for your help," Louie said.

"Before I let you go," Katherine said, "do you need me to contact anyone for you? I mean, authorities or something? What if your power goes? Or your phone? Have you contacted anyone else, like the Red Cross?"

She was edgy now, tapping her pen on the notepad, bobbing her feet in her designer shoes, nibbling at the side of a thumb. This was an emergency, wasn't it? Not just a story?

She was this guy's lifeline, his only contact with anyone right now, maybe ever again.

"I'll be fine," Louie said. He sounded so calm that Katherine stopped moving. "I think the Red Cross or whoever has their hands full in other places. No one's coming here, but that's alright with me."

"You must have lost people," she blurted. "Family?"

Louie was silent and Katherine thought he'd hung up. "Hello?"

"I'm here," he said after a moment.

"I'm sorry," Katherine said. She clutched the phone with a clammy hand. Oddly, she was now feeling like maybe he was *her* lifeline. When he hung up, she would be all alone in the office, possibly in the entire building. Without any windows nearby, she couldn't see down to the street. Maybe she was the only one on the block, or in New York.

She realized she was panicking. This was quite unlike her. Even when she'd taken those pills, it was with total composure. She'd gone about her day like it was any other and ended it by sorting through orange bottles of expired medications in her bathroom and popping the pills one by one into her mouth. Once she'd resolved herself to her task, the shaking inside had diffused into something that felt like happy. Kind of like how Louie sounded now.

She heard scuffling as he shifted his phone, and then a wholly unexpected sound. A bag crackled open, followed by the wispy fizz of a soda can popping open. She heard what sounded like a potato chip crunch. Here she'd thought he was upset, probably mourning the loss of someone close, too emotional to reply to her question, and he was helping himself to a snack.

"Hello?" she repeated. She knew she must sound irritated but realized she felt something else too. Amusement?

"Sorry," Louie said around what seemed to be a mouthful of chips. "I haven't eaten anything all day. Well, except for coffee. I wanted a bowl of cereal, or maybe some scrambled eggs with biscuits and gravy, but can you believe there's already no milk? In this entire town, not a single carton of milk that's still good, unless you count almond milk, which I don't."

Katherine choked on a short laugh. Louie laughed a little too.

"Sorry, I'm sort of freaking out a little bit over here," Katherine admitted. "You just told me that an entire town has been wiped out by the flu, and now you're talking about food. It's all a little hard to digest. No pun intended."

Louie stopped crunching. "Are you sick at all?"

"I never get sick."

"Well, that's good I guess."

"Listen, I'm sorry, but I should go. I was only supposed to come in to get my things from the office here and then go back home to work."

"What was your name again?"

"Katherine."

"Katherine, it was real nice of you to take my call."

"Thanks, Louie. If you feel unsafe, be sure to call someone. Someone else, like the authorities, I mean."

"Sure," he said. "I guess it was dumb to call a newspaper. I just thought it was interesting, kind of special."

"Or go somewhere," Katherine continued. "To a bigger town maybe?"

"Right, I'll do that. Thanks again, Katherine."

Katherine hesitated and then hit the button on the phone to end the call. As anticipated, without Louie on the line, the silence had a pulse. She dialed her boss's extension. Cradling the receiver to her ear and letting the phone ring, Katherine stood to peer over the cubicle wall. The heavy shadows in the offices made her nervous. They suddenly reminded her of the city's conservatory garden at night. She'd attended an evening fundraiser in Central Park once, and as beautiful as the warm lights were among the greenery, and though she was surrounded by guests and music, everything fell away as she watched the shadows watch her. The bushes had become people shifting uneasily in the breeze. The inky well at the foot of the fountain became a dark orchestra. Katherine peered closer at the corner office across the aisle. With its potted trees and lonely ferns, it could be the garden at night. She'd left that party early.

The voicemail greeting in her ear brought her back to reality. "Seriously?" she said aloud. The sound of her own voice calmed her. She ended the call and tried another extension. No one picked up there either.

Feeling pursued by the silence and more anxious by the moment, Katherine hung up the phone, shoved her clock and water bottle in her purse, and flung it over her shoulder. "The hell with this," she muttered. "I'll call someone when I get home." She soothed herself with chatter as she walked down the aisle. "The CDC. Or Hazmat. FEMA. The freaking army! Whoever."

She was halfway to the elevators when she turned to jog back to her desk. She'd forgotten to take the notepad with Louie's information on it. Although she wasn't sure what she could do with it if no one would pick up a damn phone, she stuffed the pad into her purse.

Louie might be the only person who could relate to how she felt in this moment. As she trotted through the cubicles, she felt a bit like the last person on Earth. This thought persisted in the elevator on the way down.

When Katherine emerged from the building, she still expected to see the New York she knew, or even a New York in crisis. Sidewalks bustling, people with bags and boxes of groceries or emergency supplies. Hands waving for taxis, others grabbing for handles. A crowd to sweep her toward the subway. But there was no one on the street. Sharon was gone. She thought of Louie again and how he would know just how she felt.

CHAPTER THREE

Ten days later

WHEN KATHARINE LEFT HER OFFICE after talking to Louie, she'd embarked on the worst commute of her life. Working her way back from the city to New Jersey, she focused on stories she'd heard from Sharon and other older coworkers about 9/11, after terrorists had flown hijacked planes into the heart of New York, telling herself that if they could get home without losing their minds, so could she.

She'd heard Sharon's story so many times, it was as if it were her own. High-heeled shoes bought from her first paycheck at her very first job in hand, Sharon had followed all the others in Midtown trying to escape the smoky air. It took them hours to arrive at the GW, where each step across the bridge brought them one step closer to home and one step farther from the toxic plume filling the streets behind them.

Terror about future attacks and a communal bond would come later when they learned more details about what had happened. That day, Sharon was one of a determined herd, moving toward safety, to home and sanctuary, away from the unknown. Katherine longed for home too, but there her comparisons ended. When she'd emerged from her office building, she found the strange silence on the street filled her with an unspoken thought—she could be heading home to die. An unknown attacker had not struck the city. Rather, a vicious strain of a common illness was leaving its skeleton intact and ravaging its lifeblood instead, killing it along with its inhabitants more effectively than any blow could do, from the inside out.

The empty seats on the PATH train now felt sinister. A whole town in the Midwest had died. Had that many people already died here? Like Louie's town, only how many times over? How long would it take to really notice that thousands of people were gone? Katherine boarded the ferry in Hoboken, which was still running, though already much emptier than during her earlier trip. She stood staring at the Hudson among a few other shell-shocked passengers, who, like her, were probably wondering how the sun could be shining on it like nothing was wrong. The bus ride that followed normally took forty minutes, but this time the trip was twice as long, punctuated by screaming ambulances and interrupted by barriers in the streets that hadn't been there earlier.

On edge from the uncharacteristic, masked silence of the others on the bus, Katherine shortened her usual ten-minute walk to the co-op to half that time. Turning the corner onto her street, she saw National Guardsmen dropping out of a military truck. Her brisk pace became a full out run, high heels and all. She didn't stop until she'd jogged up three flights, slammed her apartment door, and turned over all three locks.

At first, she was filled with purpose. She made phone calls, connecting with a few coworkers and even someone in the Tips department. No one's heart was in it, though. They murmured excuses and assurances, promising to pass along the information about Louie and his town, all while Katherine slowly killed her cell phone battery. She was down to 20 percent life before she realized she'd left her cell phone charger behind in her cubicle drawer. Cursing her bad luck, she risked calling Sharon to confirm she'd arrived home safely. When her eyes fell on her world clock, she cursed that too, as if it were at fault for her leaving behind an item of greater importance. What did it matter anymore what time it was in Tokyo?

Katherine didn't think she'd be able to sleep that night, but she did, and she dreamed of a dark garden. The sound of a terrible heartbeat chased her as she ran over old, flat stones, her hands brushing tomato plants while tall cages of peppers loomed overhead, confusing her. It was unlike the conservatory garden she remembered when awake, but also more familiar. She stopped suddenly, realizing that the heavy heartbeat was her own, vaguely aware that she was asleep in her bed and that she was dreaming. Settled, she bent down to explore the greens. When she stood, it was daytime, and the stones were warm under her feet.

The next day, she awoke feeling calmed by the dream, until she learned that the entire city was going into full lockdown. Though it was already too late for that.

Katherine watched CNN constantly over the next few days, leaving the TV on even when she slept for fear she might miss something. The media started calling the flu "Juanita." The virus had hit the planet like one big hurricane, and so, in the spirit of naming hurricanes, this one earned a name that called to mind the Spanish flu of the early twentieth century. Katherine personally found the name racist, reminiscent of when people called Covid the "Kung flu," but there was little time for public outrage about the moniker. Juanita was studied briefly, determined to be a viral cocktail of bad, and then promptly killed the scientists who had studied her. In short, she was a novel virus presenting all the symptoms of influenza but spread in ways they'd never seen a single strain do. They called her a biotic crisis. They called her a mass extinction event.

Republicans argued she had been born in a lab, a weapon set loose by America's enemies. Democrats thought she might be another evolved variant of a SARS virus, hitting the world harder because it had been weakened by Covid-19. The fringes at both ends thought that every viral monster in recent history had teamed up to make a super virus that would clean up the planet. They all agreed that this was the big one, and the fringes were right about one thing—Juanita was spreading too fast. Soon, there were no Republicans or Democrats left on television to debate the subject.

This time, the government hadn't even begun to talk "vaccine" before it seemed like everyone was in some stage of respiratory disease. News anchors had barely reported about ventilators or diminishing hospital capacity on the nightly news before people were no longer *going* to the hospital. After a few days, no one was news anchoring either, for that matter. No one was talking about essential workers and the supply chain breaking down, because once Juanita truly made landfall, within days there *were* no essential workers and no supply chain. No one was shipping, no one was receiving.

Everything just stopped. No more military trucks. No more humanitarian efforts. Young, old, and healthy alike, swept up like an island in a hurricane. And there Katherine stood, looking out her apartment window, like the last palm tree in the wind. She waited for the sun to break through. She waited for someone to tell her what to do after the storm, and eventually, when there was nothing more to see, she turned off the TV.

The pregnant silence became plain silence. Katherine wasn't sure about New York, but nine days after she'd left her office building, New Jersey was devastated, wiped out, if her own neighborhood was any indication. She'd watched people dressed like astronauts seal doors with thick orange tape from her apartment window until there was nowhere to take bodies anymore.

Katherine paced through the living area of her tiny apartment, controlling the room with a fingertip. Touching a vase here, slightly shifting a polished picture frame there. In here, the world was pristine, structured to cradle her in normalcy as the world outside changed without her consent. Life was ending everywhere, would never be the same, could never be the same, but here she wore pressed slacks and a blouse, though she wasn't going to work or even outdoors.

Katherine's meticulous control over her surroundings hadn't extended to realistic preparation for what was happening. She'd gathered no water, food, flashlights, or batteries. She hadn't looted hand sanitizer, wipes, or toilet paper. Instead, she'd quarantined at home, not venturing out even for essentials.

Yesterday, she had heard her neighbor pace above her, hushing her baby while she heaved terrible, racking coughs that made Katherine wince. Later, the pacing stopped but the crying went on. Katherine wondered whether she should go up there to help, break down the door if she had to. Maybe the infant wasn't sick yet. Maybe the baby was immune. Maybe it just needed a diaper change to stop its crying.

Anxiety about seeing the dead mother—and she must be dead if the baby was screaming like that—of even opening the apartment door that hadn't been opened in a week or entering that awful hollow stairwell, paralyzed Katherine. Early that morning, the wailing had stopped, and Katherine hated herself for feeling relieved.

As she'd done the day before, she finished her inventory of the apartment and then settled with her address book at the desk by the window where it caught the midday light. This was her "new normal." Her new routine, trying to find out who was still OK while also silently cursing her stupidity for failing to keep her old-fashioned contact list more current. Her cell was dead now, and all her saved contacts had died with it. Luckily, she still had a landline, something her job had required for remote work. Though work was officially done now, and she had been forced into early retirement, she considered this daily task just as important as her old day job.

Brownouts rolled through her neighborhood frequently now, so Internet access had gotten sketchy. They would become blackouts soon. Then the battery backups for the grid would probably fail, which meant her landline would fail soon too. She worried about this even as she recognized that she hadn't reached anyone in two days.

Katherine started with the A's in her address book and began punching in the numbers. Each number dialed, each ring, followed by dozens of other rings, nourished her despair. No one was answering. She hit on a few voicemails in the A's and B's. Her first time through, she'd gotten disconnection notices in the C's section—not a surprise, as many of the C's were for the Coburns on her father's side of the family, and most of them had moved or died years earlier anyway. Her mother's side of the family, which would also have been in the C's if she'd ever written their information down, was nonexistent too. Katherine didn't have any living relatives that she knew of, no cousins or nieces or nephews. Fortune, or misfortune, had taken her family members well before Juanita arrived. She skipped the C's and tried the D's.

When she arrived at E, and at Sharon's name, she felt a fluttering in her chest. She knew this number by heart, and she called it more often than any other. Aside from when she'd telephoned Sharon to make sure she'd gotten home safely from the office, she hadn't spoken to her since the city shut down.

She dialed and waited, folding and pressing the edge of the page down, hoping but not praying that Sharon was still healthy and would answer this time. On the fifth ring, she heard a click. It was no longer ringing, but she didn't hear a dial tone either. Or a person.

"Hello?" Katherine said into the silence. It was the first time she'd used her voice in a while and it sounded raspy like she was sick. She cleared her throat and tried again. "Sharon?"

After a beat, she heard Sharon reply. "I'm here."

"Oh, God," Katherine gasped, so excited to hear another voice, especially Sharon's, that she could barely hold the phone. "I've been trying you since Tuesday! How are you?"

Sharon's voice was stoic. "My mom passed last night," she said, but then she burst into sobs.

Katherine waited for the tide to pass, unsurprised to feel tears on her own cheeks.

"I'm so sorry," she said when Sharon's cries became sniffles.

"I went over on Wednesday to take care of her. She was sick, but not that bad, so I brought her back here with me. It was better that way, with the cats, you know. I couldn't leave them. And for a day, I even thought she might be getting better. But last night, her fever just wouldn't break, and I could hear her breathing starting to sound different, you know, like rattling, like the death rattle, isn't that what they call it? And then she just went. God, I was reaching for her soda. I wasn't even looking at her."

"I'm so sorry." Katherine seemed unable to say anything else.

"Ally hasn't moved from the scratching post since yesterday afternoon, and Clarence started puking this morning. I can't get him to eat or drink anything," Sharon continued, referring to her two tabby cats, littermates, her only children. "And now the power is out. I don't know what to do."

"You can come here," Katherine said. "If neither of us is sick by now, we must be immune. If I haven't gotten it in this old apartment building with its shitty ventilation, I probably won't get it at all." The moment she suggested it, she knew it was pointless. Sharon wouldn't leave her mother's body there alone or leave her cats behind to trek to Katherine's place. She knew it was selfish to even ask.

"I wish I could…"

"I know," Katherine interrupted. "I understand. I know that you won't want to leave right now."

"It's not that." Sharon's breath hitched before she said, "I'm sick too."

Katherine pressed her forehead to her palm, swallowing slow, deep breaths. Sharon was the only person she had left.

"Yeah," Sharon said after a beat. "Sucks, doesn't it? It only took like two days before I started to feel it."

"You don't sound sick," Katherine moaned.

"I checked my temperature an hour ago. It's low-grade still, I think, but it's 100.2. And I feel all achy and tired. I could barely lift my head this morning."

"It could be stress. The stress of all this. It doesn't mean you have it," Katherine insisted. "It could just be regular sick."

"Maybe. But we shouldn't risk your getting sick, anyway. You don't really know you're immune. I'm sorry, this sucks," she said again.

Their conversation was interrupted by a spurt of loud, rapid-fire knocks on Katherine's apartment door.

"What is that?" Sharon asked on the other end of the line.

"Jesus, someone's knocking on my door," Katherine whispered.

"Don't freak out. It could be those body management guys, maybe?" Sharon ventured. "They were in our neighborhood a few days ago…"

"I don't want to answer it."

The knocks came again, louder.

"Can't you look out the peephole?"

Katherine stood and tiptoed over to the door, listening. In a low voice, she said to Sharon, "A good idea if I had a peephole. Wait." She pressed her ear to the door. She heard a woman's voice, hushing and whispering, followed by the fussy whimper of an infant. "Oh! I think maybe it's my neighbor from upstairs! Hold on, OK?"

"Call me back," Sharon said.

"No! Wait! What if I can't get through to you again?"

"Katherine, it'll be fine," Sharon said with authority. "Just answer the door and call me back. She probably needs some sugar or something."

"Funny," Katherine retorted.

The woman knocked again.

Katherine put her free hand on the doorknob. The other still clutched the phone, though Sharon couldn't help her.

Again, more knocks, followed by a desperate plea. "Please, I know you're there. I heard you! Please."

Katherine twisted the knob, her adrenalin pumping so hard that the pull against the engaged locks shook the door. "Oh," she gasped, her own action scaring her. Katherine flipped the locks and tried again. This time, it opened.

The woman's eyes were red from crying, but the color blooming around her nose and mouth was something else. She had a fever. Katherine knew it instantly.

Instinctively, she moved back.

"No, wait," the woman cried. She pushed into the doorway. Thoughts of immunity gone, Katherine shrank from the infection weeping from her mouth.

"Stay back, please," Katherine warned. "You're sick."

"I've been walking for hours trying to find someone," the woman explained.

"I thought that you were the lady from upstairs."

The woman shook her head. "There is no one else in this building. I know. I've been going from door to door. Please, you have to help me."

"I can't help you. I'm not a doctor. I'm sorry, you have to go."

"I understand you're not a doctor. Don't worry, I know I'm not going to get better. But my daughter…" She gestured to the baby bobbing in a sling around her neck. "She isn't sick. I need you to take her."

Katherine looked at the little girl's fat cheeks, rosy but not fevered. "No, I'm sorry, I can't."

The woman unwrapped herself from the sling and shoved her child at Katherine, pressing farther into the room. "You have to. Don't you get that she'll die, and she's not even sick?"

Katherine tried to fend her off. The wireless phone in her hand clattered to the floor. The sound startled the baby, who began to fuss. "No, no," Katherine was saying, but the woman was shrieking now.

"Just take her! Please, God! Her name is Ana. Take her, please."

Katherine was still pushing the bundle away when the woman started to press kisses to the baby's cheeks. "Momma loves you, Ana. I'll always love you."

She was saying goodbye, and this terrified Katherine. "No! Stop that. Stop saying that! I won't take her."

The baby was blaring now, her mouth wide, her face red like her mother's. The woman howled along with her, saying over and over, "Take her, don't drop her. Please, please. Her name is Ana." An anti-tug-of-war ensued. The woman was trying to shove the baby into Katherine's hands. Katherine was trying to refuse without letting her fall. Every time she tried to steady the baby in her mother's arms, the woman tried to let go.

"You have to. You have to. I love you, Ana," the mother cried. Then, with wide, surprised eyes, she began to vomit a burst of ugly brown fluid. It spurted like strands of watery pudding onto the baby's white jumper and the pink sling still wrapped around her. It splattered onto Katherine's hands, white blouse, and floor. It just kept coming, and the woman fell to her knees, heaving and nearly dropping her daughter on her descent.

Horrified, Katherine staggered backward and slipped on the vomit. As she fell to her bottom, her left leg crumpled beneath her. Her soiled hands found no purchase, skidding on the slick floor so that she fell to her elbows.

The woman continued to hack, and then she was coughing and gasping for air. The baby slid from her slackened arms into the rivulets of vomit. The woman, gagging on her breath and tears, rolled onto her side and began to convulse.

It seemed to take no time at all before she was still, and Katherine knew she was dead.

The baby wasn't crying anymore, struck into silence by the abrupt fall. She kicked at her sling. The phone that had fallen from Katherine's hand bleated angrily, left off the hook for too long. For the first time since this had all started, Katherine began to weep.

CHAPTER FOUR

K ATHERINE LUNGED FOR THE CORDLESS phone to stop the noise. Once it was off, she dropped it and reached for the infant on the floor, who was trying to cry but seemed too powerless to do so. Katherine picked the baby up and gingerly bounced her, but she seemed listless. Her gaze was glassy. Katherine mentally scrambled for what to do next but seemed incapable of getting past one overpowering thought—her clean, safe apartment was corrupted. Worst of all, she'd sensed the mess coming the moment she heard the knock at the door, but she hadn't been able to ignore the compulsion to open it. (There were three messes actually, because she also now had a baby she didn't know how to care for and a dead body in the hallway.) Somehow, this felt like her own fault.

She was trying to get a grip when she heard a ringing. She searched the room for the phone with her eyes, too shell-shocked to realize it was still in her hand. She stared down at the baby in her arms and then at it. For a scary moment, she couldn't connect the ringing with the device. It might just as likely been coming from the baby's parted lips. In a rather disconnected way, she finally answered and was vaguely surprised when the horrible sound stopped instantly.

"Hello?"

"Jesus, Katherine. Are you OK? I thought you'd call me back."

"Yes, I think so."

"You don't sound it! Is that a baby crying?"

Katherine looked at the baby cradled against her body. She still seemed dazed, though she was making short, raspy cries now. Katherine sighed and sank onto a kitchen chair. "Her name is Ana."

"Is someone there?"

"Not anymore. Just me and Ana."

"Katherine, I tried calling you all night. The phone's been busy. What the hell happened?"

Katherine stared down at the baby. It somehow made things better. "A woman came and died on my floor."

She heard Sharon's sharp inhale. "We're fine," Katherine continued. "The baby will be fine. I just need to... I don't know what. What do you mean, you were trying to call me all night? It couldn't have been more than a few minutes..."

"You need to hang up and call 911, Katherine. Now, Katherine."

"Stop saying my name, Sharon," Katherine said wearily. "I'm not freaking out. And no one's going to come, if anyone even answers. I don't think they will. The mother, she would have tried that before she...gave her baby to a stranger, don't you think?"

"Well, what are you going to do?"

"I don't know. I have to clean things up. And then, there's a baby bag. I guess I'll try to take care of it. Her. I don't know why she's starting up this crying again, dammit."

She tried to hush the infant and thought about how she didn't want this responsibility. It was hard enough worrying about herself right now. Then she thought about the baby's desperate mother and her painful, messy death. If she was going to get sick eventually, Katherine didn't want to go out like that. On a stranger's floor. Or worse, alone. Before she could censor herself, Katherine blurted out, "Everyone is gone here, Sharon. I don't know what's the best thing to do, but if I'm going to get sick, I know I don't want to be alone. You shouldn't be either. And I don't know the first thing about taking care of this baby if we don't get sick. You've got nieces. I know you can show me what to do if you're not too sick. Her mother said Ana is immune, and she must be, right? The little ones all went fast. Surely, she'd be sick by now."

Sharon was silent for a long moment. "I didn't get sick right away."

Katherine was ready to plead her case, but Sharon continued. "But I'll help you for as long as I can. Bring her here."

Katherine looked at the vomit, which had dried into crusty pools by her door. Her gaze shifted to the window. It was light out. Like morning. It was a good thing that she was going to Sharon's. She still really didn't feel right. "It's so strange," she murmured. "It's like it just happened a few minutes ago. Were you really trying to call me? Is it morning?"

"There you go again. Come on back. Get ahold of your-self, girl," Sharon said, her voice firm. "You were flipped out. In shock. You've probably been sitting there for hours, or plain passed out. But you're good now. I'm going to help you. The baby probably needs to be fed and changed. Then you'll cover the dead lady with a blanket and get your ass over here."

Katherine eyed the dried vomit on her hand, the one curled around the baby. It had formed a brown crust under her nails. She cringed. "I need a shower."

"Forget a fucking shower. Just get here. You can take a shower here."

"Should I bring anything with me? Stop somewhere?"

"Stop somewhere? For like, a bottle of wine and a DVD?"

Katherine almost smiled at Sharon's disgruntled tone. It sounded so normal, and it was helping. She could feel herself coming back. "I was thinking more like for a manual. *What to Expect When You're Expecting* or something. Not a DVD. No one has DVDs anymore."

"Great, now she's joking," Sharon said, but she seemed relieved. "Just bring yourself and the baby. If we need supplies once you get here, we'll go out together. Be safe."

"I will."

Katherine hung up the phone and set it on the table. Had Sharon really been trying to call all night? The baby fell silent again as Katherine sat motionless in the kitchen. Moments passed until, belatedly, she realized that she was still sitting. She stood and immediately had to put a hand flat on the table to steady herself. She'd never felt more tired in her life.

With Ana cradled against her filthy blouse, she moved as though in a fog. She'd never held a baby before. Perhaps that was unusual for a woman in her thirties, but she had no close family to throw baby showers and first birthday parties.

Her closest friends were like her—child-free. Apartment life and commuting to New York were hard enough with a dog, let alone a kid. At the office, when coworkers would pop in during maternity leave to show everyone their new bundles of joy, Katherine always managed to avoid the commotion with a meeting, or a phone call, or even a fictitious appointment. She wasn't a baby person.

But this wasn't so bad. Not nearly as bad as she thought it would be. That solid little weight reminded her of her arm and body. It rooted her to the room. In an unexpected way, it was reassuring.

Ana's cheeks were blotchy. There were little crusty spots on them and around her nose and between her eyes. Her lips were dry and cracked, and God, she smelled something awful. The baby had probably been wet all night. Katherine carried her over to the apartment doorway, which was closed, the diaper bag lying just inside, blessedly free of vomit. "Thank God," she muttered.

"Let's get you changed," she said. Ana was still trying to cry but seemed to be growing tired of the effort. "We're good now," she added, warming up to this baby-talking thing since it seemed to be helping her to keep calm too. "We're going to clean you up and get a little food in you, and then we'll go see Auntie Sharon. Won't that be nice?"

Katherine sat on the couch and laid Ana down on the white cushion. She dug around in the bag and catalogued its contents. It was crammed full of baby stuff and very heavy. She spared a moment's pity for the young mother who had lugged it all over town, trying to find help, all while carrying Ana, but avoided thinking about the body that must be lying outside her door. She tried to focus on the girl instead, who seemed to be gearing herself up to make more noise.

After locating baby wipes, Katherine wrestled for a few moments with the vomit-crusted sling and jumper. When she removed Ana's diaper, it was decorated with an impressive display of colors and smells unlike anything Katherine had ever encountered in her life. She wondered absently if mothers were immune to this, or if they had some kind of olfactory love filter.

She soon realized using baby wipes was like trying to sweep a kitchen floor with a hand whisk. Katherine went to get some paper towels and came back, doing her best to dab and not rub Ana's irritated bottom and back. Her skin was flaming red, and Katherine couldn't quell the guilt that washed over her at the sight of it. This poor creature had defecated all over herself, and because of Katherine's inability to deal with trauma, she had lain in it for hours. She must be starving too.

When Ana's bottom was mostly clean, Katherine followed the paper towels with the baby wipe. Ana suddenly pulled from some well of impossible strength and issued a few loud, lusty cries. Her tiny little mouth looked physically incapable of making such a sound. Realizing the moisture from the wipe probably stung, Katherine dug through the bag until she found a tube of ointment.

"See here, Ana baby?" Katherine said. "We've got some cream for that. It's going to make it all better." She dabbed it carefully onto the baby's diaper rash, and she quieted to fitful, abbreviated cries. Katherine fumbled with her dirty onesie for a few minutes, and soon Ana was naked but for a fresh diaper. Katherine would worry about clothes later. For now, she was back in the bag, searching for the bottle she'd seen earlier. The baby's lethargy, punctuated by cries unaccompanied by tears, worried her. Ana must be dehydrated. She found the bottle partially full, and contemplated it for a minute, swirling the liquid around inside as if that would reveal its secrets. Would this be enough?

Crossing the kitchen, she carefully skirted around the mess on the floor, to the microwave. She knew to heat up the bottle and check the temperature on her wrist—she wasn't completely ignorant about how babies should be handled—but she would have to find some formula at the store for future feedings. There wasn't a can or anything in the bag. She stared blankly at the dark microwave for a few moments before recalling that the power was out. Room temperature it would be, then.

Thirty minutes later, Ana had been fed. Or somewhat fed. She'd kept pushing the nipple out of her mouth, which frustrated Katherine to no end because she knew the baby *had* to be hungry. Ana was clearly only a few weeks old and most certainly used to eating every few hours. Fortunately, the baby lacked the strength to resist, and Katherine persisted until she'd drunk a few ounces.

Katherine knew she had done all she could for the moment. Dressed now in unbelievably tiny, clean clothes, Ana was ready to go. Katherine stuffed some of her own things in her old college backpack, washed her hands and arms, and changed her own clothes. Aware now that a blouse and dress pants were not accessorized well with "baby," she opted for a pair of navy shorts, her alma mater T-shirt, and tennis shoes.

Like during her exodus from her job, Katherine was certain she was probably leaving something of importance behind, but there was no time to waste. It might take hours to get to Sharon's house, and she refused to travel in the dark. She must leave now.

She swung on the backpack, slung the baby bag over one shoulder and across her chest, and took Ana up into her arms. She left the apartment without a glance and swiftly stepped over the body outside. She hated goodbyes.

At the bottom of the landing, Katherine was relieved to find an abandoned stroller. Obviously, Ana's mother had left it to take the stairs. The elevator was impotent without power. It was decades old, badly in need of an overhaul, and always broke down anyway. She would not miss it.

Katherine emerged from her apartment building expecting the landscape of an apocalyptic drama or zombie flick. Or maybe something slightly more biblical, like fire and brimstone. Perhaps a blanket of dead black birds baking on the pavement in the summer heat. Something straight out of one of those same films didn't seem so far-fetched these days, everything considered. Instead, she found a mild summer morning. The sun was warm, and the breeze hinted rain, though there were no clouds that she could see. Other than the absence of pedestrians and cars on the usually busy street, it felt like any other day. It did not match the unease that covered her like an invisible cloud, that overpowering feeling that this was the end of the world, and she was alone in it.

Katherine pushed Ana in her stroller as if they were merely out for an afternoon adventure, and only a block from home, she realized that things weren't as bad as she'd feared. Fire and brimstone aside, at the very least she had expected to spot a few dead bodies, cars left in the middle of the street, or even gangs of unruly survivors looting and pillaging with rifles slung over their shoulders. But as she continued down the street undisturbed, she admonished herself gently, reminding herself to stick to the facts. The illness killing so many wasn't killing them *instantly* while they were sitting in traffic or shopping at the corner store. It stood to reason that people had gone to die at home, or to the hospital, if they were able. Their cars were parked. Their doors were locked. If there were any unruly gangs foraging about, they were either stealthier than the average Hollywood zombie or more efficient looters than she gave them credit for. Nothing appeared broken into or scavenged. Either no one wanted to risk catching illness for a free TV, or death moved faster than bad intentions.

Katherine soon discovered she wasn't the only survivor in the neighborhood. As she walked down the empty block, she could tell it wasn't wholly deserted. She sensed a few people in their homes, detected the shifting of a curtain twice. When she turned the corner onto Main Street, she felt the pressure of someone's gaze tracking her movements just before she spotted the old man on his porch.

She made eye contact before she could help herself and instantly wished she hadn't. Now she couldn't ignore him. Should she say hello, give him a polite nod like it was any other day? Should she make believe she was a mother taking her daughter for an afternoon stroll and walk right on by? He saved her from indecision by speaking first.

"Hey, there." The man rocked easily in his chair, his spindly legs revealed by a pair of neat boxer shorts, the rest of him covered by a flannel shirt buttoned up to the top. His spiky white hair poked out from underneath a very old, very worn Brooklyn Dodgers cap. Katherine slowed, but before she could respond, he pulled a hanky from his pocket and hacked into it. She was on the sidewalk, nearing the end of his walkway, but even still, the man raised his hand. "I'm sick here," he warned.

Katherine, who had no intention of approaching the stranger anyway, was still happy for the warning. It gave her a reason to keep her distance and keep walking.

"Is that Ana in there?" the man asked.

She stopped short. "You know her?" Katherine replied hopefully.

"The mother came by here yesterday, trying to find someone to take her, pushing a stroller just like that. But I told her I'm already sick. Besides, I wouldn't know the first thing about taking care of a baby. Lucky for her, looks like she found you."

Katherine nodded and glanced down at the girl. "I don't know much about caring for a baby either," she said.

"The mother?"

"Dead."

The man stopped rocking. "But you're not sick yet?"

"No." Inside, Katherine quailed at the word "yet." In all this time, she hadn't truly worried about getting sick herself. Her fear had always been about being vulnerable to the machinations of whomever survived, or worse, being left to survive on her own.

"Well, maybe you won't be," the man said kindly. "The baby's not sick, and they're the ones who get sickest the quickest. Babies and old people like me. Some people must be immune."

"I hope so," Katherine murmured. "I don't suppose you know, but are any of the buses running? I need to get to Paramus."

The old man laughed. It was a harsh, raspy sound that turned into a wet cough. He raised his handkerchief to his mouth again. When the spasm had passed, he said, "I doubt there's enough people around here to fill one, if there's even a person around to drive it. But you don't need a bus." He swept his hand out toward the street. "It's like a car buffet out there. Walk right up and help yourself. I'd give you mine if I still drove."

Katherine blushed. "Well, I didn't think of that," she admitted.

"I've been sitting here all afternoon just fantasizing about what kind of car I'd take and where I'd go. I think I'd look for a nice little Corvette that I could drive as fast as I wanted, all the way to the shore. I still might," he said, fingering the brim of his ball cap. "I'm even wearing my special hat for the occasion. I usually only bring it out to show the grandkids, but what the hell does it matter now?"

Katherine smiled tentatively. "I suppose a little joy ride sounds like fun, but I honestly wouldn't know the first thing about hot-wiring a car."

The man waved a hand at her. "Are you kidding? Just walk into a house and take the keys. Who's going to stop you? My neighbor over there, two doors down," he said, pointing, "they hauled him off to the hospital two weeks ago. House is empty. Bet you'd find his car keys hanging on a hook somewhere. He's got a piece of shit foreign car in his garage. Not your dream car if you can have any one you want, but it'd get you to Paramus, and I bet you a million dollars no one is going to come looking for you if you borrow it."

Katherine eyes flickered uncertainly up the street to where he had pointed. "Really? Just walk in?"

The old man smiled. "If you're going to be one of the survivors, you better start learning to act like one."

"I was just thinking to myself how this isn't at all like the end of the world, how you see it in movies, you know?" Katherine mused. "Lawlessness and all that."

"It will be," the old man predicted. Again, he motioned toward his neighbor's house. "Go ahead. Jimmy Barnett was an asshole anyway, if that makes you feel better about it. You're saving that baby there. The least he could do is give you his ride."

CHAPTER FIVE

L OUIE STOOD AT THE KITCHEN sink. Before him were a white plate and Pyrex dish poking above the water line like remnants from a shipwreck. His gaze shifted to the coffee cup in his hand, which was empty. He was holding it near his chest as if poised to drink. This was new.

Other than the cup, this was a familiar scene after one of his suicide attempts. When he died, conscious thought and time stopped, like being in a deep sleep. Sometimes he experienced pictures and sensations that felt like dreams, and then he would find himself here in his kitchen, alive and well in his black T-shirt and plaid pajama bottoms, the sink full of water. It didn't matter how or where he'd died. He always arrived here, and it was always morning.

The dishes were always the same, ones he owned and had used many times, but not the ones he'd used and left there the day before a death. A white plate with the green flower border, his mother's pattern—"crazy daisy" or something like that. A brown glass baking dish, a fork and a butter knife, and a fading water glass with cartoon figures on it, one his mother had bought from the gas station many years ago when he'd begged for it, ninety-nine cents with the purchase of five gallons or more.

Though Louie would not admit it aloud, the reason he continued to try to kill himself even though it seemed impossible was this exact moment. It sometimes rewarded him with a puzzle piece for his mystery. Why these plates? Why his kitchen? What new things would he find, like this plain old coffee mug? For everyone else, time went on, and the next day came as usual. For him, it felt as if no time at all had passed, though he would always learn later that it had.

After the attempt with the drain cleaner, which had done nothing but clean out his bowels, as rightly predicted by Chet, Louie tried several other chemical cocktails as well as that half-baked scheme involving heat exhaustion. That only managed to make him more popular around town when the neighbors realized that crazy Louie would do any chore they needed in the 100-degree heat for free, just to see if it would kill him. The requests to drive people places, fetch groceries and prescriptions, and take dogs for walks had increased considerably in his small town as the flu swept through it and more people stayed indoors.

Once it took hold, however, they stopped altogether. Louie had walked from house to house in the downtown area, knocking on doors and breaking windows where he had to. He found everyone dead. He'd known that's how it would be before he'd begun, but he had to be sure. After canvassing the town, Louie took Chet's old Ford pickup from behind the general store (Chet had lived above it for thirty-two years until just the week before) and drove to the outlying small business farms and Amish areas.

All he found were bodies, though as in town, some of the animals were still alive. The chickens were alive, but most cows and horses were dead. All the cats were dead, but some of the dogs were alive. It made absolutely no sense. Lucky for him, he loved eggs, preferred chicken to beef, didn't know how to ride a horse, and had always wanted a dog.

Louie pulled out the stopper in the sink and watched the water drain. If only it were this easy, he thought. If only he could just find the right plug and pull it, and it would all be over. For the millionth time that summer, Louie wondered why, if there was a God, He didn't just pull the plug on him.

He sniffed the coffee cup on the counter where he had set it, just to be sure. There could be a lingering odor from whatever might have been in it, and that would be a clue too. He smelled nothing.

Louie dried the dishes with a checkered towel. They were clean, as they always were when he awoke in the kitchen, no matter what he had left in the sink the day before. That alone was almost enough reason for him to kill himself *daily*, so he'd never have to handle a dirty dish or pan, only dry the clean ones. He stowed the items away, and his thoughts moved from the macabre to the lady at the newspaper he'd spoken to a week ago. Katherine. *Is she still alive?* he wondered. *Is she sick yet? What is she doing right now?*

No reporter had called him back. No emergency workers had appeared at his doorstep. He wasn't surprised. If there was anyone left to help, surely they'd prioritize the big cities, where there were more survivors. What could his small, vacant town offer but Louie himself? And the world didn't have time for curiosities anymore.

It would be safe to assume Katherine had died before telling anyone about his town, except his dreams told him different. He had dreamed of her every night this week, and awake or asleep, such a fate for her didn't feel right. He didn't know what Katherine looked like in real life, but the strange knowing of dreams told him the woman was her. From the shadows of his vegetable garden, he'd watched her circle his house each night, exploring, searching for a way inside as she brushed a porch chair, a windowsill, a panel of glass delicately with her fingertips, as if she could unlock secrets with her touch. He observed her from a distance that felt like thousands of miles away. Other times, he was so close that when he woke, he could smell her on his clothes, and knew she wasn't sick, and she wasn't dead. The moody feeling from his dreams would linger throughout the day, but eventually faded until the doubts came back. *If she isn't sick, if she isn't dead, what is she doing?*

When he finished with the dishes, Louie pulled on a pair of boots and carried a bucket out to the well. Despite the mysterious water in the sink, he in fact had no running water when the gennie was off, like it was now. In the beginning, he had used the twenty or so gallons still in the storage tank to clean dishes, flush his toilet, and shower. When that ran out faster than expected, he'd found the hand pump that had gotten him through the blackout of 2003, when half the country had gone black, skipping parts of Michigan but leaving Louie's town in the dark and summer heat for a week. When it was inserted into the deep well twenty feet away from his back door, Louie could pump about ten gallons a minute of fresh water with it. And that was just fine by him these days. His Hostess belly had disappeared under his waistband, and he wasn't wasting the gas in his generator on water he could summon himself with a little elbow grease.

Louie felt his arms and neck turn red in the bright sun. He ignored it, of course. Skin cancer probably couldn't get him, and besides, the hot rays felt good. He hefted the bucket around to the side of the house. Before he rounded the corner, the dogs began to bark. They had heard him and knew his routine. Louie set the bucket down and unlatched the fence to his small corral. It had been empty of goats and pigs since before he was born but was now home to twenty-six dogs. He shimmied inside and began filling the metal trough he'd appropriated from a farm up the road. The sun and dogs had drunk it dry since yesterday, and Louie decided that from now on he'd need give them water twice a day.

For the next half hour, he went back and forth with buckets until the trough was filled to the top. He'd relieved both the general store and the Walmart in Alpena of their bags of dry dog food, nearly a truckload of them. Hauling two into the center of the corral, he sliced them open with a box cutter.

The dogs descended on the food like seagulls on a hotdog. Louie knew most were still half-starved. For some, it had been a week or longer without food after their owners died and before he'd found them. On his first sweep for human survivors, Louie had collected all the orphaned dogs he could. On the second, he didn't bother searching for people anymore—he was just rescuing dogs. A few died within a day, but the tough ones hung in there. Labs, Collies, mutts, and the rest of them were ones he couldn't identify but that looked fancy. He'd always wanted a dog. Now he had twenty-six.

When the dogs had been sufficiently supplied with food, scratches, and nuzzles, Louie moved to the chicken coops. He'd expanded them considerably to accommodate as many hens as he could, rescued from his neighbors on a third circuit through town and country. On the same journey, he'd taken any coops that weren't affixed too. He couldn't take all the chickens in the county, of course, so the ones he couldn't bring with him, he set free. There were currently several roosters strutting through his yard, and the rest of the community's fowl were clucking all over town.

Louie did his usual check and found only six eggs from more than three dozen chickens. It wasn't uncommon for chickens to stop laying eggs or to slow down during the summer, especially during very hot days or weeks. However, he suspected a good number of them were just plain stressed. He cooed and clucked at them like his mother would have done and spread around pellets and oyster shells. Maybe he'd find more eggs tomorrow. Until then, he'd have a nice little omelet.

With canines and fowl fed and happy, Louie made his breakfast and then did his other chores, which included cleaning his clothes and himself, picking vegetables from his garden, and tidying the house. Once everything was set on the home front, he set off to do his "away" chores.

The truck was old, but it wasn't rusty and ran well. It was better suited to scavenging than his own car, so Louie felt little guilt about taking it from his buddy at the general store. As he cranked over the engine and pulled out of his driveway, he tried not to think about Chet. He'd never taken the man up on his offer to have a beer out on the porch, joined him in a fishing tournament, or gone down to the community center for bingo that Chet's daughter's ladies' group organized. Instead, he turned down Chet's invitations, preferring to wallow in self-imposed isolation.

Louie had cursed his small town for its nosiness, for how when his mother died, the local paper had done a story about it and tried to make the national news. She had been the first woman in their town to get coronavirus and the first to die from it. Women his mom's age baked him lasagnas and casseroles composed of different kinds of Campbell soups. Some used his mother's own recipes, showing up on his doorstep clutching their Pyrex dishes and wearing colorful facemasks they'd sewn from quilting scraps, as if poor executions of his favorite foods would comfort him instead of reminding him of her more.

The men at the funeral home had clapped him on the shoulder, offering trite phrases like "this too shall pass" and "she's in a better place now," even as they wore their masks under their noses or down around their chins. They still didn't believe in the virus, not really, even though his mom had just *died* from it. They didn't have a clue what he was feeling or know what place she had gone to either.

Louie had cursed the whole town because he couldn't make a single move—before or since his mother's death— without someone knowing about it and talking about it. He couldn't even walk down to the store and have a conversation with Chet without every customer after him that day learning his business. (Chet sold groceries, but his stock-in-trade was gossip.) Chet had been the nicest of them all, and

Louie understood conversation was just natural currency in a small town.

Now he could drive for an hour and not find a single opportunity for chitchat, a handshake, or even a friendly wave. This should be depressing as hell. It shouldn't make him happy. But it did. In fact, as he turned the block in Chet's truck, he heard himself whistling Rihanna's "Umbrella" song. It had been a long time since he'd done that.

He had something to do every day now, and he could do it in peace. Everything just seemed a little brighter, except for when he thought about Chet. It wouldn't have been so bad if Chet had survived the flu. And maybe his daughter too. She was a bit old for Louie, and probably a little too good for him, but with everyone else gone, Louie might have stood a chance.

Chet's dog, Clark, sat beside him in the old Ford. Louie reached over and patted the dog's rump, which he'd turned toward Louie so his paws could perch on the windowsill. His impressive tongue was unrolled, flapping in the wind.

"That's a good boy," Louie said to the big dumb golden retriever mix, who had more enthusiasm than sense. Clark came as a package deal with the truck, and connected him to a man who had been kind to him when others weren't. This gave Louie a soft spot for him. Thus, Clark was the only rescue allowed in the house, and the only one with his own La-Z-Boy recliner.

Louie and his dog rumbled down Main Street. Its two stoplights no longer blinked, not that stoplights meant anything to Louie anymore. He rolled through toward the southern city limits and the Marathon gas station. As was his habit, he kept his eyes peeled for humans. Unlikely as it was, maybe he'd find a cute female survivor passing through who wanted to team up.

Leaving town permanently was something Louie refused to consider. He sometimes thought about settling on an inland lake where he could fish every day—fish would be a nice little addition to his diet—but leaving the security of his home for an unknown destination and unknown people seemed crazy to him. Hell, he probably wouldn't risk straying from home to find *known* people. Louie wasn't good in groups.

He pulled the car into the gas station and cut the engine. Clark bounded through the open rear window into the truck bed and met Louie at the tailgate, tail thumping like a drum. Louie opened the gate and the dog leapt onto the hot cement, all dancing eagerness to watch Louie collect his empty cans, all but one of which he had also pilfered from his neighbors.

The pumps had stopped working when the electricity went out, so Louie bypassed those and walked fifty feet with his cans jangling to an aluminum plate in the ground. It was roughly one foot in diameter, hot and shining in the mid-afternoon sun. The plate gave access to the underground tanks—a veritable fountain of youth for his gas guzzling generators and vehicles. Last week he had come by and opened the plate, pulled the lock, and run a ten-foot tube down into the tank, and now he found the hand pump lying on the cement just where he'd left it, still attached, the tube squeezing out between the panel and ground. Open for business.

As he dropped to his knees, he enjoyed the thought that he was now getting free gas from the very place that had laid him off the summer before. Louie had worked at this garage and station since high school, and in a way, he was now the last employee standing.

He'd get a gallon of gas for every five or six revolutions of the handle, but it would take time to draw it up to the top. He vowed to himself, again, that he would search harder for propane generators. Honest work was good, but he'd get tired of pumping gas every day quick enough.

Louie lifted the panel and reached down into the hole to check that the hose was still in place. Finding everything secure, he set to work, rotating the jerky lever, feeling it hitch in his grip like he was grinding sausage. If he kept a good pace, he could fill his first two-gallon container in just under a minute. The other three empty cans sat at his feet, and there were ten more still in the bed of his truck.

"You intend to pay for that?"

Louie nearly knocked over the can he was filling, so absorbed was he in his task and so unprepared to hear a human voice. As it was, he kicked the empty cans next to him, an explosion of sound that echoed across the deserted gas station and set Clark to barking. Louie stared at a man he didn't recognize approaching with a hand on the gun at his waist.

Straightening, he noted the badge hooked into the band of the man's jeans, opposite his holster, and said, "Not exactly, Officer."

"That would be a crime," the man responded. With his thick hair and wide shoulders, he presented like a typical cop to Louie, probably in his thirties too, strong and capable in the second decade of his career. But the way he stared him down made Louie feel like a truant caught out of school.

"I see it as severance pay," Louie replied awkwardly. "I used to work here."

The stranger removed his hand from his weapon but kept a cautious distance. Clark ceased barking. "Even if you still worked here, I doubt employees get free gas when they want it," he replied evenly.

"Just trying to get by, sir," Louie said. "I'm the only one left around here."

The cop assessed him for a long moment, then bent to scratch Clark on the head, keeping his gaze fixed on Louie until the dog drew his attention with a dramatic fall and roll, lifting his legs into the air. The man chuckled softly and bent to rub his belly while Louie silently cursed Clark for welcoming the stranger before Louie had decided if it was safe.

And if it isn't? Louie berated himself. *What exactly will you do, tough guy?* He answered himself immediately. If the cop tried to mess with him, he'd reach for the lighter in his pocket. They'd both go up in flames, but Louie would be standing at his kitchen sink this time tomorrow. The only thing that might give him pause would be Clark, the little traitor. He didn't quite deserve to be doggy barbeque. Yet.

Louie suppressed the urge to call Clark to his side, as if the turncoat would even obey in the middle of his apparent ecstasy. Instead, he said, "I have a feeling money doesn't mean much around here anymore."

The cop considered this for a moment. "I suppose you're right." He stood and gestured to the cans. "Running a generator?"

Louie nodded. "A few."

The cop moved forward and extended a hand. "Devlin Kelly."

Louie wavered, having never liked cops much. He was sure they were waiting to catch him doing something wrong, like this one had just done. Also, handshakes had gone out of style two years ago. He shook the man's hand anyway. "I'm Louie."

Devlin glanced at the dog staring up at him adoringly. "And this guy?"

"Clark," Louie said. Wasn't this guy ever going to leave?

"Louie and Clark, that's funny," Devlin said. "Like the explorers."

"That's Louis and Clark," Louie said, thinking it wasn't funny at all because his name wasn't Louis. "Where'd you come from, anyway?"

"Green Bay," Devlin replied.

"That's what, a good 300 miles or so from here?"

Devlin nodded.

"Cheesehead?"

Devlin shrugged. "More of a Brewers guy."

"I try to be a Lions fan, but…" Louie shrugged. Not much point in talking sports anymore, was there? Most of the Lions were probably dead already. If he felt like making a joke, he might add that the other half were probably just playing like they were.

As he stood there awkwardly, Louie suddenly realized Michigan wasn't anywhere near Mister Officer Devlin Kelly's jurisdiction, and the cop could probably do jack squat about him borrowing a little gas. On that thought, Louie crouched to resume filling his gas can. "Long way from home," he said after a moment. "So how is it you're not wearing a uniform?"

Although carrying the badge and gun, Devlin was in jeans and a white cotton shirt. Despite the lack of uniform, he seemed every inch a cop. This guy wasn't a bum, not like the town sheriff who in April had taken to putting a dummy in his patrol car to deter speeders while he napped in his office. Devlin didn't look like he ate his dinner at the Donut Stop.

"Because it's too damn hot for a uniform, that's why," he answered, watching Louie fill the can but not voicing further objections.

"What are you doing over here?"

"My mom was living in St. Ignace. She passed two weeks ago. Flu."

"Sorry," Louie said automatically, glancing up. He might be antisocial, but he knew his manners.

Devlin accepted the sympathy with a nod. "After that, I came down through Cheboygan intending to see a cousin near Alpena—" He broke off, and Louie understood at once. The cousin was dead. Everyone was. And there seemed no point heading back the way he'd come.

"I thought maybe you were, I don't know, on assignment to find survivors or something."

Devlin shrugged. "I suppose I am now. My sister is down in Toledo. I haven't been able to reach her, so I thought I'd keep heading south."

"So just passing through, then?"

Devlin smiled slightly. "Trying to get rid of me?"

Louie tried to match his smile. "I might need to break more laws."

"If you're the only one around, I guess it doesn't much matter anymore." Devlin sighed. Louie followed his gaze down the road, and they watched the dust stirring across the pavement for a long moment. It had been blacktopped over just the month before, and on hot days, one could still smell the newness of it.

"I can't believe it…it only took a month. This thing has just, I don't know, taken over, hasn't it?" Suddenly, Devlin didn't seem so tough anymore, and Louie felt a stab of pity. Just because all of this was a refreshing change to him, didn't mean normal people weren't still reeling.

Throughout their conversation, Louie had been filling, and he stopped now that his containers were full. He wiped his sweat on his shirt sleeve and marched them back to his truck, pleased when Clark followed him. He noted a white Tahoe parked on the other side of the Ford. On the door, he saw the letters "CPD" written inside a gold star, with "Cheboygan Police" under it in gold lettering.

Devlin was right behind him and must have noted Louie's inspection. "I ran out of gas and didn't have a pump. Borrowed this one."

Louie stopped, and this time he didn't hide his interest in Devlin's badge, wondering what else the man might have "borrowed." Devlin smiled easily. He produced a wallet from his back pocket and flipped it open, revealing his Wisconsin State Patrol ID. His face matched his picture, and Louie relaxed.

Louie gave a wry smile. "Borrowed? Yeah, I've been doing that a lot myself lately." He plucked at one of the full cans with a fingernail. "This here is borrowed too."

Devlin laughed. "OK! You can take the cop out of the country and all…"

Louie flipped up the tailgate. Eight gallons would do for now. He would come back later when he could steal in peace. "Well, I guess I'm off then," he said. "Anything you need for your trip, Officer Kelly? I can pump some gas for you if you'd like."

Devlin eyed Louie for a long minute. "It's Devlin. And how about a cold beer?"

Louie pulled into his driveway and watched in the rear-view mirror as Devlin followed in his borrowed Tahoe. Being sociable was a strain for Louie, who tended to do best with his own thoughts, but what was he supposed to say when the man asked for a beer? No? He had already told the man that he had generators. He had a cold ice chest and no excuse not to invite him back, other than that he simply didn't want him here. Besides, the cop might be the last person around for a while, and people went crazy after a time if they didn't have someone to talk to.

Louie climbed out of his car and held the door for Clark, who lumbered after him. They walked back to the Tahoe.

Devlin swung his door shut and said, "Hey, you mind if I let my dog out?" He glanced at Clark.

"You got a dog in there?" Louie peered into the police car.

"He's crated. It's hot, and even with the windows open…"

"Yeah, sure, whatever," Louie replied.

Devlin walked to the back of the truck and released the hatch. A moment later, he rounded the vehicle with a Belgian Shepherd on a long vinyl leash looped around his fist. The dog was a mottled black and brown, beautiful, muscled, and full of enthusiasm. He was straining from his lead, almost hopping on his two back legs, and whining excitedly.

"Been cooped up a while?" Louie asked, watching Devlin control the dog by leaning back against the leash.

"He thinks we're going to work."

"He a cop dog?"

Devlin nodded. "This is Keno."

"You can let him run around a little," Louie offered. "Burn off some steam."

"He's always like this. Always ready to go. I'll throw the ball to him in a bit, but K-9s are alphas. He'd be too much for Clark there."

Louie looked down to his own feet where Clark sat on them.

"I'll just keep him close for now, let him settle. He'll figure out we're off the clock in a bit."

Louie, feeling awkward, said, "How about that beer, then?"

Devlin followed him to the backyard. The penned dogs scented Keno instantly and began to bark.

"Stop that," Louie admonished them, though he appreciated that not everyone welcomed the stranger with open arms. He cast an accusatory glance down at Clark, who blinked back guiltily.

Louie led Devlin to the wood porch off the back of the house. The floorboards had started to go soft and the whole thing needed stain badly. His mother would have asked him to hang red, white, and blue swags on it for the summer and fill the empty boxes on the rails with impatiens. He pointed to a pair of twisted bark rocking chairs where she used to smoke unfiltered cigarettes after dinner, pinching tobacco from her tongue and washing away the taste with lemonade. Ignoring the ghost in his mind, he tried to focus on the person actually there. "I'll just grab us those beers," he said. The dogs were still howling and jumping at the gate.

"One of these looks just my size," Devlin said, taking a seat. Keno lowered himself at his feet on command, but with a nervous whimper, like he'd rather be chasing someone or something than lounging in the shade. His paws were down but his haunches lifted eagerly. Devlin patted them down, urging the dog to settle.

Louie went into the kitchen with Clark. The breath of cold air from the refrigerator calmed him momentarily, and he paused to enjoy feeling the trickles of sweat on his neck turn to shivers. "Labatt Blue?" he called.

Devlin leaned in his chair to peer through the screen door. The rusty screen and the afternoon sunlight conspired to make his brown hair turn copper. "I don't care what it is if it's cold."

Clark settled under the kitchen table and appeared content to stay there, safe from the K-9 cop and the stifling heat. Louie envied him. He snagged two cold beers and rejoined Devlin on the porch. He tried to seem hospitable. What if the man wanted to, what, join forces? What if he asked a bunch of questions?

Louie wouldn't have minded the company so much if Devlin Kelly had been a good-looking woman. (Or a bad-looking woman. Louie wasn't really picky.) Anyone else really who could appreciate all he had done to set himself up here in comfort, who could see the safety he could provide. Devlin would recognize none of these things. He was a cop, probably even trained for the end of the world, and Louie had no desire to play the sidekick.

The beer bottles clinked together, reminding Louie that as soon as this business was done, he could return to the gas station and fill his cans. Keno lifted to stand, but Devlin grunted a command, and the dog settled again. Louie handed Devlin the beer and settled in the other rocker. He dug his keys from his front pocket and popped the top with the bottle opener on his ring. He leaned to take the cap off

Devlin's beer, but Devlin had already twisted it off and was taking a long pull.

Louie stuffed his keys in his pocket. In his mind, he heard a high school bully call him a pussy for not pinching his hand on the twist-off cap.

"This might be the best beer I've ever tasted." Devlin sighed. "It's been days since I drank anything cold. This could be ice-cold piss and I'd probably enjoy it."

Devlin swallowed more beer, observing the yard. His gaze lingered on the dog corral. A few of the rescues milled around the gate but most had retreated to the shade of the shed roof. "All of those yours?" Devlin asked.

Louie shifted uncomfortably, drawing Devlin's attention. "Just a question," Devlin said.

"Neighbors' dogs," Louie admitted. "I rounded them all up. I'd hate to see them starve."

Devlin nodded. "I thought Keno was special. I haven't seen any other dogs."

"It's weird. Some of the animals get it and some don't."

"Any guess on the percentage of dogs that are survivors?" Devlin asked.

Louie shrugged.

"I ask because it seems people are the same...most get it. Some of us don't."

"You're wondering how many survivors there are," Louie surmised.

Devlin finished off his beer and set it on the porch. "More like how many there will be. The flu's still going on. Some of us who are healthy now will still get sick later."

"You've gone from Wisconsin to Cheboygan to here. In all that way, how many people did you see?"

"I saw some cars near St. Vincent's. That's a big hospital in Green Bay."

"Was there anyone at your police station?"

"Ours is a small, remote location. A homebase for refueling, just a few desks… But no one had been there in more than a week when I was still checking in every day. Some were home sick, I think. Others just drifted away. Not much appetite for a job that we could assume didn't pay anymore. I finally realized no one was coming back. Figured it was time to go."

"After Wisconsin? How many healthy people did you see driving around?" Louie asked.

"Between Cheboygan and here, none."

"No government workers? Relief efforts?"

"I haven't seen anything like that. We're not following the same playbook as Covid. There wasn't time for organized efforts." Devlin reached down to pat Keno, who had finally lowered his chin to the porch. "But you and me, we make two, so by my count, at least some people are still healthy. For now. Maybe more than we think if we're proportional to dogs." He nodded toward the corral. The dogs were milling around in the sun, having lost interest in Keno.

Louie shuddered. *Healthy, for now.* The thought that the man sitting across from him, seemingly well but possibly carrying deadly germs, could be dead in a week gave Louie the creeps. These days, he didn't fear death. But his fear of germs, of things he couldn't see, that was always a very real thing.

As if he had read Louie's mind, Devlin said, "Don't worry. I've been exposed for weeks without so much as a sniffle."

"This might be a real dumb question," Louie murmured. "But what's next, do you think? I mean, you found me. What if you find others? Do you have a plan?"

"Not a fucking clue. Right now, honestly, I'm just focused on family. If my sister is alive, I imagine I'll stay put. Try to set things up nice for us, like you have here. Wait it out and see if things get reorganized."

Louie struggled with how to word his next thought, a first for him, because he usually just blurted out whatever he was thinking—a character flaw that probably explained why he was alone most of the time. Before the flu, that is. "I guess I kind of thought 'cause you were a cop that you'd be, I don't know, out doing your civic duty. Trying to gather people together. Organize. Reorganize, like you said. Who knows if there's anyone in a greater position of power to do it?"

Devlin's eyes slid away.

Louie cleared his throat. "I'm not trying to say you're not doing your job."

Devlin's gaze jerked back to Louie.

"Well, shit," Louie said with embarrassment. "That came off sounding even worse. I guess I'm out of practice already."

Devlin forced a laugh, but his eyes had narrowed. "Hey, it's not like on TV. I'm a cop, but I'm also a human being. With a family. With the same fears you have. Of course I want to do what I can to help anyone I run across if they need it. If I see someone breaking a law, a law that's still important," he amended, "my instinct is to do what I can to maintain the peace, protect others. But hey, there's no rule book on this stuff. A big ass chunk of the population just up and died. My job doesn't seem as important to society as it was a month ago."

"Sorry," Louie mumbled. "I didn't mean to say you have some kind of responsibility. The way you came up on me at the gas station, well, you did seem a little 'on the job' to me."

"Habit," Devlin said flatly. "And I didn't realize that this town was gone." He glanced at the dogs in their pen again. "Obviously, there's no need to worry about rationing…"

"So you're not going to arrest me if I tell you that I've been 'borrowing' what I need all over town?" Louie asked, attempting levity.

"I suppose there's no one left to miss anything, is there?"

Louie shook his head, trying to appear mournful about this fact that strangely delighted him.

"In that case, you have an unlimited supply of beer, right?"

Devlin didn't drink too many beers, and Louie was relieved that Devlin was finally climbing into his stolen Tahoe when they heard the CB radio crackle to life.

"Can anyone hear me out there?" The voice was fractured by static.

Devlin, in mid-hoist, jerked his gaze to Louie and grinned. "Guess we're not the only ones around here after all!" Landing in his seat, he snatched up the radio. He palmed the microphone like an expert and said, "This is Officer Devlin Kelly. I hear you, over."

"I read you," the voice returned.

There was something else now…maybe two more voices, or three? Louie strained to hear through what sounded like several people trying to talk at once.

Devlin waited until he heard silence and then pressed the button. "A little trouble hearing you. One at a time please, over."

"Sorry," the voice said again, clearer now. And male, to Louie's disappointment.

"Hey, there. What's your name and how many in your party? Over," replied Devlin.

They heard a few clicks and waited.

"I'm Grider from Dayton," the man finally said. "I've got a lady named Adra and her sons William and Jayden with me that I picked up near Alpena in my rig, and we just bumped into Scott who was heading east on 32 until his truck broke down. He's got three buddies with him from the Hillman area. They're crammed in my bunk now, and we're heading west on the 32. Where are you? Over."

"I'm Devlin from Wisconsin, and I'm here with Louie. We're near Atlanta. Michigan. Over."

"We're only about two miles, maybe three, from Atlanta, over."

"Standby."

"We're listening."

Devlin turned to Louie. "I hate to ask, but are you up for some company?"

Company was the last thing he wanted, but how could he say no? "I guess so," he muttered.

Devlin lowered the CB mic. "Up to you, man. I get it if you feel like you're fine here alone."

"Would they stay here?"

"I don't know. I can offer to take them with me."

Louie shrugged, resigned. "Well, if you can take them with you."

Devlin turned his attention back to the radio. "Anyone sick in your party, Grider? Over."

"Not a one. Over."

"We're OK too. We've got electricity and food. You're welcome here, over."

After a beat, Grider returned. "Lead me there, Big Bear."

"Standby." To Louie, Devlin asked, "You mind if I stick around a while longer?"

"Long enough to gather your own supplies for the road, I suppose. You're not going to eat all my food, are you?

"Not my intention," Devlin said. "The guy said he was up from Dayton, didn't he?"

"So?"

"Maybe he passed through Toledo on his way."

"Would that make a difference?"

Devlin plunged his free hand into his hair. "I don't know. Probably not. Even if he tells me the whole fucking city is dead, I'll want to see for myself. But…"

"But it would help to know how urgently you need to get there," Louie finished for him. He eyed Devlin's wild hair for a moment. "Fine, then. I'll go hide the beer."

He turned back to the house, leaving Devlin to guide the Grider party to his previously peaceful, wonderfully underpopulated ranch. As he passed over the porch, Louie picked up their empties and muttered to Clark through the screen door. "Guess we need to make the place ready for guests, Clark. *More guests.* As if twenty-six dogs…actually *twenty-eight* dogs," he qualified, "if we count your sorry ass and that Keno, plus Officer Devlin Kelly, weren't enough." He tossed the bottles in a garbage can full of others. Taking measure of the burning sky, he saw that the sun was about an hour from setting. There were storm clouds gathering but he didn't think the rain would come until dark. "And now rain. Perfect."

Louie stomped into the house, picturing twenty-eight muddy dogs. The door thumped behind him. He knew he would have to burn off his pique before Devlin came around. For reasons he couldn't articulate even to himself, he didn't want the other man to see how affected he was by the idea of others joining them. Wouldn't that seem odd? And more than anything, Louie never wanted to appear odd. Fitting in was his game, and that meant reacting to things like the majority of other people did. If Devlin joined up with this Grider guy, if "normal" meant wanting to be with others, then Louie would play along.

The house was tidy, but Louie ran a sponge over the kitchen countertop anyway, scrubbing at scratches and stains that had been there since he was a boy, simply to kill a few minutes and expend his nervous energy. He was indeed hiding the beer in the crisper drawer when Devlin knocked on the door a while later. Louie opened it to Devlin and his dog, Grider, and eight other strangers.

"I'd like to keep the big door closed with the air conditioning on," Louie said by way of greeting as they filed past him through the kitchen and into the living room.

He hoped the message was clear. *In case there are any questions, this is Louie's house. And Louie's house has rules.*

"Sure, Louie," Devlin said. He was fighting to keep Keno from taking off down the hallway after Clark. "No problem." He motioned to the big man beside him. "This is Grider. That's his big rig out front."

Grider had the appearance of a man hard-working his way through life, toward both retirement and a third chin. Probably in his late fifties. Louie sensed no threat to his ego and moved forward to accept Grider's offered handshake.

"Hi," he mumbled in the direction of the truck driver's thick wrist.

"Thanks for having us," Grider said. "Everyone was hot as hell in my truck." He motioned to the black woman behind him, who had her hands on her sons' shoulders. "This is Adra, William, and Jayden."

Adra seemed nervous to Louie but was pretty in her capris and scarf-covered hair. He flipped an awkward wave to her and the boys. She said quickly, "They're ten and twelve. I promise they won't be any trouble." The boys stared at Louie, their faces mirroring the unhappiness he felt about more people to navigate.

Another tall man stepped forward with his hand out. "Mike." After a firm shake, he pointed out the others. "Scott, Tim, Chris." The four men were all thick-necked, sunburned, and not unlike the guys who'd tripped Louie in the hallways in high school. These were good old boys who'd probably made all the teams, fucked all the decent girls, and gotten scholarships to schools with good football programs even though their grades sucked. The kind of boys who asked if that prom suit came in camo. They all had brush haircuts.

Louie managed another awkward wave in their direction. Everyone was staring at him. He supposed he was expected to say something like, *Welcome, everyone!* Or *mi casa es su casa!* What came out was less eloquent. "It's going to rain. I hope you have camping equipment."

CHAPTER SIX

KATHERINE WOULDN'T BE DRIVING JIMMY Barnett's piece-of-shit foreign car after all. As advertised, it was a car buffet out there. Why settle for meat and potatoes when you can have all the dessert you want?

Though it made logical sense, right and wrong still warred within her. So she thanked the old man kindly for his helpful advice, walked unhurriedly down the block as if she were an upstanding citizen, and when she turned the corner out of sight, began scoping around for her new car. Katherine could hear the man whistling from his porch, which meant he probably would hear the engine rev in the quiet of the neighborhood a few minutes later, but there was nothing to be done about that.

What a gorgeous car it was, washed and waxed, waiting for her under a fancy cover in a nearby garage. A sporty little green Jaguar with all the bells and whistles. It was perfectly impractical for East Coast winters, but when the weather turned cold, she could exchange it for any other one she wanted.

It required real discipline to control her speed. Katherine slid her palm over the sleek wooden gear shift, feeling the car respond effortlessly no matter how she pushed it. She figured it was born for speed, and like her, wanted to feast on the open buffet of road stretched before it. But she found herself easing off the gas. To balance out her thievery, Katherine heeded the traffic laws, even though she was the only driver on the road. Besides easing her conscience, she hadn't actually driven in years. She didn't even have a license. It would be just her luck to lose control and careen into a telephone pole with no ambulance to call.

She halted at a stop sign and glanced in the rearview mirror. Baby Ana was asleep in her car carrier, which popped straight off the fancy stroller for just this purpose.

"I know this is silly," she said aloud, "but stopping at all the signs makes me feel more normal. And I have precious cargo."

The baby didn't stir, and Katherine was grateful. She was doing her best to baby talk them both through this, but the tiny burden in the back seat already weighed on her. Was this temporary? Or was she a mother now?

Her name is Ana.

Mommy loves you.

She hated herself for feeling ambivalent about this little girl, whom someone else had cherished deeply. For the millionth time, Katherine wondered why she'd been born without the baby gene. A thirty-something woman with no prospects for a child of her own should be secretly delighted to have a baby dropped on her. Adoption was an expensive, complicated thing, and here she was, free and clear, with a healthy little baby who needed a mommy. Yet Katherine couldn't help but resent the situation. She'd never wanted a kid. She was career-focused, independent—a modern woman.

Or she had been one. In the blink of an eye, she'd gone from wonderful, imperfect Katherine, free to be full of quirky flaws, to responsible…what? Foster mom? Guardian? Survivor.

The more Katherine worried, the faster she drove. It was only ten miles from her Bergen County apartment to Sharon's suburb in Paramus, and her fears that the short trip might take hours if the streets were clogged turned out to be unfounded. Between Katherine's speeding and the Jaguar's smooth acceptance, it took only twenty minutes. When she arrived, Sharon was waiting on the stoop of her brownstone, her hair a puffy masterpiece, wearing yoga pants and a T-shirt. Not dressed for company, but then, Katherine wasn't company. She was her new roommate.

Sharon came down to the curb.

"Nice ride. Did we get a raise?" she said.

Katherine walked around the luxury car and opened the rear passenger door. "We got Jags for our last bonus." She pointed at Ana. "Management gets free babies too."

Sharon's eyes lit up when they fixed on the baby, out-shining the grief beneath her levity. Katherine rolled her eyes internally. Sharon's face was comical. She had the baby look.

Before Katherine blinked, Sharon was cooing and moving in on Ana, releasing her from the carrier with impressive speed and cuddling her against one large breast. "And who is this?" she sang. The girl blinked up at her.

"Her name is Ana," Katherine said. Though her tone was steady, in her mind she screamed it like Ana's mother had once wailed it. *Her name is Ana! Take her. Her name is Ana!*

"I sure didn't get one of these for Christmas," Sharon said in the same singsong voice. "Must be nice to be management, don't you think, Ana?"

"God, Sharon. You're not going to talk like that from now on, are you?"

Sharon laughed. "Sorry. Baby talk just comes naturally."

Katherine tried to ignore the unintentional jab. Even women who merely *wanted* children had maternal skills she didn't possess. She reached into the car for the baby bag and her suitcase, then pressed the door closed. She didn't slam it, but it sounded loud in the empty neighborhood. No one on the sidewalks or porches here, cars all snug in their garages.

"I think anyone still well is hiding out," Sharon said, seeing Katherine assess the street.

"Maybe," Katherine said noncommittally. There was a smell here, like walking past a dumpster in New Orleans. But this wasn't leftover food rotting in the bin.

"You think they're all…dead?"

"I don't know." Based on the smell, probably. But she said, "Maybe. It seems to work fast. Everyone in my building is gone for sure. And do you know anyone who, even two weeks ago, wasn't sick or who didn't know someone sick?"

Sharon's eyes lowered. Katherine remembered her dead mother was still inside. "I'm sorry," she said. "About your mom."

Sharon focused her attention on the baby. As though she were talking to Ana, she said, "I moved her next door to Mrs. Radcliff's."

"Oh."

"I couldn't have her here with us. Not with a baby here. And I couldn't bear to leave her outside. Mrs. Radcliff passed a few days ago, and they haven't picked her up yet. I figure when they do, they will take Mom too…" Sharon croaked the last words toward the brownstone.

Katherine followed her. She wanted to ask her how she'd managed the move by herself, but realized it was an insensitive question. At least now she understood why Sharon looked like hell. Her wild hair. The comfy pants. She'd been dragging a dead body, and she was sick besides. "How are you feeling?"

"Not too bad yet, I guess. Scratchy throat, hot eyes. Tylenol is working on the fever so far. Nothing I would have called out of work over," she said, starting up the stairs. "By the way, I let the cats out," Sharon added over her shoulder. "Not sure if they can survive it, but they definitely have it too. I'm putting food out. They're still eating." *For now.* Setting her cats loose into the neighborhood had to have been almost as traumatic for Sharon as the death of her mother. Her cats were her children.

"I'm sorry, hon. Oh, that reminds me…" Katherine said, pausing at the stoop. She slid her mask up over her nose. It had been dangling around her neck like a cloth necklace, so familiar after two years of Covid that wearing it again barely bothered her.

"It's too late for me to worry about catching it," Sharon replied, waiting for Katherine to follow. "But I'll wear one for you. It's just inside on the table."

Katherine waved the thought off. "Forget it. You've touched everything in the house, and your mom too. I doubt my mask will do much to protect me, but I'll wear it anyway. It's not a big deal."

"Are you sure you want to stay?" Sharon asked.

Katherine wondered if she was suggesting that she leave Ana and go. She almost asked but said instead, "At this point, what does it matter? Even if I avoid getting it, I'm not going to survive long on my own anyway." She thought about her empty cupboards, her lack of toilet paper. It sounded terrible, but the benefits of being with Sharon outweighed the risks. Being alone again was worse than dying.

"What about Ana?" Sharon asked. "If she's not immune...I mean, babies and old people get sickest, right?"

It was true. Sharon was sick, and Katherine's survival instincts weren't going to get her far. So what chance did Ana have? None. Even perfectly healthy, the baby couldn't survive on her own. Once they were gone, she would starve to death.

This thought was much too morbid to share on a hot day after the day they'd had, so she said, "If we're going to get it, we'll get it. But since we can't mask her, I guess let's just mask ourselves and hope for the best."

Sharon's mouth turned down, but she said, "Up to you," and then turned to carry Ana inside. She'd resumed her lyrical conversation with the baby, slipping on a mask and whispering words behind it to Ana that Katherine couldn't hear.

Why is it up to me? asked Katherine in her head, trailing behind them. *I'm not her mother. Didn't I just prove that? Wouldn't her mother be the first person to insist upon masks, just in case?*

They entered the cool foyer. Katherine lagged behind while Sharon disappeared into the depths of her home. Katherine entered the small sitting room, noting that her friend had kept most of the mauve-and-knit décor. Sharon had inherited the building a few years earlier after her Aunt Patty had a fatal stroke. A windfall, but not without its drawbacks. Sharon's mother had been fine with her daughter inheriting her only sister's brownstone as long as she didn't make changes—an ongoing battle between them, likely right up until a few hours ago.

Katherine dropped the baby bag and suitcase onto a rug and sat down, sagging into the oversize sofa. She felt like she was in a cocoon, safe from all the drama for now. She poked at a needlepoint pillow. "You don't have anyone upstairs, do you?" she called to Sharon after a moment.

"Not since Jenny and Greg moved out. I've been keeping up with it on my own." Three different tenants had occupied the third-floor converted suite since Katherine had known Sharon. Though her friend was loathe to admit it, Katherine knew that even a paid-for, free-and-clear brownstone was expensive when it came to taxes and utilities.

"I guess it wouldn't be convenient to have tenants right now anyway," Katherine remarked. Sharon had drifted back into the room with Ana over her shoulder, and now the conversation stopped when Ana gurgled and then vomited onto Sharon's shirt.

"Oooh," Sharon gasped.

It should have sounded like dismay, but instead it came off more like astonishment or delight. As in, *Oooh, baby vomit!*

Before Katherine could register her own disgust, Sharon had already rushed to the kitchen to fetch a hand towel.

Sharon came back into the room, swiping at the baby's jumper. Ana seemed to be working up to a cry. "When did she last eat?"

"Just before we came over," Katherine said. Had she done something wrong?

"Her lips are really dry."

"I noticed. That's why I fed her before I left. I thought she was dehydrated."

"She definitely looks dehydrated. That would make sense if she hasn't eaten for a while…"

Sharon was avoiding mentioning "the incident"—meaning Katherine's little loss of time when she had apparently been freaking out—but it seemed they were both thinking about it.

"I'm not sure why she threw up," Sharon continued. "Hopefully it's just some regular tummy upset. Maybe after not eating for a bit, she drank too much too fast? But then you'd think she'd have thrown up right away…"

"Don't ask me," Katherine said. "I have no idea what's normal."

"We should get her some supplies anyway. Maybe some Pedialyte. There can't be much in that bag."

Katherine shrugged and stood. "It'll be easier for me to just get what she needs than for all three of us to pack up and go."

"Alone? I thought we'd go together."

"It's not exactly a zombie apocalypse out there, Sharon."

Sharon tried to laugh. "Well, what *is* it like? I haven't been out for a few days, and that was only straight to my mom's and back."

"It's like a regular day. Except someone came and took up the people."

"That sounds bad."

"Well, I did see an old guy on his porch, but aside from the fact that he was sitting in his underwear, it was OK. I didn't see anyone else though. No zombies."

This time Sharon did laugh. "Go then."

Katherine was halfway to the Jaguar when Sharon called after her. "Hey!"

Katherine paused.

"Don't forget infant diapers, infant formula, and Pedialyte. And maybe some more food for us. Canned stuff. Stuff that will last. And maybe milk if it's still good."

"Got it."

Katherine began walking toward the car again.

"Hey!"

Katherine turned to Sharon, now standing in the doorway with baby Ana.

"Come back soon."

Katherine had just belted in and was muttering to herself when Sharon slid into the passenger seat with the baby in her arms. Sharon's cheeks were damp now along the top of her mask, probably from fever.

"Seriously?"

"I changed my mind. I don't want you to go alone." She seemed to be trying for nonchalance.

Katherine stared. Did Sharon think her moral compass was so broken that she would just leave them?

Sharon settled into the seat and belted herself and the baby in together. "I just want you to be safe," she said, which irritated Katherine even more. She knew Sharon wasn't saying what she really thought, that Katherine was only capable of thinking about Katherine.

"Like hell," Katherine snapped, jerking the gearshift to drive. "You think I'd leave you? Really?" When her friend didn't answer, she added, "Aren't you worried about going out with a fever? Infecting other people?"

"You said all the people are gone."

Katherine followed Sharon's directions to the market in Little Ferry and tried not to think about what was really bothering her. *Could* she and the beautiful Jaguar have run away together?

They pulled in the parking lot. Sharon got out and went to the back for the stroller. Watching her in the rearview mirror, absorbed with the baby and not yet realizing that Katherine hadn't gotten out of the car, Katherine's heart thrummed as she thought about how much she wanted to pull the car away. Now. Just drive.

She didn't want a baby. And she didn't want to watch her friend slowly die. All she wanted to do was drive until New Jersey was a memory. She closed her eyes and imagined herself in a safe place. It was a verdant garden, somewhere unknown to her, flourishing under a hot sun. She was picking vegetables and tucking them into the folds of her sundress, feeling the heat on her shoulders like a lifeforce, watching her hands disappear in shadows cast from her sunhat. She could even smell the dirt and the breeze stroke across the soil. Birds wheeled suddenly into the sky, startled by a man carrying a tall glass of iced tea. A strong man who wasn't sick.

Sharon knocked on the window.

"You coming or what?"

She was eyeing Katherine distrustfully.

Katherine glanced down and realized she had actually shifted the car into reverse rather than park, and she hadn't turned off the ignition. She did those things now, nodding to Sharon. Climbing into the weak afternoon sun, she wished it was hot as it had been in her mind a few moments ago. But it couldn't be, because New Jersey wasn't her safe place. It never had been, though she'd lived here her whole life.

She followed Sharon to the Village IGA. The door wasn't locked, and the bell chimed overhead to announce their presence to a nearby rack of candy bars. Katherine tried to assess the threat level. If one had a vivid imagination, it appeared like the setting of a zombie apocalypse movie, the kind that Sharon both loved and feared with equal fervor. Except this setting wasn't spooky. There were no other shoppers, and the lights were off, but it was just a store.

Sharon let out a slow breath. "Thank God."

"You sure you don't want to check the aisles for monsters? Vampires, or zombies maybe?"

Sharon drew Ana closer. "Sorry if I'm a bit edgy. All those horror movies," she said. "I never pictured I'd be one of the survivors, you know? I always thought I'd be one of the first to go, taken out in a blaze of gory. You've got to admit this is crazy."

"Blaze of gory. You're such a nerd." Katherine noted Sharon's blotchy cheeks and the sweat beading at her hairline. She seemed worse than she had twenty minutes ago, when they'd been admiring her fancy new car. "What's crazy is you out shopping. You should be resting."

"I feel better than I did this morning," Sharon replied. She eased the baby from her stroller and laid her in the top basket of a shopping cart like she was putting her down for a nap in a mine field. Ana blinked her listless eyes at the metal bars.

"She's not looking too good." Sharon sounded worried. "The mom said she wasn't sick? That she's immune?"

"That's what she said." Katherine shrugged. "I don't know. I think she just needs to eat more."

"Let's find the baby stuff, then."

They rolled through the aisles, noting the items were all neatly arranged on their shelves. "I don't get it," Sharon said. "How is all this stuff still here? I thought everyone was dropping like flies and there were no deliveries."

"Maybe it got stocked one last time, but there was no one around to shop."

When they came to the baby supplies, Katherine stared. Like the other sections, this one was generously stocked. The sheer number of choices overwhelmed her. Not long ago she'd been a modern woman, basket over her arm, dodging the house moms pushing carts shaped like toy cars and passing over the baby and pet food aisles. This was foreign territory.

She touched a package of diapers, her fingertips lightly tapping out a question.

"Not those!" Sharon said.

Katherine's hand jerked. "What's wrong with these?"

"Too big. We need infant ones."

Katherine considered this for a moment. Abruptly, she knocked the diapers to the floor. She eyed the shelf artistically before knocking a few more packages down. "Clean up in aisle seven!"

"What'd you do *that* for?" Sharon exclaimed.

"I'm looting!" She swept an arm over one shelf, brushing more items onto the puffy pile below. "This is how one loots! It's kind of fun."

Sharon fixed her with an amused glare. "Are you losing it?"

Katherine giggled.

"When you're done raping and pillaging the grocery shelves, please try to remember that I'm dealing with enough crazy right now," Sharon huffed.

"Oh, please. We need to lighten up. The world hasn't ended yet."

Sharon placed a gentle hand on Ana's belly in the shopping cart and gave Katherine a look as if to say, *Who can joke at a time like this? We have a* BABY *now.* Katherine heard the unvoiced thought, even the gooey emphasis on the word *baaaaaaby* that Sharon would use. She rolled her eyes. "Whatever. How about I get for food for us and you shop for Ana?"

"Yes, exactly what I was thinking."

Katherine snagged her own shopping cart and began to explore her inner thief. She stocked up on baked beans, corn, anything that would last. As she explored, the sun slipped behind a cloud as if it were going to rain. The generous, arched windows spanning the walls at the front and sides, which under normal circumstances probably made the IGA feel like an outdoor farmer's market, now had the opposite effect. They effused gloomy daylight, the shelves and displays in front of the windows casting dark shadows that made her nervous.

Though it seemed strange to do so, Katherine shouted, "You still good over there, Sharon?"

Sharon was several aisles away, likely perusing baby supplies as if she were registering for a baby shower.

"I'm here," she answered. "Finally starting to get weirded out like the rest of us?"

Katherine ignored her question and asked instead, "Do you want tuna?"

"Like fresh tuna steaks or like tuna in a can?"

"Am I over here with cargo pants and a fishing rod, Sharon? Your choices are tuna in a can and tuna in a pouch."

"I don't really care for tuna," Sharon replied. "But it's good protein and you don't have to cook it, so stock up, I guess."

Katherine swept the cans of water-packed fish into the cart. She thought about leaving some for others who might come along but resisted the urge. Now was the time to put themselves first.

"Well, doesn't this just suck," she heard Sharon say a few moments later.

"What?"

"End-of-the-world sale and the snacks are almost completely wiped out."

Katherine came down to the end of her aisle and spotted Sharon wheeling toward her, checking out the remaining merchandise.

"Yeah, there's some real geniuses out there. Leave all the canned goods, baby supplies, and important stuff, but God help us if we forget to loot the fucking pork rinds," Sharon grumbled. She left her cart and disappeared down the aisle. A moment later she reemerged with a fist full of little bags. She lifted them happily. "Pork rinds! This is the last of 'em."

Katherine grinned and reached toward the display rack next to her. "I don't eat pork rinds, but look, peanuts and cashews!"

Sharon joined her. "It's weird. No one seems to have stocked up on anything obvious. I mean, we're not exactly on the ball in getting supplies. I still don't understand how there's even food on the shelves." She motioned to Katherine's cart. "Why so many batteries left? And bottled water?"

Katherine turned a slow circle, taking a quick inventory. With the exception of maybe fresh fruit and dairy products, which probably wouldn't have been delivered lately, there did seem to be a suspicious abundance of everything else. "We must be the only ones healthy enough to shop."

"The flu doesn't work *that* fast," Sharon murmured. "My mom was sick for several days. I could have gone out and gotten her some groceries any day, if she'd needed anything. It's like everyone was in denial or something. Like it would all just be here waiting for us. Nothing at all like how it was with Covid. Remember what it was like trying to get toilet paper?"

Katherine remembered floating through her apartment with a dust rag trying to clean the fear from her mind. Denial seemed likely. She said instead, "If it doesn't work so fast that there's been no time for shopping, maybe deliveries have been coming in as usual? Maybe today is the first day the store is closed. Or maybe they had lots of inventory, and up until recently, the manager was still stocking the shelves? Who knows?"

Sharon shrugged. She pointed over Katherine's shoulder and said, "There's my next stop."

Katherine glanced behind her at the white counter at the rear of the store and the cheerful blue sign above it. "Hometown Pharmacy?"

"Yeah, let's hope no one cleared that out."

"Tylenol is back that way. And if you're thinking you'll find something prescription, like Tamiflu, I'm sure it's all gone."

"I was thinking about something a little stronger."

"Like?"

"Like, I don't know. A little OxyContin?"

Katherine would have laughed if she hadn't first caught the shame on Sharon's face as she turned away from Ana. "Sharon! You want to get high?"

Sharon shrugged. "Not *high*, exactly. But if I'm going to die from the flu, I'll be damned if I'm going to suffer." She met Katherine's eyes. Katherine saw the expression Sharon usually adopted before a meeting with her boss. "Tylenol, my ass."

This time Katherine did laugh. "Fine, let your opioid flag fly."

Behind the counter, rows of unclaimed prescriptions waited in wire baskets on shelves. It was dark and window-less back there. Sharon tried the little half-door to the back and found it locked. She felt around for a slide lock and found none. "It has a key-card slot," she said with surprise.

"Climb over it," Katherine suggested.

Sharon touched Ana in the cart. "Maybe you should."

"For Christ's sake. You think I can't take care of her for five minutes?"

"I'm sick," Sharon insisted. "You climb."

With a huff, Katherine brushed past her and threw one leg and then the other over the door, her shorts riding high on her thighs as her toes reached for the tile floor. Once behind the counter, she bent to read the tiny labels. "I don't see anything good," she complained after a moment.

"Keep looking. Pain killers and antibiotics," Sharon encouraged.

"Antibiotics don't work on flu viruses." Katherine said. "You know, this is the first time I've actually felt like a thief. Canned goods are one thing, but it feels really wrong being back here."

"I won't tell."

"There's no one around *to* tell," Katherine said. She tossed a few prescription bags onto the countertop. "These might work. No Oxy yet, but a few here might be antidepressants. One feels like an inhaler. That would be good."

"There's a back room," Sharon suggested, beginning to sift through the bags herself. "And don't just think about stuff for the flu. Think long term. You could need antibiotics or penicillin or whatever at some point. Get it now before someone else does."

Katherine entered the small stockroom. She was squinting at a rack of white bags with tiny labels when she heard the front doorbell tinkle. "Shit," she hissed, and snatched whatever she could carry. She returned in a rush, her hands full of goods. Fumbling, she dropped them onto the counter.

Sharon's eyes were round and frightened. They had been caught! She was casting around for a place to hide.

Katherine waved her behind the counter. Sharon plucked Ana from the grocery basket, and Katherine prayed the baby wouldn't choose this moment to wake up. Sharon was up and over the partition like she'd just stolen the Lindberg baby, and falling to her knees, pressed next to Katherine on the floor.

They heard voices move through the store, catching tones but no words until the speakers had reached the pharmacy.

"I told you," a girl said.

They heard the rustling paper of a prescription bag.

"So what? We don't know if it's the good stuff," a teenage boy replied.

"The good stuff," the girl sneered. "Like you know anything about good stuff."

"Knock it off, you guys," an older-sounding male said. "Let's get what we need and get the fuck out of here. This place isn't right."

Katherine and Sharon's eyes met under the shadow of the countertop. "Stay here?" Katherine mouthed. Sharon nodded.

"Nothing about anything is right anymore," the girl sniffed.

They heard the rattle of pills as someone rifled through the bags.

"Whoa. Party."

"Good. Take them and let's go."

Katherine began to rise. No way she was going to let anyone make off with their stash. Sharon needed it. These people just wanted to get high.

But Sharon's fear was working against her self-preservation. She grabbed at Katherine's arm, shaking her head. "No," she whispered.

Katherine shrugged her off and stood. The trio of pilferers had already turned away, their fists full of bags. Katherine was so angry, she couldn't speak, like in a dream when she tried to scream or to hit someone. Her mouth worked soundlessly. She wanted to shout, to tell them Sharon had the flu and needed those pills. She wanted to tell them that was *their* "good stuff." What came out was less articulate. "Hey!"

The girl dropped her bags on the floor. The boy jumped like he'd been goosed. The third, a grown man, whirled around and crouched, ready for a fight.

Katherine held her hands up stick-'em-up style. "Whoa. It's OK." She focused on the man. "We don't want trouble."

His stance relaxed, but Katherine still felt danger. He had dark hair and dark eyes, his body tall and solid. Faded ink spread up the side of his neck, probably more hidden on his arms by dark swaths of hair. But it wasn't his appearance that felt dangerous. It was his expression. He measured her up like an obstacle, like she was a wall to break.

"My friend is sick and those are ours," Katherine said. She sounded calm, surprising herself, because along with her unease, the anger was still there, throbbing below the surface in her throat and eyeballs. She pulled Sharon to her feet. Sharon had Ana in a death grip. "We're not trying to get stoned. She has the flu. We need those."

All three of the newcomers pulled away, putting a few more feet between them. The girl, long blonde hair tangled in the straps of her backpack, edged toward the boy. The teenage boy, matching hair curled around large ears, tugged the mask under his chin up and over his nose. His fingers went back to the strap of his backpack, bloodless where he clutched it.

"You don't need them," the man said. "If she's sick, nothing helps. She's dead."

"Lee," the girl gasped behind him. "Don't say that." She crossed herself, a prayer, a shield from disease.

"I'm not dead yet, Mister. I'll take every cocktail of pills I can get first." Sharon had found her voice, and Katherine heard a flicker of her old spirit.

The man just shrugged and turned away. The girl trailed after him. "Lee," she entreated, tugging at his shirt. "We don't have to take all of it, do we?"

Lee kept walking. The girl turned and scooped up the bags she had dropped on the floor. She tossed them onto the counter. "At least take these."

The younger male had stayed behind, hovering near a rack of thermometers like a stray dog trying to determine if it was safe to approach. "You really sick?" he whispered to Sharon.

Sharon leaned forward. "Do I look it?"

At the sight of her red, watery eyes, his own eyes fell. "Here, take these too," he said to her chin. He put his bags back.

"Thank you," Sharon breathed. "I swear, I need them."

"Wait," Katherine said as they walked away. Eying their dirty packs and walking shoes, she got the feeling they weren't local, just out for a day of shopping but transient. Searching. Lost. "I don't want to sound like the neighborhood watch here, but are you kids safe? Do you know that guy?"

"Lee?" the boy said. "He's our mom's boyfriend."

"*Was* our mom's boyfriend," the girl said.

The boy lowered his eyes, and Katherine understood that their mom wasn't waiting for them at home.

"And we're not little kids," she added. "I'm fifteen and he's seventeen."

"If you need help, we have a house."

Katherine glanced at Sharon. Was she inviting them to, what? Join up?

"We're fine," the boy said to them. And to the girl, "We're fine."

But she hesitated, tempted. She eyed the baby. "Ricky."

One word, but the way she said it stopped him in his tracks again. "No, Mack. They're sick."

"Just me," Sharon insisted. "Katherine seems fine, and the baby is too, even though both of her parents were sick. As far as we know, all the babies have died, but Ana, she's OK. That means something. My whole upstairs apartment is empty if you need a safe place to stay. I usually rent it out, but no one's there. We can help you. Share supplies."

When the kids wavered, she continued, "Sure I'm sick, but at this point, how many people do you think you're going to find who aren't? We can mask. Be safe. It's a big house. If your mom got it but you didn't, you're probably in the clear anyway." Sharon turned to Katherine as if to ask for support in convincing them.

Katherine wanted none of it, but she wouldn't challenge her in front of the others. She was a houseguest herself and knew this wasn't up to her, but no way she'd be offering anyone a place to stay if it were. Why was this so important to Sharon? Sure, there was benefit to the kids to come with them, but what was the upside for Sharon, Ana? For her?

"Safety in numbers. We can take care of each other..." Sharon was saying when the older man came stomping back. He held two red handbaskets containing dry goods and the remaining pharmacy bags.

"What the hell? Are we swapping recipes here?" He spotted the bags on the counter. "What's this?"

"We're leaving them, Lee," said the girl.

"Mackenzie," Ricky hissed.

"The fuck we are," Lee said.

The strangers stared at each other for a long, tense moment. Katherine felt the unspoken battle being waged among them—dissention among the ranks, reassertion of authority, feminine foot-stomping, and perhaps a slight shift of power. She hoped it was all moving toward a consensus that they should leave the pills and go it alone but sensed it wasn't.

"They have a place to stay," Mackenzie said. She hitched her backpack higher on her shoulder. "We're going with them. We'll share the medicine. Share food." The dissention.

"No. We're not," Lee said. "We already know they're sick." The assertion of power.

"My mom didn't leave me with you so you could boss me around. She wanted you to take care of me. What if something happens to you, huh? What if it just takes awhile and you get sick too? Ever think of that? The more of us together, the better." The feminine foot-stomping.

Ricky shifted in his chucks. He seemed intimidated by Lee but was throwing his loyalty in with Mackenzie. *Mack.*

"They *are* the first live people we've seen in a week, man." And there it was. The shift of power.

Lee pointed a finger at each of them in turn. "A dead woman, a probably dying woman, and a baby. More people for me to take care of, that's what this is."

Katherine bristled. This guy had no idea what she'd been through today, without any help from him. And Sharon, she'd lugged a dead body to another house! She was strong in every way that counted. "It's getting late," she said. "I don't know if joining up is the best idea either, to be honest. We don't want anyone else to get sick." She ignored Sharon's wounded expression. "But if you're coming with us, we'd better get going. Ana needs to be fed and changed, Sharon should be in bed, and I don't want to be roaming around after dark. It's creepy enough around here as it is." She climbed over the half-door and held Ana while Sharon did the same.

"We're coming," Mackenzie said. She walked to Lee and eased one of the baskets from his hand, holding his gaze.

"Whatever," he said. The word was surrender, though his tone said otherwise. "We have to sleep somewhere tonight. But tomorrow, we keep with the plan."

"The plan was to find people," Ricky mumbled.

CHAPTER EIGHT

LOUIE STOOD AT THE DARK bay window, peering through the glass into his backyard. He was not hunched to the side of the window, peeking around the swag of his mother's frilly curtains. He wasn't on his knees, spying over the window molding. But he felt like he was peeping all the same.

Right on time, he thought, realizing his voice was sarcastic even in his own mind. He watched a figure tiptoe across the yard in the moonlight to a tent opposite her own. Adra was sleeping with Chris. She usually waited in her tent for an hour or so after her boys switched off the lamplight in their tent. Her own lamp would switch off next, and five minutes later, Louie would see her creep to Chris's tent, pawing at the nylon door like a cat.

No sound came from the tent, and for this Louie was grateful. Watching their shadows twist was bad enough, but hearing sounds of ecstasy, and wondering if William and Jayden could hear them too, would have been worse.

The town had gotten smaller, a lot smaller, but his sex drive hadn't diminished. Here Adra was doing it with a seventh of the eligible male population in Atlanta (Grider was too old and didn't count in his book)—and yet Louie still had the odds stacked against him. He reminded himself that he had never been considered eligible by any of the women he knew before and recalculated the size of the male population to six. A deadly flu outbreak didn't seem to have changed the natural order. He was still a loser.

Louie stiffened. He was no longer alone.

Devlin came in behind him, and now Louie felt spied on.

"Need something, Devlin?"

The man opened the fridge and banished the shadows. He helped himself to a bottle of water and shut the door, bringing back the darkness. "Air conditioning," he said flatly.

Louie watched Devlin drink. "You know it was dragging my generators. If I hadn't turned it off days ago, we'd be out in this heat collecting fuel."

"Fucking heat," Devlin grunted. He scraped a chair back and tossed himself into it. "I thought the rain would have cooled things off. Now it's just muggy. I can't sleep in this shit. Everything feels wet."

Devlin's cursing had grown exponentially with the heat wave. Somehow, this made Louie feel a little better. Devlin could try to take control of Louie's house all he wanted, but when it came down to it, he was just another man sweating his balls off.

"I can't believe the crickets either," the cop continued. "It's like everything that eats crickets died. If I weren't afraid I'd cook myself in my sleep, I'd shut the window."

Grider shuffled into the kitchen. He wore only boxer shorts and a ball cap. "Tupperware party?" he asked. He moved straight to the fridge for a bottle of water. Louie would rather be alone than watch how easily these men helped themselves to his life, but he liked Grider well enough. He was an easygoing guy, sort of funny, a loyal type like Clark the dog, wagging his tail at everyone. And Grider was a follower, which was just fine. Louie had always been a follower too, though he didn't want to be one anymore. Now more than ever, Louie wanted to be the hero.

Grider made a sound like he'd dropped something heavy when he lowered onto the chair next to Devlin. He flipped his hat onto the table. A shock of sweaty hair shot from his thinning scalp. "Any reason why we're sitting here in the dark?" he asked.

Louie joined them at the table. "It's the middle of the night, and it costs too much to turn on the lights."

Already the idea of money had shifted in their minds. They knew he meant it cost too much gas or propane. Too much human fuel expended to gather it.

"We don't need lights to hear each other complain," Devlin said. "I take it you can't sleep either?"

"It's hot as Hades in that room," Grider replied.

"That was my mother's room," Louie said. "She always complained about that too. The windows face west. The sun sets into it."

"Better than sleeping out in a tent. Nothing worse than waking up in a closed tent in the morning, with that sun shining straight on top of you, trapping you in the heat," Devlin said.

Louie watched the two men tap their water bottles together. A week ago, the adults had flipped for sleeping spots. Devlin and Grider had won bedrooms. The others drove to the Walmart in Algonac for tents, tarps, and sleeping pads. The tarps had turned out to be prophetic. The rain had barely stopped since, though it had done nothing to relieve the heat. If anything, the rain seemed to turn into steam when it met the ground, making moist air that made Louie feel like he was drowning. The thick smell of wet dog in the air was almost unbearable.

"The hottest summer on record. It's gotta be. What are the chances of that, with all of this going on?" Grider grumped. Louie had noticed that he rarely referred to the flu as the flu. "All of this" was as close as he came to talking about the pandemic. Devlin, in contrast, seemed to want to talk about it all the time.

"This is bullshit, Louie," Devlin said. "We've got to turn the air on, just for a little bit."

Louie, who actually didn't mind gathering fuel, even in the hot sun, said, "It's too hot to get more fuel. The last thing we need is someone with heat stroke. No hospitals, no doctors…"

"I know," Devlin interrupted. "But we need sleep too."

"We need to be smart about this."

"Damn it!" Devlin crunched his empty water bottle in his hand and flung it at the garbage. It missed by a wide margin, and Louie had to hide his smile. Devlin was fun to rile. He hated that Louie had control. Devlin could make all the decisions he wanted about what he and the others would do during the day, what they would salvage, how they would prepare for moving on. But it was Louie's house and Louie's generators. They both knew it.

"You're killing me, Louie," Devlin said. There wasn't much heat left in his voice. It had gone the way of the water bottle.

You're killing me, Louie. The words echoed in his mind after Devlin and Grider had gone back to their beds. Devlin had it wrong. Louie was killing Louie. Every night he scratched his itch. Sometimes he went into the bathroom and flicked open a wrist. Other times he went back to the idea list, like the night he'd sat with a plastic shopping bag over his head there in the kitchen. Anyone could come in and discover him, which would be a nice little experiment, because so far he hadn't actually died in front of anyone. What would they see the moment he died? Would he vanish? Or would they find him dead and then alive again in the morning? He wondered if they would value his invincibility or if they would be afraid.

In Louie's mind, this was one of several puzzles he needed to solve. The first and most obvious had to do with the sink full of suds and dishes. Why was there something different there every time now? The second, and certainly the one on everyone else's minds, was how the flu had killed so fast.

Given that it needed a host to survive, the flu was mighty cavalier. When the group returned from the Walmart trip, they'd reported no survivors. They didn't see a single car. In just one week, it was like they were the only ones left. Was it a coincidence that everyone was dying the summer Louie had become immortal?

One final mystery plagued him. What was his connection to this woman, Katherine? Why was he still dreaming about her, always here at his home, on the porch, in the garden, drifting through his subconscious like a memory? If it meant she was still alive, should he stop trying to kill himself? Was he meant to find her?

But he couldn't stop. Not only did he crave more clues, but destroying himself by night always brought Louie a measure of relief in the morning. He felt more focused after he'd *suicided*, the term he'd come to use in conversation with himself. As in, *I think I need to* suicide *tonight*, or, *I wonder if anyone will find me if I* suicide *myself on the couch. Maybe I should just walk into the bedroom and* suicide *myself right in Devlin's face.*

Suicide was no longer a noun for Louie. It was a verb. A therapeutic one. It made him think of those cutters on the talk shows. Wasn't that what they did? They cut themselves and the pain released their sadness, or anxiety, or whatever bad thing they were feeling? He imagined they felt the same surge of pleasure he did, like an orgasm of relief, except maybe they also felt fear about what would come next, and he didn't have that anymore.

A teenage girl, well, she might worry about not waking up in the morning if she cut a little too deep. Or worry that if she did wake up, she'd be photoshopping scars off her skin on Instagram for the rest of her life. But Louie didn't have scars. Suiciding was just like going to sleep, the deaths themselves the fastest-acting sleeping pill ever. He would dream good dreams, and then he'd find himself at that sink, floating in happiness like bubbles on the water. Pure and light, untouched, and fully rested.

And, bonus, he always did it first thing after lights out, so *he* never slept in the stifling heat. Screw Devlin and his sweaty balls.

CHAPTER NINE

"You're not going over there to poke at a dead body," Katherine said. She was sitting on the couch with a book, her feet curled under her, reading Mackenzie's stony face. If she hadn't happened to ask where Mack and Ricky were going, the teens would be next door by now, seeing things they didn't need to see.

"You can't tell me what to do. You're not my mother."

Oh, how Katherine had learned to hate that phrase. She knew the teenager missed her mom, and the key word there was teenager—didn't they rebel over everything?—but if she heard *you're not my mother* one more time…

"And you're not my daughter, Mack," Katherine said. "So I don't have to treat you differently than anyone else."

Mack sniffed. "I hate this! Every time I have an idea, a good idea, I get totally shot down. If it's not *him* telling me no," she waved a hand toward Lee, who was slouched in his recliner, "it's you! The only person who goes along with anything is Ricky, and that's just 'cause he's bored."

Ricky moved from the doorway and flounced onto the loveseat. "So bored," he moaned. "Obviously! You know you're bored when a dead body sounds more interesting than hanging out with the live ones here." He glanced at Lee.

"Read a book, Ricky," Katherine said, waggling her paperback at him. "And it's morbid and inconsiderate of Sharon's feelings to go over there," she admonished Mackenzie. "Why would normal, nice kids even want to see that?"

Ricky had flung his arm over his eyes. "Who said we were normal?"

Mack made a face at him. "Not helping, Ricky. Seriously, Katherine, I just need to check for two seconds! Not to gawk at her. Just observe, like, scientifically. If I were a scientist..."

"Oh, wait, you're a scientist now?" Ricky interjected, uncovering his eyes to mock his sister with fake surprise. "Didn't know we were going over there to do some *sciencing*, I would have brought my microscope. I can be a scientist too!"

Mack snatched Katherine's paperback and flung it at her brother. He deflected it easily, laughing. "Fine, I'm not a scientist, Jerkface," she said to him. "And since we agree you're not my mother," she added to Katherine, "what are you going to do about it if we go over there?" She marched over to the doorway. "Besides, Sharon won't even know if no one tells her!"

Katherine was moving to stand when Lee rose from his chair. "Sit your ass down, Mack," he said. It was bad news when Lee's voice was quiet. Ricky stopped smiling.

"You're taking her side?" Mackenzie looked hurt. "Really?"

Lee and Mack's eyes met. "After everything, Lee?" Mack asked after a pregnant pause.

Lee butted heads with Katherine constantly, mostly to entertain himself. It seemed they'd all figured out in the last week that Katherine valued control, and she was easy to throw off balance. All she wanted was to keep things as normal as possible, and Lee delighted in keeping her on edge by making things as abnormal as he could. Why was he suddenly agreeing with her? Katherine wondered. It was enough to make her question her own judgment.

"We don't know what grossness is lurking over there. For all we know, you can still get sick. You are not going, not on some stupid ass theory you got from a dream," Lee said.

"It's not a stupid ass theory," Mackenzie sniffed. "It makes sense!"

"What theory is this? And keep your voice down, Mack," Katherine interjected. "Ana…"

Sadness flicked over Mack's face. They all knew there was something wrong with Ana.

"Will you actually listen to my theory, Katherine? For real? Not like Lee, who barely listened before he laughed in my face?"

Katherine shifted to make room on the couch, resigned. "If it will help me understand why you're so hell bent on going over there, of course. Explain."

Mack joined her, pulling a pillow onto her lap like a buffer. "I had a dream that bees were filling up my bedroom. Not this bedroom, *my* bedroom. At home. I don't know how I knew, but I just knew that if one of them stung me, I was dead. I couldn't move or one was going to sting me."

"We've heard all this," Lee sighed. He had flopped back into his recliner. Making a stand had sapped his energies for the moment.

Ricky retrieved Katherine's book from the floor and began to thumb through it, ignoring them. He must have heard the theory already too.

"Katherine hasn't heard it," Mack snapped, turning to her. "When I woke up, there was a bee outside my window. It's the first bee I've seen in weeks. You haven't seen any, have you?"

"No, but I haven't been looking for any either. Why would I be looking for bees?" Katherine asked.

"Forget that for now. So, my dream got me thinking. I had a dream about bees in our backyard too, in the garden, a few weeks before my mom died. And then in real life, my mom was stung by a bee in the garden just before she got sick! It's like, all connected!"

The word garden snagged Katherine's focus for a moment. Was Mack having dreams like hers? Ones that feel too real to be dreams, that felt strangely prophetic?

Katherine dreamed about the garden so often now that it felt very personal to her. Her private refuge, the smells of earth and growing things far removed from the dark brownstone and the growing odor of decay infusing the neighborhood. When she closed her eyes at night, she escaped to that place.

The thought that Mack might have dreams of the garden too suddenly struck a chord in her that felt a lot like jealousy. And there was the house too, with that big wide porch…

"Well?" Mack asked.

Katherine snapped to, realizing she'd woolgathered so long that Mack had fallen silent. "Hon, I think you're in mourning. So it makes sense that you'd be having dreams about your mom. It doesn't mean that there's a bee conspiracy or that a bee killed her. Just coincidence."

Tears spilled from Mackenzie's eyes, and she swiped at them with the heels of her hands. Katherine had noticed that Mack hated to show any weakness. She didn't want Katherine coddling her. Katherine didn't consider herself a coddler, but Mack didn't know that.

"I just have this feeling. Bees have been disappearing for some time. Ricky was telling me about it a while back, before all this started. He read about it online. Something about the world ending after the bees were gone."

"In four years," Ricky said from behind the paperback. "Einstein predicted it."

"Ricky probably told you about bees disappearing right around the time you dreamed about them in your backyard," Katherine suggested.

Mack continued, undeterred. "What if they're like, fighting back or teaming up with the virus? You know, for their survival? Stinging people and somehow making them vulnerable to the virus. Or maybe even spreading the virus! I mean, everyone knows we're destroying the Earth." Katherine started to interject, but Mack plunged on. "There are two dead bodies next door, maybe with some answers. All I want to do is see if I can find a bee sting mark or signs of swelling or something."

"You'll find plenty of swelling, I bet. Bloated, dead swelling." This from Lee in his typical cutting fashion. Everything he said rubbed Katherine raw. Sharon's *mother* was over there. He was sitting here scratching himself in *her* chair.

Mack held her ground. "I'm not asking anyone else to go with me, Lee. I just want to go check things out."

"Have you talked to Sharon about this?" Katherine asked.

"She'll just say no."

"No, I mean, did you ask her if she's been stung by a bee?"

"I…no," Mack faltered. "I mean, I didn't want to say anything about anything. I really don't even want her to know if I go over there. It can't help her."

On that Katherine agreed. Nothing could help Sharon. A cocktail of pills relieved her symptoms a bit, but she was getting worse each day. She had lasted longer than her mother, but that didn't mean anything. Sharon's mother had been old. Sharon was young and vital. At least, she had been.

"I'd rather you upset Sharon a little by asking her a simple question about a bee sting than risk upsetting her a lot, if she finds out you examined her mother's body," Katherine said. "Come on then. Let's go ask her."

Katherine rose and Mack followed, though with reluctance. "I…"

"What?"

"What if it's still catching?"

Behind them, Lee chuckled. "You're still afraid of getting sick from her, but you'll go play with a diseased body, eh?"

"Well, we don't know if it's still, like, *active* in a dead body. But it's definitely active up there," Mackenzie said, pointing to the ceiling.

Sharon had been quarantining herself on the second floor since Lee and the kids joined them. That way, no one had to wear masks, and Sharon didn't feel well enough to leave her bedroom anyway. When Ana grew sicker, she joined Sharon in isolation, though none of them were certain if the flu was the cause of her distress. The baby didn't have the "classic" symptoms, yet she was taking only an ounce or two of formula. She rarely cried. Her eyes were dull. She hadn't perked up at all since coming to the brownstone.

"None of us have gotten sick so far from Sharon," Katherine said. She frowned at Lee, knowing even as she did so that he would probably ignore her. She didn't like it when he said things about diseased bodies. It felt disrespectful even out of Sharon's earshot. "Though I doubt staying away from her is going to help in any case. If it's really the flu, the germs were all over everything before we even got here. If we could get sick, I think we'd be sick by now. Just wear your mask and you'll be fine."

"Like a scientist!" Ricky said as they left the room.

Katherine and Mack went to the kitchen. "Let's get some dinner for her and take it up together, alright? It's going to get dark soon."

Mack nodded and moved to the pantry. After a moment of peering at the shelves, she said, "Crackers and something from a can again?"

Katherine was shuffling through a drawer for the can opener. "That's about all we've got to work with now." She found it. "Why the hell aren't we just keeping this out? I keep leaving it by the sink and someone keeps moving it!"

It was candles and lanterns by night and can openers and cold food by day. The convenience snacks were already being rationed. The end of the world gave everyone the munchies, and they'd burned through half their stash before good sense hit them. An unopened bag of chips stayed good much longer than the fresh fruit and vegetables.

Even with rationing, food kept disappearing. Katherine glanced at the trash basket, filled with open cans. How many more had they gone through since just yesterday? She had no idea teenagers ate so much.

Mackenzie came to the counter, her mouth full of crackers from the box under her arm. In the other hand she held a flat can of tuna. "This OK?"

"I think there are some little packets of mayo and relish in there. And we can add some carrots and celery too. Let's try to do it up nice for her."

Mackenzie gave her a wobbly smile. "This sucks, doesn't it?" The angry teenager from before was gone, but Katherine knew this girl well too. This version was emotional and edgy, ready to cry whenever she felt unsure. Shaky whenever it struck her how vastly their lives had changed. Katherine understood. None of them had been prepared.

Katherine took the can from her. "It could be worse." Sharon wasn't eating much these days. She considered splitting the can, leaving part of it outside on a dish for Sharon's cats, even though the last plate had remained untouched. It's what Sharon would want, to share her portion.

"How?" Mack asked, digging into the cracker box.

Katherine sighed. "I don't know. I just get the feeling it could be much worse."

"We could get swarmed by bees." Mack said, shuddering delicately.

"There's that."

"We could have no food and starve to death," Mack said around the crackers she was chewing.

"Yep."

"We could be alone," Mack said.

"Or sick and alone," Katherine rejoined.

"Is this making you feel any better?" Mackenzie asked.

"No, you?" Katherine snagged the box of crackers from her.

Mack frowned at the box. "No."

"Worst-case scenarios are usually my forte. I'm always thinking worst-case scenario. It gets me through the tough times," Katherine confessed. She set the crackers out of Mack's reach and turned to open the tuna. "But these days, I don't know. Thinking about how much worse things could get just makes it…"

"Scarier."

"I was going to say depressing."

Mackenzie went back to the pantry and disappeared inside. She said something Katherine couldn't hear.

"What was that?" she asked when the girl returned.

Mack tossed a few packets of mayo on the countertop. "No relish."

"Oh, well." Katherine reached for a bowl from the shelf above her. She'd give Sharon the whole can. The cats would have to fend for themselves if they were still out there fending.

"But that's not what I said. I asked why God is doing this to us."

Katherine stopped in mid-motion. "I don't believe in God."

"Oh," Mack said, and turned away.

When the food was ready, Katherine followed Mackenzie up the staircase with a dinner tray.

Mackenzie carried a lantern. It was unlit for now but would be necessary in another half hour. Twice Mack skimmed her moist palm against her baggy shorts, the same ones she'd been wearing all week, refusing to go with Katherine to scavenge for new clothes. The action brought Katherine up short.

"You don't have to be nervous. You're going to see Sharon, not the Wizard of Oz."

Mack paused to glance back. "We don't know for sure that we can't get sick, though, do we? We thought Ana couldn't get sick, but she did. It could just take longer for some."

Katherine motioned for Mackenzie to keep moving. "There's nothing we can do about it now. Sharon and her mother have been in every room of this place. And besides, we don't know what kind of sick Ana is."

They reached the top of the stairs, and Mackenzie hesitated again. "What now?" Katherine asked. She felt like she was constantly reassuring everyone else. It would be nice to be soothed for once.

"Did you really mean that before? About not believing in God?"

Mack plucked at the oversize flowery blouse she had taken from Sharon's closet. Her golden hair was long and pretty even in the heat, her big eyes wide and white in the partial shadows. For the first time, Katherine realized how young Mackenzie really was. For all her assertiveness, her loud opinions on everything from sleeping arrangements to bathroom use, she was only a scared teenager.

"I meant it, but I'm sorry if that bothers you. I won't say it again."

"It makes me afraid for you."

"Don't be," Katherine said. "There's enough to worry about these days."

She began to move down the hall toward Sharon's room, but Mack stayed put. "What's more important than worrying about our souls? I worry about my soul all the time. Lately, I worry about it a lot more, actually…"

"I don't believe in all of that. I respect that you do, but…a nice girl like you doesn't need to be worrying about her soul anyway. You shouldn't believe you're bad when you're not."

"You don't have to believe."

"I know, I know. God believes for us."

Mackenzie looked wounded. Katherine hadn't meant to sound sarcastic, but it was hard not to. Was this really happening? End of the world, only a few people left on the entire eastern seaboard, and she was living with Little Miss Jerry Falwell.

That probably wasn't fair. Mackenzie meant well, but Katherine thought it best to shut the door on this conversation for good. If not, she'd be sharing a bathroom with a door-to-door Bible salesman for the rest of her life.

"I'm sorry. I don't mean to be glib. I just don't believe in what you believe in."

"Can I pray for you? I won't try to change your mind, I promise. But my mom…she would have wanted me to witness to you, and if I couldn't do that, to pray that God will keep you safe."

Katherine squeezed her eyes shut, as if doing so would seal her lips too. A dozen cynical retorts sprang to mind, but she knew she couldn't say them aloud. Maybe if Mack hadn't mentioned her mother… Instead, she held the tray in a white-knuckle grip and said evenly, "I appreciate that you want to pray for me, Mack. Thank you."

She pulled up her facemask and pushed inside Sharon's bedroom, half-hoping the teenager wouldn't follow. Mack did follow, though, taking a mask from her pocket and sliding it into place. Katherine didn't think there was a point to wearing one for her own health, but whenever Sharon called, she put it on just in case. She didn't want to infect the rest of the household. Mack wore one because if Sharon hadn't been stung by a bee, there were greater, unseen things to fear.

Katherine had been Sharon's sole caregiver this past week, and she was used to seeing her friend huddled in the big four-poster bed, burning from fever with the quilt wrinkled at her feet. Tonight Sharon wasn't where Katherine expected. She was sitting in an overstuffed chair, feet on an ottoman, Ana in the stroller next to her. Sharon moved it back and forth with her foot as she stared straight ahead, unblinking.

"Hey, girl. Are you feeling better?" Katherine asked. She set the tray on the small round table in front of her friend. Sharon continued to watch the gathering darkness. "The same," she said. "I was thinking, Katherine, when I die, will you take me next door and lay me with my mother? She's on the bed in the guest room. I pulled some begonias from Mrs. Radcliff's and laid them in her hands. You could do the same for me."

It had been like this for the last two days. Sharon was obsessed with death. Understandable, given that she was dying and knew it, but Katherine still resented it. Life as Katherine knew it was over, even if she didn't get sick. She was trying to mourn her own losses, and here was Sharon saying things like, "Will you lay me with my mother with begonias in my hands?"

It was in that moment that Katherine realized she needed to leave. When Sharon died, she could go. Mackenzie and Ricky would survive with Lee. She realized that now. The insertion of Katherine and Sharon in their lives had been a momentary distraction. They would carry on as if they had never met. Mack would still be stubborn and opinionated, driven to find answers and meaning in everything. Ricky, thoughtful and loyal, would ground his sister to reality, encourage her when needed, and tease her when she was lowest. Lee, cynical and strong, would complain even as he defended them with his life.

Ana, well, the jury was still out there, but she suspected when Sharon went, Ana would follow. The two seemed tied by a thread Katherine couldn't see or understand. Days when Sharon seemed improved, Ana gurgled and kicked, making faces at things Katherine couldn't see. When Sharon's cough made it sound like she only had hours left on this Earth, Ana lay in a thrall, immune to tenderness.

"Whatever flowers you want," Katherine assured Sharon, arranging the dishes. She had a role to play too, hers a duty to keep Sharon calm. "But let's not go there now. I've got dinner here for you, and Mackenzie wants to talk with you."

Sharon dragged her eyes from the window. Her lip curled at the warm tuna salad, but she tried to smile. "Tuna, huh?"

"Hey, you're the one who told me to put it in the basket, remember?"

"Looks good," Sharon said. At least she still made the effort to humor them. "How have you been, Mackenzie?"

Mack hovered near the doorway. "Sorry I haven't been up. I didn't want to bother you."

"Come on in. I won't bite."

Mack eased into the room. "Not exactly what I'm afraid of," she admitted.

"I understand. Believe me, if I was young like you, I wouldn't take any chances."

Somehow Sharon's understanding of Mack's discomfort relieved the tension. Mack slid into the chair opposite her. "I like your room," she offered. It was all pastels and heavy wood furniture, awful in Katherine's opinion, but Sharon accepted the compliment with far greater pleasure than a sick woman should take in anything.

"I used to hate it. It reminded me of old people. Now I find it kind of comforting, like my aunt is still here. Some of the things, like that lamp there, were my grandmother's too. It's nice to be surrounded by family."

Mack twisted her hands on her lap, and Sharon seemed to realize what she had said. "I'm sorry, kiddo. I know you can't be with your mom's things. I'm sure you miss your house, your bedroom."

Mack nodded.

"Well, we're your family now," Sharon said. "When I'm gone, this will all be yours."

"Really?" Mack breathed.

"What did you expect?" Sharon asked. "When I go you'd have to leave?"

Mackenzie glanced at Katherine. "I kind of figured since it was your house and you invited us, when you, *you know*, that we'd be moving on."

Sharon's head scarf was askew. Her lips and eyes were fevered, puffy with heat and pain. A light nightgown, just about the only thing she could tolerate on her fevered body today, clung to her middle, where sweat bled through. She picked it away from her skin absently. "I can see how you would think that," she said. "But if you want to stay, stay. I imagine Katherine will be leaving soon enough."

This surprised Katherine. She'd been bent over the table, lumping tuna onto crackers and only half listening. "What?"

"I think disease is making me kind of psychic," Sharon said. "I can just see how it's all going to shake out."

"You're closest to God right now," Mackenzie blurted.

Sharon nodded, seemingly reassured by this explanation.

But it terrified Katherine. "Stop talking like this, Sharon. You're not psychic, and you should be thinking about getting well, not expecting the worst."

Mack resumed wringing her hands, perhaps worrying for Sharon, perhaps worrying that she might have started an argument.

"I've had more than a week to think about dying," Sharon said. "I'm not scared anymore, and I'm not kidding. I feel like things are really coming into focus. I realize that you only came here for me, Katherine. You might have thought that you came because you didn't want to be alone. But the truth is, you're better alone, and you would have been just fine. You've always been like that. The tough cookie in the office who gets everything done twice as fast going at it solo."

Katherine sat on the bed, the plate slick in her hands. The room was hot, as if Sharon's body alone heated it like a woodstove. The way Sharon was talking made her uncomfortable too—so calm and, in a strange way, enlightened. This wasn't her Sharon. Her cursing, cynical Sharon. The Sharon she knew was a fighter. "I'm not leaving," Katherine muttered, even though she'd thought about leaving a moment ago.

"You will," Sharon insisted. "Which is fine. I can see how you'd want to move on. Though I do worry about Ana…" her voice trailed off, not so much a weakness of her body as perhaps a signal that she didn't like her train of thought. Sweat had begun to dot her fuzzy hairline and her upper lip, but she continued. "I'm not sure what you're going to do about her yet." She lifted her hand to the stroller, again nudging it into a gentle rock.

"We'll take care of her," Mackenzie said. "You shouldn't worry about anything."

Katherine could see that Mack liked Sharon. Even when she was in this maudlin mood, Mack was in awe of her. Thinking of Mack and her evangelizing before, Katherine wondered what Mack would say if she knew Sharon was a lesbian.

Sharon's glassy eyes fixed on the girl. "I'm sorry, sweetie. I don't mean to freak you out."

Mack shrugged. "S'OK."

Sharon's foot stilled on the stroller. She didn't have the energy to continue.

"You need to eat," Katherine insisted. "You need to keep your energy up." She stood and put a garnished cracker in Sharon's hand. "Go ahead."

"My mom always said to starve a fever," Sharon replied. "I'm really not hungry anymore."

"Eat it anyway," Katherine said. "Wives' tales aside, Mack made the effort to make it." Katherine gave Mack an encouraging nod. "Mack wants to talk to you about something too, remember?"

"Sorry, Mack. I'd forgotten. Here I am rambling on." Sharon nibbled at the cracker and fixed her swollen gaze on the girl, showing interest for the first time in something besides death and its consequences.

Mack was about to start when Sharon coughed around the cracker crumbs, spraying them on her chest. When she started to wheeze, Mack said softly, "Never mind. I just wanted to say hi."

CHAPTER TEN

OUIE WAS JUST STARTING TO think the day
was going alright when he realized everyone was
totally fucked. The heat had finally broken a bit,
they'd spent the day successfully gathering (now he didn't
have to listen to Devlin's incessant bitching about that for
a few days), and he'd just settled down for a nice dinner of
Frosted Flakes and powdered milk. The diabetic dinner of
champions.

Then Adra's two boys came in. "We're hungry," they
complained. Of course they were hungry! For kids who
didn't do much but sit around and grow taller, William and
Jayden were always hungry. Louie's own mother would have
told him to hush up and just be hungry for a bit if he'd come
in her kitchen asking about dinner when he'd only just had
lunch. *Feeling hungry never hurt no one, Louie.*

The boys slumped down at the table on either side of
Louie, as if they were the ones who had been out "shopping"
all day. Instead, they'd been sleeping on the couch when
he and the others left and were still there when the adults
returned.

Like everyone else, the boys had overcome their shyness. They acted like Louie's house was theirs and rarely asked for permission to touch his things.

"Is there any left?" Jayden asked. He reached for the open cereal box.

Louie grunted around his spoon but said nothing. Jayden peered inside, shuffled the contents, and muttered, "Thanks for leaving some."

The boy set the box down and sneezed. And then sneezed again. Three more times.

Louie's eyes jerked from his floating flakes to the boy. Red eyes, a little moisture beading on his brow, and there— another sneeze! His attention flicked to William, who wasn't sneezing but resembled his brother, like he'd gone ten rounds with Tyson. He was slouching on the table and staring at the cartoons on the back of the cereal box with disinterest.

Louie's chair scraped against the floor. In his haste to rise, it tipped over and landed with a loud crack. "Jesus Christ!" he exclaimed. "When were you going to tell someone?"

Jayden looked defiant. William ignored him.

"Answer, for Christ's sake!"

Devlin came in from the living room, his hand floating to his hip as if his gun were still holstered there. It wasn't. "What'd they do now, Louie?" he asked, righting the chair.

Devlin's calm demeanor only enraged Louie more. "Look at them!" He waved a finger in the air between the two kids. Devlin's eyes bounced from one boy to the other.

Realization was dawning in his eyes as Louie barked out "Adra!"

Devlin dropped onto a kitchen chair like a boxer on his stool. As if Tyson had done him in too. All the air had been punched out of him.

"Adra!" Louie was stomping through the house now, slamming doors open. Adra had started taking afternoon naps in Devlin's or Grider's rooms.

Grider came in from the back porch looking harassed. "What the hell's gotten into him?"

Devlin breathed into his hands. "They're sick."

Grider floundered, gurgling up a sound that could have been question or denial.

Louie strode back in the kitchen. It was bad enough he'd let these strangers into his house. *His* house. But they'd brought their germs with them too. Just the thought of the invisible disease crawling across his kitchen table, over that cereal box where the boy had pinched it between his fingers, oozing into every fiber of the damn house, made disgust bubble in his gut. His haven, the only place in the world that was his, and it was infected. At that moment it didn't matter that he couldn't get sick and die. All that mattered was that he'd been betrayed.

He grabbed Jayden by his shirt and swung him toward the door. The boy, bewildered, tripped over his sneakers. Devlin and Grider sprang at him at once. "Louie, no!"

The three men and boy were grappling in the middle of the kitchen when Chris shoved through the back door with Adra behind him. She started screeching, and Chris plunged into the fray like it was a brawl at a barn party. Asking no questions and eager to join in, he went behind Louie, slung a thick arm around his throat, and jerked hard, dislodging him from the others. He swung him around, and Louie had to catch the wall to keep from falling.

Normally he would have been too insecure to fight, but his fury was still on him, and he charged at Chris with his fists up. Chris, the opposite of Louie and exactly the kind of guy who would fight, cracked him in the nose, and he went down.

William was now sobbing into the box of cereal, and Adra rushed to him, Jayden in her wake. "What did he do to you?" she cried. "What did you do to them?" she flung at Louie.

Louie staggered to his feet and swayed against the wall, pressing the heel of his hand to his burning nose. He examined his palm and saw red snot smeared on it. His pulse throbbed behind his eyes, and for a split second, he thought maybe he would have a stroke, at long last, and that would be it. "They're sick," he sniffed, deflating slightly as the fluids leaked out of him. "When was someone going to say something?"

Chris, who'd been angling near Louie like he might be ready for another go, turned toward the boys with an expression of pure horror. Chris might be a dumb prick, but he knew what *sick* meant, and at the moment, it was more important to him than a nightly bang with the kids' mom. "Adra?"

"They're not! They're not, Chris. It's nothing. They're tired is all!"

"For how long?"

"They're not sick!" she insisted. Her wide brown eyes swept the room frantically, seeking an ally. She settled on

Devlin, who was leaning against the refrigerator. "Devlin, they're not sick. Please!"

He thrust his hands into his hair and stared at the kitchen tile. "If they can get sick, after all this time, any of us can still get sick," he muttered. Devlin wasn't losing it, but he was close.

Louie saw his fear and felt a gleeful tingle. *Mr. Big Cop is finally growing a brain to match his machismo*, he thought. Before Devlin could start to waver, Louie broke away from the wall and said to Adra, "I want you out. Now."

She staggered back to the screen door as if he'd physically pushed her.

"Come on, now. Let's just all calm down for a minute." This from Grider, who shuffled in the corner, hands shoved in the pockets of his faded overalls.

Now that he'd said it, though, Louie felt a surge of relief. He'd never wanted to open his house in the first place! Now he finally had a reason to make them go. "If you don't like it, Grider, you can go too," he said. "All of you! You can fuck off out of my house."

"Let's just talk this through." Devlin straightened up until they all could see the lawman again. Damn, Louie thought, gone with the brains and back to the machismo. "Adra, come back," Devlin said. "Come on. Let's sit down together and talk about this."

He led Adra and the boys back to the table, and Louie's fading, hot fury morphed into something new—a deep, cool rage. *This is how it's going to be?*

In the calmest voice he could manage, Louie said to Devlin, "You're overstepping, officer. This is my home. You're just a guest. All of you, just guests."

"Louie," Devlin said. It was the way he said it that needled Louie, drawn out, like he was being childish. *Come on now*, he seemed to say, *we share our toys*. Meanwhile, Grider was considering Louie carefully, as if he were meeting him for the first time and had just now noticed the horns spouting from his head. He probably thought Louie was crazy. Louie hated when people called him crazy. Especially people like Grider who didn't think thoughts of their own, who just went along.

Mike, Scott, and Tim—three more guys whose judgment hinged on what Officer Devlin told them to think—had come in through the front door behind him by now, hovering like they were waiting for the crack of a starting pistol. Louie felt surrounded.

"Gang up on me all you want," he hissed. "But this is *my* home. They were guests, and now they're…" He struggled for the word. "Squatters! Trespassers. That's what they are now." Louie retreated past Scott and Tim to the living room. Germs were probably crawling all over his sofa where the boys had lounged all day, so he went to his bedroom instead, hands held up to avoid touching anything, like a surgeon heading into the operating room. He slammed the door with a snap of his hip.

He sank onto his bed and saw that his fingers were trembling. They couldn't just stay when he told them to leave. Could they?

He rubbed his hands on his jeans, over and over. Underneath that concern, another sickening feeling made his stomach turn. He would never be the hero now. Not after this. Because a real hero wouldn't say the things he'd just said, even if they were the right things.

All this time letting them stay, being the good guy and giving them refuge, wasted. Erased. Now he was the jerk. He was the asshole. But wasn't he *right*? And didn't being right make a difference?

Sometimes it is better to be kind than right, his mother would have said, and he would have frowned and nodded but not really understood what she meant, because lying and saying someone else was right when they weren't right wasn't very righteous either. These were the social complexities Louie always failed to understand.

He tried to weigh his options, to understand his choices, because his mother had also always said *Life is made of the choices you make, Louie. And if you don't like your life, make better choices.*

He could deal with the kids being sick and let them stay. Not a good choice in his mind, but a choice. It wasn't like letting them stay would make him sick or make them better, but he could still *choose* it. But even if he could apologize his way out of their being mad at him, the very act of giving in would hand all the power over to Devlin. Louie would have no say anymore if he backed down, and they'd all know it.

He could also just pack up and leave. Let them all spread their dirty germs to each other, dumb and sightless, until the very end of them! But then where exactly would he go? He turned his attention to his bedroom window. He'd only ever lived in this house, slept in this bed, fell asleep each night gazing out this same glass at the garden he'd known all his life. When the window was open and a good breeze came in, he would drift off smelling earthy soil, wet and rich from evening watering. As dry as it was in this heat, he thought he could even smell it now, and this calmed him.

He'd picked vegetables from that garden since he was old enough to learn to cultivate seeds himself, to start them in little plastic cups that would sit on the dining table for weeks in the spring, waiting until the ground was soft and warm enough, growing from green fuzz to something more that would feed them through the summer. His mom would sometimes part those rows of cups down the center to make room for one of her jigsaw puzzles or to iron his church shirt, and Louie would grumble until she was finished and he could line them in their ranks again like toy soldiers.

His mother had died in this house. Then, like a good son, he'd tipped the little brown box full of her ashes into that very garden, down by the asparagus. Louie had loved his mother but hated asparagus, refused to eat it, so this was the best spot in his mind for her remains to feed the greens.

Even the ridicule he'd faced over his bumbling suicides over the last year, the scornful looks from the regular church-goers, the scolding looks from the people who'd known his mother, and worst, the pitying looks from everyone else—none of it had ever driven him out of town. Nothing should have the power to make him leave the place he loved. The actual injustice of it was too much for Louie to seriously consider this option.

He could kill them all. That was a choice! The maddest choice of all. He'd burn the house down with everyone in it. He'd be fine in the morning, and the garden should be OK, though Louie paused now to wonder about the house itself. Could he return to the sink in the morning if the sink was gone?

When he found himself there after one of his suicides, the things that had happened the day before had still happened. It was not as if his mistakes had been erased. Still, he might have to experiment a little to make sure the inanimate objects in the kitchen reset themselves when he did…

Louie stopped short in his thoughts. Jesus, what was he thinking? Maybe the heat really had gotten to him. Or maybe he was crazy after all, like half the town thought before the flu made them think about something else. He wasn't a killer!

Unless killing himself counted.

CHAPTER ELEVEN

"I'M SORRY HONEY, BUT I'VE never been stung by a bee. As far as I know, my mom hadn't been recently either."

Mack slumped in her chair across from Sharon. "It was just an idea," she mumbled.

"It's good that you're trying to figure this out," Katherine said. She was sympathetic to Mack's need to make sense of things, to regain control, even if only to understand what was coming for all of them.

Mack gave Katherine a weary smile. To Sharon, she said, "I'm really sorry we bothered you."

Sharon started to reply but broke into a series of coughs that racked her body and lifted her spine from her chair. Katherine felt those coughs in her bones. How much longer did Sharon have? A day? Two at the most? Her eyes were starting to shrink in her head, her cheek bones protruding after a solid week of vomiting.

Katherine tried to skip the sympathy. She knew her friend hated it. Instead, she asked, "Does Ana need a change?"

Sharon continued to cough in sharp spates that sounded like the *rat-tat-tat* of a rifle, but she shook her head. Sharon didn't trust Katherine with Ana, which would soon be a problem if Ana outlived her, because Katherine hadn't yet learned anything about baby care. Katherine made a move to peek into the stroller, and Sharon looked fierce, such a contrast to her earlier Zen-like state that Katherine nearly stepped back from her. The two women stared at each other for a long, uncomfortable moment.

"Mack, why don't you go downstairs and see what Lee and Ricky want to eat?" Katherine said at last.

"Sure. Sorry again, Sharon." Mack made a quick escape.

"What was that?" Katherine demanded when the girl was gone.

Sharon, recovered from her coughing fit, had sunk back into her chair. It swallowed her whole. "What was what?"

"That look! Ana's not your daughter or your property. And she's sick. Why won't you let anyone else care for her?"

To her surprise, Sharon seemed like she was about to say something vicious but appeared to catch herself.

"What?" Katherine asked.

"Never mind."

Katherine clenched her jaw. "*What?*"

After a pregnant pause, Sharon said, "No one else comes up here, Katherine. It's you I don't want to care for her."

Despite herself, Katherine felt injured. "What am I, a monster? Is that what you think? I'm incapable of taking care of a child? You're ridiculous."

Sharon said nothing. The silence was unsatisfying. Katherine couldn't leave it alone. "We're friends. We've been friends for a long time. Why don't you trust me?"

Sharon just blinked. Finally, she said, "Sit down. There's something I need to say to you."

Katherine sat in the chair Mack had occupied. As if it would prevent Sharon from saying hurtful things, Katherine began her own tirade. "What? Is it because I don't have a mother? Or siblings? Because I've never wanted children? Because I got the promotion over you, Sharon?"

"She doesn't have the flu," Sharon said.

"She's sick…"

"Yes, but I don't think it's the flu."

"Spit it out, Sharon," Katherine snapped.

"I think it was the formula you gave her. Or it might have been breast milk in the bottle. Spoiled, I think, either way. I don't know what you were doing for hours, passed out or…whatever…but if that bottle was sitting in the bag all that while, it would have been bad by the time you gave it to her. It wasn't even refrigerated. I'd guess she tried to refuse it. Babies have instincts for that. It probably tasted awful too, full of bacteria.

"She wasn't sick when her mother left her with you, but I believe she got sick after you fed her bad milk. And without medical knowledge to get rid of whatever bacterial infection is growing inside her, she's been getting more and more dehydrated since. It's why she can't cry."

"No," Katherine faltered. "It's more likely the flu."

"It isn't. She doesn't have the same symptoms as me. No diarrhea or vomiting since the first day. I've been sick and getting sicker, it's harder and harder to keep anything down. She just lies there. She's not crying, not shitting, not drinking unless you force it. I've tried small bits of penicillin in her formula. I figure there's not much to lose at this point, experimenting, and at times I even thought it might be helping her a little, but she will hardly take the nipple now. She's weak, and I can't get enough in her. When I try to force it, I can see her curl up on herself. It's obvious that her tummy hurts."

"If she has the flu, it will make her tummy hurt. And the flu would make her dehydrated. We knew that. That's what the Pedialyte was for."

"It was too late for Pedialyte," Sharon insisted.

"God, you sound like you want it to be my fault!"

"Of course I don't."

"Then why did you even tell me? I can't do anything about it now, Sharon. Except feel like a shit. I didn't know what to do. She was crying. I knew she hadn't been fed. There was a bottle there, so I did what I thought I was supposed to do. I was trying to take care of her!"

"Well, you can understand then why I've taken over her care. If I can just get her to take to a bottle, get some more penicillin in her, and some Pedialyte, maybe she still has a chance."

Shame washed over Katherine. A dying woman thought she was a better caretaker to this little baby than her, a smart, healthy adult. Was she right?

"And what then?"

Sharon didn't pretend to misunderstand. "Then I'm going to have to give her back to you. I doubt Lee will take her, and the kids can't unless he lets them. So I guess it's got to be you." Sharon coughed again, then pressed on. "It's not like I think you harmed her on purpose. Or even that I'm judging you for not knowing about baby formula. But I've been thinking. What happened that day? I mean, did you really pass out for hours? An entire day? I called and called.

Your *lapse* is the reason the bottle went bad. Why didn't you hear the phone?"

Katherine had wondered the same thing. She stood and paced away from the carriage. "I don't know. I don't remember. I was…overwhelmed, I guess."

"What if you get 'overwhelmed' again?"

Katherine stopped at the window and peered past her reflection in the glass to the empty street below. "I'm overwhelmed now," she murmured. "But I'm still here." She turned from the window to meet Sharon's eyes. "Overwhelmed and still here! I stuck. I've been sticking."

"And if you decide to take your life again?" Sharon asked bluntly.

"Sharon!"

"What?! Don't give me grief for bringing it up. It wasn't long ago that you were *joking* about it. Joking about it!" For a moment, she seemed more exasperated than sick, her fevered eyes alert. "But it's never been a joke to me, now or then. Somebody actually needs you now. It's not just about Katherine Coburn, who sometimes gets bored and decides life isn't fun anymore and swallows a handful of Valium. Will having someone dependent on you keep you from checking out?"

Katherine turned back to the window. "Whatever. It wasn't Valium."

"Christ, whatever it was. Did you or did you not want to live anymore?"

"The reality of everyone up and dying kind of casts a new light on things," Katherine retorted.

"Sure, but what about when everyone is gone and it's just you and Ana, day after day? Won't you start to wonder why you're keeping the two of you alive? For what purpose?"

"It's like you think that I'm this horrible person."

Sharon sighed and settled back in her chair, fatigue beginning to strain around her eyes again. "I'm too sick to listen to you feel sorry for yourself."

Katherine couldn't speak for a long minute. The time had come to tell Sharon the truth, but the words were dry in her throat like old crackers. The thought shifted her attention to Sharon's dinner plate on the table, ignored as she dug for the truth, the crackers growing staler and tuna crusting over in the warm room. "I didn't do it because I was bored," she said at last.

Sharon leaned forward. "Then tell me why you really did," she said. "We don't have time for bullshit."

Katherine came back and sat across from Sharon. "Do you remember I put time off on the calendar to go to Vegas?"

Sharon nodded. "Yeah. You never took the trip though. Came in to work that Monday like you were never going on vacation."

"I was supposed to get an abortion that week." Katherine hitched a jagged breath. "There was no trip, obviously," she added. "I made it up."

Sharon shifted in her chair, wincing as if her bones were grinding against the cushion. She *had* lost a lot of weight. But Katherine suspected Sharon was pained by more than her body just then. Katherine had said the A-word, and she knew that despite Sharon's penchant for creative cursing and the naughty sense of humor that had once bonded them at work, she had been raised in a Christian, pro-life family.

"You had an abortion?" Sharon asked finally. "Wait, back up. Who? When did you even get pregnant?"

"Erika's bachelorette party. I went home with the dancer."

Despite the circumstances, Katherine almost wanted to laugh at Sharon's mouth gaping and closing like an astounded fish. Had she told her this, sans the abortion part, back when her friend was healthy, she had no doubt that Sharon would have high-fived her and then bemoaned her own rotten sex life.

Katherine continued. "But no, I didn't get an abortion that week. I didn't have to. I lost it. In a bathroom stall at work the Friday before, if you want to know." It was the first time she'd told anyone, not even her gynecologist who she'd evaded after it had happened. Telling Sharon now was a sick relief, like vomiting into a toilet after too much alcohol. Getting it all out would feel better. The rest of her story came out in a wave. "I was only a few weeks along. I've always been very regular, so I knew right away that I was pregnant. Plenty of time to consider my options. When the miscarriage happened, it was just like a bad period really, and that was that. A few cells in a tissue, but they totally turned my world upside down."

"And this is why you...you know? Did it?" Sharon asked gently.

"I'd made the appointment with the doctor, but you know, I wasn't positive if I was going to do it for sure." How to explain to Sharon the conflict she'd felt, knowing an abortion was right for her but felt wrong? "It was still kind of just an option in my head. The appointment written on my calendar was still something I could ignore if I really wanted, like missing yoga or canceling a teeth cleaning. So there I was trying to figure out if I could really have a baby when I'd never wanted a baby, if I was going to show up for my appointment, and then in a split second, the baby made the decision for me. And once it was done, I just felt…"

"I can see how that would be depressing. The hormones. Terrible. I understand, Katherine, really." For the first time in a long while, Sharon was looking at her like a friend. How amazing that talking about abortion was the thing to remove the judgment from her eyes.

"No, it was more than that. I felt *responsible*. Like I made it happen. By the very act of making that appointment, putting in for my time off, planning for it, I created the outcome before I even really made the decision. And I couldn't take it back. It's the most helpless I've ever felt in my whole life. Like my body had the right to make decisions without me. My other thought, the darkest one, the one that kept me up at night, was that maybe the baby herself had made a decision, like she knew what she was going to get for a mother and didn't want me."

"The girl who is always in control. Always organized. That's why you got the promotion over me, by the way. Katherine, always dependable."

She should have told Sharon sooner, should have given Sharon more credit that she would understand. Sharon had always gotten her and had seen firsthand at the office how much she valued control. "Exactly. I felt like I didn't have control over anything anymore, least of all myself," Katherine said. "And then this idea got in my head that there was one thing I could do to take control. I could make a choice. And that's why I took those pills. It was a dumb decision, something I thought about way less than I'd thought about the abortion. But I changed my mind, and though I don't remember it, I called 911."

"My God. I'm so sorry. I'm sorry this all happened."

"Don't be sorry. The point is, I made a choice to die, but I also made a choice to live. I still want to live, maybe even more now that life seems so precious. So many people who never wanted to die are dead. Killing myself now would be like, I don't know, mocking them. I also can't help but think that maybe there's a reason Ana's mom came knocking on my door."

Sharon nodded. "This is your second chance."

Katherine thought about this. "The idea of a baby still scares me, if I'm honest. But she's here. No choice to be made this time, whether I want to be a mother or not. So, like I said before, I'm sticking. I promise you I'll do everything I can to keep her safe."

"I wish I could be here to help you," Sharon said. "And I'm sorry I didn't trust you. I still don't know what happened in that apartment for all those hours, but at least I know you weren't sitting there trying to kill yourself. Or doing drugs or whatever. I've had some dark thoughts too." Sharon seemed poised to say more but shook off the words, seeming to come to a decision. She nudged the baby carriage toward her. "She does need changing."

Katherine accepted the chore as the apology it was and moved Ana to the bed. She thought about what Sharon had said as she began to pick at the tapes on Ana's diaper. Trust—it was a luxury now, not a given. What Sharon didn't understand was that it didn't matter whether she *trusted* her with Ana. When Sharon died, there would be no choice.

Katherine would have a baby. Choices were a luxury now too.

Her thoughts turned to Sharon's earlier comment about wishing to be there to help. "You will be here to help, by the way," she said, glancing at her friend. "I'm not letting you go without a fight. We still have bags and bags of prescriptions. Something will work, for both of you."

Sharon waved airily. "Whatever. I'm not scared. I've been dreaming about my mom. Sometimes I'm not even aware that I'm asleep, and then all of a sudden I see her, and I know she's waiting for me. It's real, I swear. She tells me it's OK. She tells me it's time for my homegoing. She tells me about who is waiting with her. Waiting for me."

The thought that Sharon might be so close to death terrified her, but Katherine couldn't ignore the excited goosebumps that rose along her arms. "I've had dreams lately too. Ones that feel real like that."

"About my mom?"

"No. There's this garden. It's all hot in the sun, and there are rows and rows of leafy greens. And there's this big wall of white trellises with giant cucumbers growing on them. They're so heavy with cucumbers and big vines that the wall of them is falling back against a fence. I think I've dreamed about it every night this week." She realized she'd been speaking in the singsong voice Sharon had used with Ana, as if she were recounting her dreams to both of them.

"The same dream?"

"Mostly," she said, reaching for the powder. "Last night there was a man with me. I've seen him before, but not his face. I can hear a baby crying on the porch."

CHAPTER TWELVE

"FAMILY MEETING," DEVLIN SAID THROUGH the door. "Come on, Louie. It's time to talk."

On the other side of the door, Louie was on his bed, looping a thin rope and squinting at a drawing of various knots. How had anyone ever come up with the idea of the noose? It seemed very complicated, but then Louie had never made one, and any knot seemed complicated to execute correctly the very first time.

Heavy knocks disturbed his concentration. "Louie," Devlin said in a long-suffering tone obvious even through his bedroom door.

Louie, who had stayed in his room all afternoon and evening, and was currently preparing tonight's suicide of choice, finally replied. "Go away, Devlin. I've already said what I wanted to say."

"The boys are outside, Louie. They're in their tent, and Adra is with them. But the rest of us need to talk. We need to figure out the best course of action."

Louie snorted. Figure out the best course of action. Some might say heeding the homeowner's wishes was the best, in fact the only, course of action.

"I'm busy," Louie returned, touching his bruised nose. He relished the slight sting. It helped him recall his anger. "You all sit out there and talk it out over a nice cold beer, and then remember that whatever you *decide*, it's my fridge that made that beer cold for you." He saw the doorknob twitch.

"I'm coming in, Louie."

Flipping his rope and booklet under the quilt, Louie pulled his pillow over the lump they made just as the door opened.

"Nobody's disputing this is your house." Devlin leaned against the doorjamb, hands in his pockets, looking to Louie like the Marlboro man from advertisements in his mom's old magazines. Cool, always watchful, always managing. Except today, Officer Devlin Kelly was trying to manage Louie with that patient, persuasive voice of his, and it made Louie want to reach for his rope and toss it right around the asshole's neck.

"Then there's no debate."

"Louie…"

"My house, my rules. If we want to be safe, anyone sick needs to go."

"We've already been exposed," Devlin insisted. He turned to acknowledge Grider, who shuffled in past him.

"Nobody's trying to say this isn't your place, Louie," the older man said. "But we can be smart about this."

Apparently the family meeting would happen no matter where he went. Louie usually liked Grider, but he didn't like him much then. "Stop saying my name, both of you," he said. "You're not hostage negotiators."

Devlin and Grider exchanged a look. It was enough for Louie to understand that Devlin had likely prepped them on how to deal with a difficult citizen. Gentle, nonconfrontational language and establishing a relationship by using the person's name certainly topped the list. So, this was a negotiation now, huh?

"There's nothing to negotiate," he added quietly.

Grider hitched up his pants and sat on the end of the bed. Louie eyed those dirty jeans, thought about where they had sat this week and how he should clean his quilt when Devlin said, "It's like I said before, we're already exposed. So what does kicking them out accomplish? They'll just die out there on the road."

Louie tossed up his hands, exasperated, because now Adra and Chris were crowding the doorway with Devlin.

"Please don't make us leave, Louie," Adra begged.

This gave Louie a small thrill, because at least someone was behaving like it was his choice. Hard on the heels of this feeling was one of guilt. He shouldn't feel good about a woman pleading with him for help. A hero wouldn't enjoy someone's distress.

"I'm not trying to be cold about this, *Adra*," Louie said, stressing her name deliberately. "I'm the only one being practical here. If we ignore the fact that you hid this from us for who knows how long, it's still true that they are sick, and we don't know whether it's going to make everyone else sick. Some of us might be immune, but maybe not. We thought your boys were, and now we know they aren't. Do you want to be responsible for Devlin or Grider or Chris getting the flu next?"

Adra looked stricken. "Of course not. I don't want anyone to be sick. But I can't do anything about that, and we don't even know for sure that William and Jayden have the flu. I'm sure regular colds still exist. Allergies…"

"Stop denying it," Louie said. "We don't have time for you to be in denial."

Grider bobbed his head. "He's right about that. For now, I think we need to assume that they've got it."

Adra shrank against Chris, who put his arm around her shoulders. "So we put them in quarantine," Chris said. When Adra stiffened against him, he added, "I don't mean that like it sounds. I just mean that we put them in a room and just one person puts food outside the door or whatever. We should limit how much we're around them. Maybe think about making some face masks."

"Not in my house," Louie insisted. Perhaps he should reconsider choice number three. He'd been too quick to dismiss it.

"They can't just stay in a tent, Louie," Adra said. "You don't know how hot it is out there."

"They could have my room," Devlin offered.

Louie turned his thoughts from mass murder to face Devlin. "No, they can't."

Grider sighed loud and long. "Well, what are we supposed to do then? Do you want them to suffer, Louie?"

He didn't want anyone to suffer, of course, but what did his house have to do with it? He hadn't created this damn flu, so why was it his responsibility? "I don't want them to suffer," Louie said aloud. "But have you thought about the fact that all of us could end up suffering?"

"It's hard to know what the right thing to do is," Devlin said. He inched into the room and leaned his ass on the edge of Louie's bureau. Why was he always leaning against everything like an exhausted cowboy? *Lazy fucking Marlboro man.*

"It is hard to know what to do and hard to make tough decisions," Louie said. "That's why I'm making it easy for you and saying it's my house, my decision. None of you have to feel guilty about a thing. I say the four of them—Adra, her boyfriend, and her two boys—go down the road to the Buckley's place and shack up there. It's close enough for help if they need it." Now that he'd thought of it, he warmed to the idea. "Yeah, it's close enough for help. We can even drop off supplies whenever. It's on the way back from town."

Adra had pulled away from Chris at Louie's mention of a boyfriend. Grider noticed and grumbled, "Christ, Adra. We all know whose tent you're in at night."

Chris, on the other hand, looked terrified.

"What, you don't want to stand by your woman?" Louie needled. He knew it was an aggressive thing to say, but the raw tingle in his nose was a reminder that Chris was a bully.

"It's not set up over there," Chris said, mostly to Adra. "How would that be any more comfortable for the kids? That's all I'm worried about."

"We could grab a few gennies from town," Devlin said. "It's not like we couldn't set it up." He glanced at Louie when he added, "It's not like we were going to all stay together forever. We'll have to spread out eventually."

Adra wasn't convinced. "You're just trying to make us go away. We don't even know if anyone is sick! Besides, what if there're *bodies* over there?"

Devlin lifted an eyebrow at Louie. The gesture seemed to say, *Can you believe she's still on this old 'it's just a cold' thing?* But Louie didn't want Devlin's comradery. After all, Devlin was the reason these people were in his home at all.

"There's another thing," Louie said. His shoulders slumped because he knew before he even said it that what was going to come out of his mouth wasn't the least bit heroic. Still, it needed saying, didn't it? "A night more out in that tent, and the boys might be too sick to move. You need to think about how long you are willing to let those boys suffer, Adra. On a farm, we just don't let that happen."

He could see her struggle to digest what he meant. When she got his meaning, Chris had to catch her arm before she came into his room. The fire was back in her eyes.

"You're the sick one, you know that, Louie?" she spat.

"Just trying to be practical here."

"There is something wrong with you," she screamed, swatting at Chris.

Grider and Devlin seemed alarmed by the turn the meeting had taken.

"Louie," Grider scolded. "Not an option."

Louie knew it was a tough choice, but wouldn't he have to consider it if he was in Adra's shoes? Wasn't it the compassionate thing?

Chris was whispering in Adra's ear, trying to calm her. To Louie he said only, "You are fucked up, man. You can't talk like that to her." He pulled her from the doorway down the hallway, and Louie thought, *Guess the family meeting is over.*

"I wasn't trying to upset her," he said. "It's not like anybody wants them to die. I was just trying to say that if she didn't want to move down to the Buckley's, while they can…

if they wait any longer for her to admit that her kids actually have the flu, it's going to be too late. They are going to be suffering, and we're still all going to be at risk of getting it on top of it."

"This isn't an ideal situation for any of us," Devlin said. "But for fuck's sake, Louie. Putting her children down like sick horses so you don't have to deal with it isn't an option for her. You should be able to see implying that would set her off. She doesn't even think they're sick!" His voice was calm, but Louie could see that red splotches starting to spread on his chest where his shirt was unbuttoned.

Grider stepped up with his big hands spread, like he was trying to talk both of them off a ledge. "Look, the idea of moving them isn't a bad one. To Louie's point, if we do it immediately, we could take one of the generators from here down to this Buckley place, and then replace yours, Louie, on our next trip to town. We can give them some of our food too. They would have eaten it here anyway, so it's no loss. Why don't we just try to focus on that idea?"

Louie didn't want to hear anymore. Nothing had been accomplished by "talking it out." They still all thought he was crazy, an asshole, even though he was only trying to bring up a rational point, and nothing had changed. He still wanted them out, and everyone else was still in the deciding phase.

Let them continue to debate. He was done. He thought again about the rope, resting just beneath his pillow, and wished for them to all go to bed. He needed some relief. And even though he'd still wake up in the morning with the same problems, he would feel restored, all of his stress going down the drain like a swirl of dishwater in the sink.

CHAPTER THIRTEEN

T HE SUN WAS HOT SO that it made the dirt smell dirtier and the plants smell like jungle. Katherine picked her way through the garden, her flipflops making soft *thwicks* against the flat steppingstones buried deep in pea gravel.

She passed cucumbers on her left and then stopped a moment to stare at a thicket of asparagus spears among a rash of grass. Something about those stalks felt meaningful. She heard gravel crunch and turned to see a man approach with a large basket full of verdant greens looped around one arm. Without looking, she knew there were carrots in there, as well as kale and spinach, small green peppers, and a few giant cucumbers. There were roses too, although she couldn't see them, snipped from a bush just outside the garden. They were for her.

She still couldn't make out the man's face, but she knew she'd met him before in a place just like this. Then, suddenly, she realized that this was a dream, and she had dreamed of him before. Afraid she would wake up now that she knew it for what it was, she said, "Who are you?"

"I'm Louie," he replied.

"Do I know you?" she asked.

Louie shrugged. "Maybe. We dream about each other a lot."

Katherine felt herself nodding. "Yes, we do. Always here." Then, "Where are we?"

"This is my garden. Yours too."

"I have a garden?"

"And a baby," he said.

On cue, Katherine began to hear an infant cry behind her. She didn't want to turn away from the man, certain that if she did, she would wake up, but the cries pulled at her, and they were waking her up too.

"I have to go," she said regretfully.

The man named Louie shrugged again. "You'll be back."

"Will you still be here?"

"Sure. I don't have anywhere else to go."

Reassured, Katherine turned away from him. She tried to see through the weeping trees that framed the garden, searching with her eyes for the baby's voice. She turned back, but the man had turned away and was talking to the asparagus.

She was walking toward the sound when she woke up.

Katherine kicked off her blanket, hot from sleep and frustrated from the dream. She had so many questions. Reality had come too soon.

Louie. Was he the Louie she had talked to that day at work? The last man in his town? Was she subconsciously worried about him, and that's why she kept dreaming about him? It seemed so real, but then, didn't most of her dreams?

She heard Ana crying upstairs and realized that was probably why she'd heard a baby cry in her dream. Like dreaming of a fire alarm or an ambulance only to awaken to her alarm blaring. Or dreaming of swimming and waking up needing to pee.

Katherine rubbed her eyes and, out of habit, sought a bedside clock on the nightstand before she realized she wasn't in her own bed and there was no electricity for a clock besides. The baby continued to cry above her. Accustomed to Sharon taking care her, Katherine waited to hear her hush. When she didn't, Katherine rose and felt for the votive candle and lighter she'd left on the dresser. It wasn't quite dawn yet and was still mostly dark in the room.

She climbed the staircase to the second floor, pausing between board squeaks to listen for Mack, who might come down from the third-floor apartment above. Hearing only the baby cry, Katherine continued.

She cracked the bedroom door. "Sharon?" she whispered.

She wasn't in her bed or in the chair where she sat most of the time but in a straight-backed chair across the room, facing the window where the sun would rise. Katherine set down the candle and moved to pick up Ana, the cries cutting off like she'd hit a switch as soon as the baby was in her arms. She crept across the room, the wooden floorboards popping, old and dry like the ones on the stairs. "Sharon?" she said again.

Sharon didn't turn, and Katherine knew then that she was dead. She stopped hard at the realization, and Ana fussed a moment like she was deciding whether to let loose another good cry. "Hush, now," Katherine said, putting her to her shoulder, beginning to dance the maternal baby dance that sometimes worked to stop the rain instead of bring it. "That's a girl," she murmured.

"Katherine?" she heard behind her. It was Mack. "Is Ana OK?"

"Stop there, Mack," Katherine said, her voice high and reedy even to her own ears.

Mack stilled. "Is Sharon OK?"

"No, honey." She started to tell her that Sharon was gone but decided too many people had died to use euphemisms anymore. "I think she's died." She heard Mack moan. Katherine walked back across the room, the boards cracking just like they had before she knew her friend was dead. It seemed wrong that things should continue on in the same way as before, even though there was one less person in the room now. She pressed Ana into Mack's arms. "Change Ana, please?"

Mack took the baby but was mute, stuck in place, watching as Katherine crossed the room, passing out of the small circle of light cast by the candle and into shadow. Katherine stroked Sharon's head with a light hand and then moved down to her neck, checking for a pulse she knew wasn't there.

"Is she, for sure?" Mack asked. "Dead I mean?"

"Change Ana," Katherine replied, nodding. "And then wake Lee."

When Mack just stood there, Katherine urged, "Get moving, Mack. Lee will have to help me with her. She wants to be laid with her mom next door."

Mack stripped Ana of her diaper on the bed as the morning light began to brighten the room. "She's not wet," she said. "There's just a little bit of dark hard stuff."

"She's not drinking much," Katherine murmured, taking the pillow from Sharon's arms and placing it on the floor.

She tugged the blanket in Sharon's lap up and over her face. It started to creep back down, and Katherine battled with it for a moment before tucking it behind Sharon's head to pin it to the chair. "Sorry, hon," she said, even as a wave of relief hit her now that Sharon's open mouth was covered.

She gave silent thanks that Mack had not come over. Sharon's face had frozen as if screaming when she died. Katherine knew it was from when the air in her lungs let go, but it would have scared the girl.

"I'll go get Lee," Mack said from across the room. Her voice was shaky when she asked, "Can I take the candle with me?"

"Go ahead," Katherine said. As Mack left Ana clothed and kicking on the bed, she stood in the partial darkness with Sharon. She should probably cry now, before Lee got there and made her feel stupid about it, but for some reason, she just wasn't ready to yet. She would later, she decided, after she finished the business of Sharon's homegoing. When she was alone and could do it privately, in her bedroom where she wouldn't upset anyone.

The minutes stretched and Katherine turned to watch the sun rise over the trees. *Too bad she missed this*, she thought, and it was this that made her cry, despite her best intentions.

"This has to happen now?" Lee said, coming into the room. "It's not even light out."

For once, his contrary nature was welcome, because annoyance cut off her tears. She swiped at her wet face and turned around. Lee was wearing athletic shorts, no shirt, and his hair was smashed to hell on one side. He rubbed irritably at the pillow creases on his face.

"I know it's early," she said. "But we should move Sharon now, before it gets hot outside."

Surprisingly, Lee nodded his agreement. Relieved, she started to thank him, and then he said, "Yeah, it already smells in here. Wow." And just like that, she hated him again.

Katherine returned to Sharon's home in the late morning, sweaty and miserable. It hadn't taken much time to move Sharon next door. Her body was heavier than her frail mother would have been when Sharon moved her, but Lee was even stronger than he looked, doing most of the heavy work. He was also inconsiderate as usual, causing Katherine to chase after his clumsy, lurching body, protecting Sharon's arms and legs from the ground and doorways. Inside, they held their breath behind masks. Lee, gagging slightly, for once kept his sarcastic thoughts to himself. He dispatched Sharon to the bedroom and staggered back to the brownstone, looking sick, but Katherine wasn't done yet. Sharon had asked for flowers, and Katherine had to make it happen. Most flowers she found were crisp, shriveled in bone dry dirt from the relentless heat. She'd walked all the way down the block to find a window box with flowers in the shade.

In the bathroom, as she scraped the dirt from under her nails with a Kleenex and wished for running water so that she could wash the stink from her hair, her thoughts turned to last night's dream. In the light of day, it had lost some of its magic. It had felt real, but it wasn't. Not really. It couldn't be. And yet, as she had closed the door on Sharon, resting on the bed next to her mom, she couldn't help but think about how her friend had dreamed of dying and felt certain she would join her mom soon. And she had. So if Sharon's dream was real, why couldn't hers be?

Sharon had those dreams *because* she knew she was dying and had specifically asked to be placed with her mother, Katherine lectured herself. That's not a dream coming true, that's a dream about something realistic happening. Even so, she had talked to her mom like Katherine had talked to the man in the garden. It might not be anything, but it *felt* like something. And what else did she have left anymore? The flu had stripped the world not just of people, but of everything, until all that was left was how she felt about it.

Katherine tossed the tissue in the garbage and went up to Sharon's room, taking the stairs two at a time. She suddenly felt like she knew just what could make this niggling feeling go away. She found Ana's diaper bag and dug into it, plunging her hands in every pocket until she found what she wanted. The yellow sticky note. She sat on the bed and stared at Louie's name and address for a long time.

After a while, Lee came in. She felt his eyes on her, but she didn't really feel like looking up. "What?" she asked eventually.

"We need to talk."

Katherine looked up when she heard his odd tone. "About?"

"Ricky. I think he's sick."

Ricky did look a bit sick, but whether it was the flu or not was unclear.

"I'm not a doctor," Katherine said, removing her hand from his forehead. "But he doesn't seem to have a fever to me."

Lee cursed under his breath as he rummaged through the nightstand looking for a thermometer. Mackenzie was searching the medicine cabinet down the hall. "There's nothing in here," she called to them. "Who doesn't have a thermometer in a freaking pandemic? My mom had like five of them from Covid. We had to take our temperatures ten times a day!"

Lee slammed the last drawer shut with his foot. "Nothing but fucking yarn."

"I know there's one around somewhere," Katherine insisted. "Sharon told me her temperature the first day she was sick." She shrugged. "I don't know. Knowing her, once she figured she had the flu, she tossed it. Either that, or she was keeping it in her bathrobe pocket. I don't remember seeing her take her temp though."

"I'm not going back over to the funky house to search her pockets," Lee said.

She ignored him as Mack came into the room. "Does he have any allergies or anything?"

"No," Ricky and Mack said at the same time.

"Besides sneezing, what else are you feeling, Ricky? Sneezing could be anything."

"Nothing, I swear," he said, sitting up from the bed where Lee had directed him earlier. "He's just overreacting!"

"We can't be too careful!" Lee insisted. "Someone just dies of the flu, and now someone else is sneezing his ass off, of course I'm going to put two and two together."

"I'm not sure math is your strong suit, Lee," Mack said. "You were the one that didn't get that there was strength in numbers. We've been much better here than we were on the road when we were just driving around doing nothing. Why are you trying to get us kicked out?"

"I've had enough of this," Lee said, leaving the room. "I'm going on a food run," they heard him call from the stairway. "And don't forget to stay away from the fucking bees, Mackenzie."

"Good riddance," Ricky said under his breath. At Katherine's look, he added, "For real, he's been such an asshole. He wasn't such an asshole when he started dating my mom."

Mack flopped on the edge of the bed. "At least I had a theory," she said, clearly hurt by Lee's dig about the bees. "Why's he like this? Sometimes he can be so nice, when it's just me and him, but then other times it's really easy to just *hate* him."

Katherine hesitated to align herself in any way with the man, but said, "Times are a little rough. He's under a lot of stress. And Mack, remember what Sharon said. You're not getting kicked out, and you don't have to go anywhere. This is your place now."

"Even if he's stressed out, it doesn't mean he has to pick on Ricky and say he's sick when he's not," Mack said. "It makes me worried about how much he'd freak if one of us actually does get the flu."

They didn't find out how freaked Lee would get because Lee didn't come back from the store. Maybe he really did think Ricky was sick, or maybe that was just the excuse that let him keep driving. Either way, Katherine tried not to be jealous as she pictured him in her stolen Jaguar purring down the open highway, flu and obligations far behind him.

Two days later, Ana was still listless with dehydration, and Katherine wasn't so sure about Mack and Ricky's chances either. Without Lee, the kids had unglued from each other and from the routines the group had once built together. Mack spent all of her time in her room praying over the baby, only eating when Katherine brought her food. Ricky had stopped sneezing, but he slept more and more.

The dreams still came to Katherine, isolating her from them, pulling her in a way she couldn't describe toward the man named Louie. On the third day, she awoke with the sound of a baby crying in her mind, but the house was dead silent.

She followed her own morning routine, rifling through the shopping bag on the counter from the trip she'd taken to the store yesterday. She'd used Sharon's mom's old Honda, the pine tree air freshener still giving a whiff of Christmas, and found the IGA in the same condition they'd left it the last time. The store had been warm inside, gnats swarming in the air, which was rank from spoiling fruit and potatoes, but there was plenty of safe food left. She loaded up, hoping that this might be her last trip to this particular store. She'd seen no sign that Lee had been there.

Now she opened a box of Pop-Tarts and picked out three foil packets, breakfast for the family. She found Ricky asleep on the first-floor sofa, even though it was now almost noon, and tucked a packet near where his hand cradled his head. He didn't stir under his drawn hoodie.

Katherine climbed the stairs to the third-floor apartment but found Mack's room empty. She dropped the Pop-Tarts on the unmade bed and backtracked, checking all of the rooms and the bathroom. "Mack?" she called, and when she got no response, "Ana?"

Katherine tried not to overreact, but it wasn't like Mack to disappear. Ricky sometimes wandered outside, but his sister preferred to haunt the brownstone, lounging in its cool shadows. And Ana, well, she didn't go anywhere on her own. Where would Mack take her? This time Katherine paid her noisy footsteps on the creaky stairs no mind, jogging back down and calling to Ricky. "Wake up. I can't find Mack and Ana!"

He swung his legs to the floor. Muzzy from sleep, he struggled out of his hoodie. "Huh?"

"Did your sister say she was going anywhere?"

Ricky snaked a hand under his T-shirt and scratched absently at his flat stomach. He'd been wearing that same shirt for three days now, and Katherine could smell teenage body odor from where she stood, activated by movement. At least his was a healthy male smell. It overpowered other odors from the neighborhood that had begun to penetrate the house.

"Nuh uh," he said. His glassy gaze slid to the package of pastries now broken under his palm.

"Go check the second floor for me. I don't think she'd go in Sharon's room, but I don't know where else she'd be. I'll check out back."

Katherine went through the kitchen to the tiny patio behind the brownstone, not surprised to find it empty. She met Ricky back in the living room.

"Nothing?"

"No," Ricky said, more awake now. "The car is still out front though. She didn't go out."

Katherine went out to the stoop, looked dumbly at the Honda parked at the curb and then up and down the street. "Where the hell…"

Ricky came up behind her. "Oh, hey, the gate's open over there," he said, sounding mystified.

Katherine's gaze jerked to the tiny iron gate at the base of the steps next door. It was an unusual detail in the row of brownstones, and she knew she had closed it before, because it had sounded like a crypt door creaking shut when she left Sharon behind. Now it was swung wide open, butted to the iron fence that surrounded the small dried-up flower bed in front of their house and Mrs. Radcliff's.

"Why would she go over there?" Ricky asked, sounding scared now. "It's nasty."

Katherine thought she might know why. She hoped she was wrong. "Go back inside, Ricky. I'll go check."

"No argument here. *I'm* not going over there."

Katherine went down the steps to the street and trailed her fingers over the gate, considering. She didn't really want to go inside either. In this heat, Sharon, her mother, and their neighbor would smell ten times worse than the last time she was there. "She better not be looking for bee stings," Ricky called from the top of the stairs.

"No, I don't think so," Katherine said.

When she went inside, shirt pulled up over her mouth, she knew where to look for Mack. She moved fast through the empty foyer, living area, and kitchen to the back bedroom. The door was ajar, and she heard the girl before she saw her. Nudging her way into the dark room, she spotted Mack kneeling, hands clasped, head bowed, murmuring prayers into the bedspread.

The bodies were on the king-sized bed, each lying arm to arm, flowers in various stages of decay tucked neatly around them. Sharon's and her mother's open mouths were silently protesting the small body nestled between them. Ana wasn't moving, her tiny arms folded, pudgy chin and cheeks resting on her chest.

Mack turned when Katherine grunted indelicately. Katherine dropped the shirt from her mouth and knelt beside the girl. She pulled her to her breast and rocked her as she wept. "I couldn't find more flowers for her."

Later, when Mack had gone silent, Katherine moved through Sharon's brownstone, collecting and packing their meager belongings into the Honda. Mack and Ricky sat disinterested on the couch, not helping, but not hindering the progress. When she was ready, she said only, "We're going to Michigan. I know someone there," and they followed her.

CHAPTER FOURTEEN

LOUIE SLEPT ON THE SIDE of the bed he'd slept in all his life, quilt kicked into a lump down by his feet, the ridge of his body a dark mass in the shadow of predawn. He didn't hear when the two men came inside the room behind him or see when they knelt in the dark alongside his bed as if they were going to pray for him. Nor did he hear the thick sound they must have heard when the butcher knife punched deep into his kidney through his back. He didn't see or hear any of that but imagined those details later.

Louie woke up when it was happening, and these details were as clear and sharp in his mind as the knife in his back. One heavy arm held him down while another continued to thrust. His last thought was that the holes they were making were going to let the stuff out of his body like slits in the top of a hot fruit pie.

He was still alive, barely, when Chris and his redneck buddies began to dig a grave for him in his own garden, lying face down in the dirt so that he could only imagine the sweat on their faces and the rich soil dusting their arms as they grunted with the effort. When he was dead and awareness was gone, he never felt what it was like to be rolled into a hole or watch the first hints of dawn disappear as he was buried.

He knew what they'd done the next morning when he was very much alive at his kitchen sink watching blood curl in the shipwrecked water. *This is new*, he thought. One, he was standing here after being *murdered* (add that to his list, and then cross it off), and two, there had never been blood in the sink before. The mug, which he'd been holding lately, was broken in two large halves next to the sink, and there was blood on and around that too, in a sticky-looking puddle.

Louie pulled out the drain stopper, and the pink water went down the pipes. The dishes in the sink, usually clean, so that all he had to do was wipe them dry, were tainted by the blood. Louie grabbed the Pyrex dish, and without thinking much about it, slammed it down on the floor. This was unsatisfying—it only cracked with a loud thunk—so Louie snatched the wet crazy daisy plate from the sink and smashed it against a cabinet. He was sweeping the counter of its tiny appliances with a stiff arm, in the midst of trashing his own kitchen, when Adra, Devlin, and Grider came in for breakfast.

"What in the hell?" Grider exclaimed as Devlin rushed Louie and grabbed his arms to prevent further damage.

"They tried to kill me," Louie managed, struggling against Devlin, who heaved him around by his shirt and pushed him down onto a chair. It tipped from the momentum, and Louie found himself rolling on the linoleum and then for a moment looking dazedly at the underbelly of the kitchen table. Devlin pulled him out from under it and covered him like a pro wrestler who'd probably be named Marlboro Man if not for the name infringement.

"If they want all this to be theirs, I'm not just handing it over nice and clean!" Louie shouted beneath him, kicking at the other chairs around the table. Suddenly Clark was in the fray, barking madly, tail whipping, uncertain if he should be protecting or playing.

"Calm down, Louie! You're not making sense!" Grider said. He tried to hold Clark back as he helped Devlin hold Louie still. "Stop it now! Adra, get this dog!"

Louie ceased fighting against the weight of Grider and Devlin as his energy started to drain, but he was still spitting mad. They'd done it in his own home. In his own garden! "Her boyfriends," he hissed. "They attacked me last night. Stabbed me right in the back while I was sleeping."

"Nonsense, Louie," Grider said, but Devlin, more pragmatic than the truck driver, rolled Louie over and pulled up his T-shirt to inspect him, revealing smooth intact skin.

"You must mean a figurative stab in the back," Devlin drawled. "Or else you dreamed it."

Louie scrambled away and made it to a sitting position, tugging down his shirt and pointing at Adra. "She put them up to it. In my own home!"

Adra held Clark by the collar, staring at Louie like she'd seen a ghost, and he realized then that this was more than just a cliché. She truly was looking at him like he was a ghost, and that meant she knew, maybe had even watched Chris and the boys do it. He didn't remember her quiet voice or the sound of her light footsteps, but by the look on her face, she'd probably been in the garden too, overseeing the planting.

With her round eyes and half-open mouth, Adra didn't look like a woman who expected to find Louie alive and well the next day, and though Grider and Devlin might take her silence for shock at the damage he'd inflicted on his kitchen, Louie knew better.

Except now he sounded crazier than ever, making accusations of murder when he wasn't even dead. Fortunately, Adra hadn't yet reached the same conclusion. If she'd only kept her cool, it was doubtful they would have believed anything he said. But she was muttering now, and she wasn't gaslighting him with denials. "I saw you," she said, pointing back at him like a wild tattletale. "I saw you, you freak!"

Louie had been called a freak before, many times and many years before he'd actually become one. The name-calling didn't faze him, but what rocked him was how he had underestimated her. She had watched her boyfriend and his bros roll Louie into a shallow grave, all right. Maybe felt his flesh for a pulse herself before they moved him from the bedroom. Louie watched her face as it fell apart. Oh, yes, she'd been part of it. Instigated it even, having the most to gain.

Adra released Clark and fled, banging out the door and yelling for Chris in his tent. Louie couldn't see what happened next, because Grider and Devlin had hauled him to his feet and began questioning him about the bloody mug on the counter. Apparently, blood without evidence of a wound concerned them. *What have you done? Who have you hurt?*

Minutes later they heard an engine start, followed by the sound of gravel spraying beneath the tires of a truck hauling ass. Louie pushed past Grider in time to see Chet's truck round the corner of the house. Chris, Adra, and the boys were in the cab, with the other three men staring at him from the back.

That night, Louie sat on his bed and calmly drew a serrated pocketknife over his wrist. Tonight's suicide felt appropriate since this was his knife and his choice. Grider and Devlin were whispering in the kitchen, sitting at the table amongst the debris he hadn't let them clean up. They were worrying, conspiring even, but Louie knew that he wasn't crazy no matter what they thought. He hadn't just trashed his kitchen because he was angry at what the rednecks had done. He wanted to see what it would look like tomorrow.

"You must have been busy cleaning last night," Grider said, pulling up a chair across from Louie. The morning sun slanted across the kitchen and heated the floor under his feet. He was reading a comic book and drinking instant coffee heated on the Coleman stove in his bedroom. Looking up at Grider, he replied, "Guess I must have."

The kitchen was clean, though only half of what he'd broken had been repaired, everything else now dry and stacked in the cabinets and the rest in the garbage can. If Grider or Devlin cared to look, they would find the Pyrex dish in the bottom cabinet with a permanent crack down the middle. The coffee mug, also in the trash bin, was in pieces. Louie hid the debris at the bottom of the can and would be happy if he never saw it again. He couldn't make sense of the blood on the mug, or in the sink for that matter—a nasty twist, which might portend something bad, something worse than immortality.

Maybe the blood meant he was running out of suicides, like a cat on his ninth life. Maybe he was getting weaker or closer to the end, though no closer to solving the mystery. He looked carefully at his wrist and thought he detected a thin red line where he'd drawn his pocketknife last night, though he couldn't be sure of the cause, if there was really a mark at all. He *had* been smashing plates yesterday.

Blood and possible scars aside, Louie was happy this morning. Some of this could be attributed to suiciding, which usually made him feel like pieces of himself had fitted back together, but mostly it was because he'd gotten what he wanted after all. Adra, her sick kids, and the rest of them were gone. It was only Grider and Devlin now, and that made it just a little easier to breathe today.

Grider leaned back in his chair, and Louie felt the man's eyes take in his nonchalance, his hand tapping against his thigh. Though Louie was actually thinking hard as he stared at his comic book, he tried to look like he was really into it, even whistling a bit. He was sure Grider still didn't quite understand what had happened yesterday. How had he and Devlin made sense of Adra, Chris, and the others' sudden, mysterious departure? Had they concocted an explanation yet for why Louie had accused his houseguests of hurting him when he couldn't prove it? Had they given a narrative to the bloody mug on the counter?

Louie didn't mind Grider's confusion. It was about time someone else had puzzles to worry about. Let him and the Marlboro Man wonder why Louie was in such a good mood after his tantrum yesterday.

As Louie flipped a page and took a sip from his cup, Grider said, "I think I'll be leaving today, Louie."

He looked up. "Really?"

"Try not to look so hopeful about it," Grider said, "and I'll try not to be offended."

Louie shrugged and looked back down at his comic. "I don't mind you so much, Grider. You were the best of them, you know. Stay if you like."

The unexpected compliment seemed to give Grider pause, but then he doggedly went on with his prepared speech. "Well, see, the thing is that we might have some family still out there. You know, if we're resistant, or immune to this thing, maybe it's genetic. So Devlin and I are thinking we'll get down to Toledo, check on his sister."

He had Louie's attention again. "Devlin's going too?"

Grider seemed to mistake Louie's sudden attentiveness for distress, explaining quickly, "Well, you know, I think he stayed longer than he'd planned. If me and the others hadn't shown up, I think he would have split by now. I feel responsible for that, thought I could repay him by sharing in the driving. Get my dirty rig out of your yard."

"Well, that would be just fine, Grider," Louie said. *Don't let the door hit you on the ass on your way out.* Grider might be the best of them, but he'd still freeloaded for days, and the people he'd brought here had stolen the truck. Chet's truck. But still.

Grider was reading his mind. "Since you're down a truck, I thought maybe I'd take you for a ride in the Tahoe while Devlin is packing up and we can find you some new wheels. I could grab a few supplies. You never know what we'll find, or not find, when we pass through the next town."

"There's not much food left," Louie said, hoping Grider's gathering supplies didn't mean wiping out the rest of anything good in town. "I mean, of fresh stuff."

"I was thinking more about guns, ammunition," Grider said. "Not everyone will be as hospitable as you were with us." He pushed away from the table, making sounds like a man ready to get moving.

Louie, somewhat mollified by the comment about hospitality—at least someone appreciated him—decided he might as well go with him. He did need a new truck.

Lucky for Louie, he lived in a Northern Michigan town where super duty trucks outnumbered any other kind of vehicle two to one. He'd only taken Chet's for sentimental reasons, and because he happened to be taking supplies from Chet's store anyway.

He had Grider drive him a few miles outside of town to Elk Ridge, where he knew Fred Murchison had good supplies on his ranch. Louie had been there several weeks earlier to get a few tools and spied a nice Ram that he would have taken if he didn't already have Chet's truck. While he was there, he'd let the horses out in the field. When he pulled up with Grider, he didn't see them anymore. The only animals left were two cows moaning in the yard.

"Hey, there's some fresh milk right there!" Grider said.

Louie tried to hide his annoyance. Grider wasn't exactly city folk (also known as "cidiots" in these parts), but he wasn't a farmer and probably didn't know any farmers either. "There used to be near eighty cows here. Those ones are all that's left, and their tits would be all infected by now from not being milked."

Grider pulled around the yard, the cows drifting closer as he got out. "Really?" he said, staring at them as if he could assess their health. "They don't just dry up?"

Louie, not being a farmer himself but knowing a bit more than Grider, said, "Not dairy cows, not high producers like here at the Ridge. A regular cow that just has milk for her calf will dry up naturally after a few weeks, but dairy ones like these need to be milked regularly or their udders rupture. Or they get an infection."

"You didn't think before about taking a cow for some milk?" Grider asked.

"Not really. I don't know much about pasteurization. The idea of drinking germs and bacteria straight from the cow doesn't sound tasty. If there was Internet, I suppose I could have looked up how to heat it properly, but not now."

Grider paused. "What do you mean no Internet? Not that I did anything more with it than use my smart phone to get directions, but I kind of assumed if I charged my cell there'd still be satellites up there doing their thing."

Louie stopped at the first pole barn. "Well, I mean, I'm sure there's still some Internet out there. It's not like it's one big machine somewhere. But the web servers in the world need power to keep it going, and even if some of it isn't blacked out yet, I personally don't have a way to access whatever's left. My Wi-Fi was down last I checked, and I don't think any Internet providers are going to send out a technician to get it back up."

"Wow," Grider remarked, and Louie wasn't sure if he was still talking about the Internet or commenting on the impressive workshop Louie had just revealed. He assumed it was the latter when Grider whistled and stepped inside. "Holy Moses, look at all this."

Fred Murchison's 40' x 40' steel-walled workshop had a much better selection of firearms than Chet's corner store, which, with the exception of liquor, sold everything from groceries and clothing to bait and used guns. And this wasn't the man's only outbuilding. He had everything you could need on or off the farm, depending on which barn you went in.

"Yeah, it's pretty great," Louie agreed. "You should see upstairs. The whole thing is one big wood shop. Fred made furniture in the winter."

"Sounds like a handy guy."

"Was. He was a doomsday prepper sort of guy too, so there's a cellar full of MREs if you get really desperate. They're salty as shit, but you could take some for the road, just in case."

"Did he die, or did he disappear?" Grider asked, moving through the giant workspace. "I wouldn't want to come up on him in a hidden bunker and get my head blown off."

"Naw, he's dead." Louie said. "He's in his recliner in the big house. Wife too. He was a hell of a prepper, but the guy never wore a mask, not even during the worst of Covid when all the stores said you had to have one. He'd just walk on in and practically dare someone to say anything, which of course no one did. I guess he was more of a freedoms guy than a thinker."

Grider stopped perusing and put his paw on a nice Winchester double-barreled shotgun on a workbench, old but well-maintained. "I'm sure Devlin knows more about weapons than I do, but it seems like this would win an argument." He hefted it onto his shoulder and pointed it away from Louie into the middle of the room, handling it like he might know at least a little something about guns.

He lowered the weapon. "With all this over here, how come you didn't pack up and move? I bet he's got a whole house generator. Plenty of room for all your dogs."

"I didn't like Fred." It was one of those things that sounded stupid when he said it out loud, but it was the truth. He wanted to live somewhere with good memories, and all he remembered about Fred was that he had a son Louie's age who had once stolen Louie's shoes from his gym locker. Gym was first period, and he had walked around school the whole rest of the day in his socks.

One of the things he liked about Grider was that he was agreeable. He didn't debate or even confront others, at least not on his own. Grider just shrugged and accepted Louie's explanation, and they moved on.

CHAPTER FIFTEEN

T HE WELCOME CENTER JUST INSIDE the Ohio border was dark, cool, and deserted. It was a fancy one, like a log cabin retreat with a huge lobby full of impressive wood beams and large windows letting in natural light. It introduced visitors to the state with a sea of pamphlets and artifacts.

The information desk was empty, but the brochure racks were full. Katherine shook her legs as she paced back and forth, pausing to study a colorful wall map. Ricky and Mack still hadn't emerged from the restrooms, but she had taken her time too. The rest stop was cooler and quieter than the car, the toilets clean.

Katherine had worried there might be obstacles to slow their progress, but the roads were disappointingly empty. In fact, the only thing slowing them down was Ricky and Mack. Katherine was itching to get moving. Their current progress put them in Michigan before nightfall. Making good time, however, necessitated being in the car, driving, heading toward a destination.

Ricky emerged, still looking a bit green. "Feeling better?" Katherine asked. The boy wasn't much for cars, as she'd learned an hour into their journey.

"I guess." He eyed the vending machines. "Maybe something salty would help. Do you have any money?"

"Sorry." Katherine stretched her arms over her head and moaned. This was the longest car trip she'd taken since childhood, and the movement made her stiff joints crackle. "Hey, does Mack get carsick too?"

"Probably, if she ever had to sit in the backseat," Ricky muttered. He moved to the vending machines and eyed them as only a hungry teenage boy could. "They've got ginger ale," he said. "You think I could just break into this?"

"Knock yourself out," Katherine crossed the big room to the door marked 'Ladies.' Mack came out looking clammy and flushed. She'd been sick.

"Did you throw up too?" Katherine asked. Behind her, she heard a lusty karate cry accompanied by the enthusiastic whaps of Ricky's sneaker against a vending machine window.

Mack nodded. She seemed reluctant to stray from the bathroom.

"I guess motion sickness runs in families," Katherine said. She guided Mack back in toward the sinks. It was darker inside but brightened by high block windows. "Splash your face a little?"

"Yeah, OK."

Katherine pulled a handful of brown paper towels from the dispenser and wet them. She handed the soggy lump to Mack. "Put this on your neck for a minute," she said.

Mack took them and sighed, but not her usual annoyed teenager sigh, or even a tired one. It wasn't a sound Katherine had heard her make before. It sounded like defeat. Suddenly Mack choked up and balled the wet napkins to her eyes, as if pressing the tears back inside.

"Oh, hey," Katherine said. She put a hand on her shoulder. "We can stay here for a little while if you need. It's OK."

Mack shook her head and moved to the sink, leaning over with her elbows on the counter, tears dropping straight into the water pooled at the bottom. She made a choking sound again that might have been either sobbing or dry heaving. "It's just a little carsickness," Katherine murmured, and for lack of anything better to do, moistened more paper towels and held them to Mack's neck, rubbing her back as the girl pressed the others over her mouth.

The soggy tissues smelled like wet cardboard, or like the brownish paper she remembered from grade school with broad lines on it for practicing her letters. *Make an O like an egg, and then crack it open to make an E*, she thought.

"It's not," Mack said at last. "Not carsickness."

"Well, it's not the flu," Katherine said immediately. She refused to lose anyone else to the flu.

"No, not that either," Mack agreed, and sighed again. She straightened in front of the mirror and poked at the smudges under her eyes. She looked like a middle-aged woman assessing her appearance, about to rummage around in her purse for lipstick or cream to cover those dark circles before heading back to the bar.

Katherine was amused by this and trying to picture Mack as an adult in the normal world.

"I'm pregnant. You don't have to say anything," Mack added, looking back at Katherine in the mirror. "I know you think I'm stupid."

Katherine felt like the stupid one. Knocked stupid. Mack's revelation was a left hook to her brain. She would have sooner believed the girl could fly than the truth, which was that somehow someone had gotten this fifteen-year-old pregnant.

She scrambled for the right questions to ask, wanting all the answers at once. "You're what? How? Who?"

Mack tried to smile, but it turned to a grimace. She bent back over the sink, heaving and swallowing silently. There was nothing to purge. Nothing in her belly except for a baby. When the spasms stopped, she replied, "I'm sure you know how babies are made. And the who, well, I think you can figure that out too."

Katherine swallowed her own bile. The end of the world left few options for the father. There were only two men in their lives, and one was Mack's brother. "Lee, then. Did he know?"

"Yeah. He knew."

Katherine turned to lean against the wall. "When did it start?"

Mack bent to splash water on her face, sniffed and then crossed to the paper towel dispenser. She yanked them out one at a time as if they were the ones who had wronged her. She swiped at her face as she replied, "Awhile ago. Since before my mom was sick."

Katherine's mind was reeling. Maybe in a lonely, end-of-the-world kind of way she could understand, in life-affirming desperation. But this? No. Lee had been doing his girlfriend's teenage daughter for months, before the pandemic even.

"He said he loved me," Mack said into the paper towels. "That she loved God and church more than him. He said that fate introduced him to my mom, but it was me he was meant for." Mack turned to Katherine. "Can you believe that crap? And I ate it up too. I thought I was so freaking sexy, pleasing a guy like that."

"It's not your fault," Katherine whispered. "Lee, that fucking bastard." She couldn't think what else to say. If Mack had been her daughter, she would have killed Lee. She still wanted to.

Mack wadded the towels and shoved them in the small bin beneath the dispenser. It was full, and they slowly un-folded, floating to the floor. She ignored them. "I didn't say it was my *fault*," she said, and that stubborn teen voice was back. "He was a jerk with a lot of dumb ideas about why we were together, but when we were alone, he was different. Sweet. Kind of immature, actually. Sometimes I thought I was more like the grownup."

"You're fifteen, Mack."

Mack cut Katherine a look in the mirror. "I know how old I am. I also know that what we were doing was sinful, no matter how old I am. He was with my mom, living with us even, and we shouldn't have done that to her. Now you get why I've been worrying about my soul. Guess it's too late to worry now."

"How far along are you?"

"A few months, maybe five?"

"Five? That much?" She should be showing by now. Katherine looked down at the girl's baggy track shorts, which revealed nothing, and thought about all the big shirts she'd been wearing from Sharon's closet. She had one on now. Katherine flashed back to all the missing food she'd blamed on Ricky, a growing teenage boy. If she had really been paying attention, Mack's pregnancy might have been obvious to her. There had just been so much else going on, with Sharon. Ana. Not to mention the dreams that made her want to stay asleep. "Does Ricky know?"

Mack shook her head. "He's been distracted by this whole world-ending thing. And even if he wasn't, I doubt he'd pick up on the signs. He might be older than me, but he's kind of dumb about real stuff, if you know what I mean."

"But Lee knew, and he left us anyway."

Mack nodded. She pulled a hair tie from her back pocket and began to comb her long strands with her fingers. "I told you, I'm the mature one in the relationship. He couldn't deal. I'm not surprised."

"I thought…" Katherine wasn't sure how to say what she was thinking.

"That we hated each other? That we fought all the time?"

"No. Well, I mean, yes, I did. But, what I was going to say is that I thought you were a good girl." She left the restroom.

"I *am* a good girl," Mack said, following behind her.

Katherine stopped. "I'm sorry. I didn't mean it like that. What I meant is that I thought you were a better girl than me. Trust me, I've made mistakes. Even ones like this, and not that long ago," she said, thinking back to her one-night stand with a stripper who had called himself Thunder, his long hair smelling like sweat and baby powder as he'd panted over top of her. If she'd had her baby, she wouldn't have known where to find the father. She'd never even asked his real name. "But I thought you were smarter at fifteen than I was at thirty. You wanted to pray for me, worried that I was going to hell because I don't believe in God, and here you were pregnant…"

Katherine's words had echoed through the large stone room. Ricky looked up from where he was gathering snacks from the floor, having successfully broken into the vending machine. His furtive look, like a raccoon caught rummaging through garbage, disappeared when he saw it was just them and remembered they were alone in the world.

"I prayed on this for a long time," Mack said stiffly. "Lee was right about this being God's will. Do you know that my mom hadn't even gotten the Covid vaccine yet? She kept coming up with excuses not to, and now I realize that was for a reason. It's all for a reason. She wasn't meant to live, and I wasn't meant to die, and neither was Lee. Why else would I be pregnant when everyone else is dying? I mean, I'm going to have a baby made from *two* immune people! How could that be a mistake? How could it be anything other than meant to be?"

"He left you, though," Katherine reminded her, but even as she said this, she remembered that his abandonment was the best thing for Mack. As stubborn and smart and reckless as she knew Mack to be, she had to remind herself that she was only a child. She was judging the girl for her choices when Lee was to blame. Mack might have thought she consented to this relationship, but at only fifteen years old...Lee was nothing more than an abuser. She should have said that first, but damn it, learning about the pregnancy had frazzled her circuits. "Look, I'm projecting. I'm the one who got pregnant once from making a dumb choice, and I know you think you made a choice to be with Lee, but you didn't. Not really. It sounds like he twisted a lot of things to get what he wanted. I think it's probably good that he's gone."

Mack shrugged. "Think what you want, but I know Lee loves me. I've been thinking about it, and I think that he kind of just flipped out for a minute. With Sharon, and then Ricky. He just got in his own head."

"I'm glad you can forgive, Mack, but Lee better hope we never cross paths again." Katherine turned to hail Ricky. "Come on, let's get moving!" The more distance she could put between them and Lee the better.

Mack touched her arm. "I'm not going with you. I changed my mind."

Katherine turned to her. "You what?"

"The minivan we saw when we pulled up, we're going to take it and go back."

"What are we doing?" Ricky said, approaching with bouquets of snack bags pinched in his hands. Orange powder around his mouth suggested he'd already started in on them. His color was back, and he looked ready to roll.

"Me and you are going back to Sharon's," Mack said, at the same time Katherine answered, "Nothing."

Ricky looked between the two. "You two aren't fighting now, are you?"

"No," Mack said. "But we gotta go back, Ricky."

"Don't be stupid. There's nothing back there. Here, take some of these." He pushed a few bags into his sister's hands.

"I've been thinking that Lee will come back, and he's not going to know where we went," Mack insisted.

"Good," Ricky said, shouldering out the main door. Katherine and Mack followed him down the path.

"I'm not kidding," Mack said. "He's going to come back, Ricky."

"And I'm not kidding when I say I don't give a crap. Lee taking off was the best thing that's happened to us in a while. We're going to Michigan, and we don't need him."

They had come to the car. Unable to fill up on gas, they'd had to switch vehicles twice, and just Katherine's luck, this one was another freaking Honda. Mack wouldn't get in. "I have my reasons OK? I need to go back for Lee." Ricky hopped into the front passenger seat and dropped the snack bags on the dash. "Shotgun," he said, and when Mack didn't move, he closed the door.

Katherine stood with a hand on the driver's door, watching her over the car. "Come on. Just get in."

"I'm taking that minivan over there," Mack said loudly to Ricky through the closed window, pointing across the lot.

"You can't even drive!" he shouted back at his sister.

"I can figure it out!"

"Oh, you know how to hotwire a car now?"

This gave Mack pause, and she considered. "There might be keys in it."

Ricky stared straight ahead, and she turned and marched across the lot. "Stupid idiot," he hissed, and got out. Had he called her a stupid bitch, Katherine would have thought he sounded just like Lee.

"What does she think she's doing?" Ricky demanded.

Katherine shrugged. "She's hormonal."

"Gross," Ricky said immediately, throwing up a hand to prevent her from saying more. "I don't want to hear about period stuff." He started after Mack. The minivan must have been unlocked, and she was already searching inside.

Katherine got in the Honda but didn't close the door. She just watched. After a few moments of Mack and Ricky sitting in the van, she knew what was going to happen.

Ricky jogged back and opened the passenger door. "Listen, Katherine. We found a key fob. I'm sorry, but—"

"I know," Katherine interrupted. "It's OK. Just grab your bags." It wasn't OK, but how could she stop them? They'd drifted into her life in that store, and even now, after everything they'd been through together, they didn't belong to her. They had chosen to come home with her and Sharon that day, and now they were choosing to move on.

She waited while Ricky collected their things from the back. He tossed Mack's pack over one shoulder and grabbed his duffle. He started to gather the snacks from the front seat, stopped for a moment, and then left her a third of them. She remembered the moment at the pharmacy when he'd seen the fairness in leaving some prescriptions for Sharon and felt a rush of tenderness.

"Ricky, you know you don't have to go? She won't go if you don't go."

He shook his hair, long strands falling into his eyes. He looked like a troubled pop star when he said, "I don't know what's wrong with her. But if I don't go, I swear she's going anyway. I can't let her go off alone."

Katherine started the car, and he closed the door. "Take care, Ricky."

"We will," he said. "Thanks for everything. Sorry about this."

Katherine shifted into drive, and Ricky started to walk away. She paused, reconsidered, and before she could stop herself, shouted to him, "Hey!"

He turned back.

"She's pregnant."

He pushed his bangs out of the way, duffle sliding to the pavement. "What?"

"It's Lee's." She waited, hoping shock could change his mind. When his mouth twisted into the stubborn look she'd seen so many times on Mack, she knew they wouldn't be coming with her. "Be careful of him, Ricky. If he's there when you get back, watch out for her." Thinking of Lee's easy anger, she added, "Watch out for each other."

Katherine rolled up the window and pulled away. She cranked the air conditioning. In the rearview, she saw Ricky hadn't moved. She braked, thinking maybe he had realized how stupid it was to go back, that if Lee never returned, he and Mack would be alone with a baby. Maybe he'd put together that if Lee never returned, *he'd* be the one helping his sister deliver that baby. She saw him reach for his duffle and turn toward the minivan. *OK then*, she thought, and eased her foot off the brake.

They had burned daylight at the welcome center, and as Katherine got closer to Louie's address, she started to worry that arriving unexpectedly after dark could be a mistake. After all, she didn't really know Louie. What if he were trigger happy? Didn't everyone in the country have guns?

A half hour away and low on gas again, she pulled to the side of the road. The sun had taken its heat with it, and the empty, dark road made her edgy. She turned off the engine and climbed into the backseat, feeling too weird to actually get out of the car and enter through the door. Pulling out a blanket from under the grocery bags on the floor, she wrapped it around her like armor, lying back and watching night fall.

Katherine had seen plenty in the city. Guys who turned nasty if she rejected their drink at the bar, the homeless man by her office who had hissed at her every morning. She'd even witnessed a mugging once, though it had never happened to her personally. She thought of herself as a tough city girl, but the wide-open fields and loud insects of the country still made her nervous.

Katherine thought she'd be in for an uncomfortable night between the strange noises and cramped backseat, but the drama of the day and the long, lonely drive overtook her. She fell asleep almost immediately.

She dreamed of Louie and picked vegetables with him through the night. When they were done, they sat together with baskets of food nestled in their laps and watched the sunrise.

"I wish I could tell you that I'm on my way," she told him. She plucked a leaf of spinach and tested its freshness with her teeth.

"You just did," he replied.

"I mean so that you'll know in real life." She chewed the green, then flicked the stem into the dirt. "But I didn't have a way to call you. And this is my dream, not yours."

"No, it's not your dream. But it's not mine either," Louie mused. "I think it's *ours*."

Katherine awoke sweating. It would be another record-setting day, already was, and the sun heat the car like a greenhouse. The daylight was reassuring, so she felt safe enough getting out now, pausing in the road to stretch, to bend and touch her toes.

She brushed her hair into a ponytail and then dug through the garbage bag of clothes in the trunk for something fresh to put on. She debated wearing her same old cutoff shorts with a fresh T-shirt but remembered Sharon's white sundress with the tiny violets on it. A strappy dress was perfect for a heatwave. Even better for meeting someone you hoped would let you in his house. She pulled it on.

Driving through the town, she noticed how normal it seemed with its two (nonfunctioning) stoplights and its even number of bars and churches, unless you considered all the people were missing. She only jumped a little when she passed a sheriff's car parked at a corner, believing someone was inside until she saw that it was only a mannequin with a hat on.

She stopped at the mailbox at the end of Louie's drive, double-checked the green address tag next to it just to be sure, and debated whether she should drive straight up the long driveway or park and walk up. Would it make a difference if she arrived on foot or if she barreled up to his front door like an invited guest?

She settled for pulling partway up the drive, and when she got out, a cloud of dust swirling at the hem of her skirt, she half expected him to already have spotted her and come out to greet her. He hadn't, so Katherine smoothed her hot hands over her borrowed cotton dress and approached cautiously. "Hello? Anyone home?"

Minutes later, she was feeling foolish. He hadn't come to the door when she knocked, and what the hell had she expected anyway? The town was dead, and he probably was too. Dreaming of him was not the same as knowing he was alive. When she woke this morning, the taste of spinach fresh on her tongue, she'd almost convinced herself that not only was Louie alive, but he *knew* she was coming.

She sat on the metal rocking chair next to the door and fanned herself with her hand. Heat bled through the porch roof like it wasn't there. Lifting her ponytail, Katherine swatted at the strands sticking to her neck. She cursed the heat and the man who had lured her here when he was just going to go off and die anyway.

Maybe he's out running errands. *Errands*, she thought scathingly. *Nobody runs errands anymore, Katherine.* Then she heard a generator kick to life like an engine. She started in her chair as if jerked from a dream. "Louie?" she called. There wouldn't be a generator running if he wasn't here. Her supposition was confirmed a moment later when she walked around the house and spotted the dogs. They began to bark. No, they wouldn't be here either.

The dogs came over to sniff her fingers between the wood beams. Her attention wasn't on them, however. She'd spied the garden gate, and she knew now that Louie was in there, beyond the white trellises blocking her view, crouched somewhere with his fingers in the cool soil.

She moved through the garden like it was her own, recognizing plants like friends. She found him near the back, sitting on a big rock. He was sifting through a basket of large greens so that she could see the shaggy top of his sandy hair. Katherine paused to watch him. She was not surprised to find that he looked like the man she'd dreamed of, and if her dreams were right about his appearance, they must be right about the kind of man he'd be too. Remembering herself, her gaze shifted to his waist to make sure he didn't have a gun. She was a trespasser, after all, and she might know who he was, but she couldn't be certain he'd know her.

When he finally saw her, she moved closer, noting that the hair curling around his ears needed cutting, and his wide eyes were the light brown she remembered. His face looked younger than she expected, open, like she'd given him a surprise gift. He didn't look shocked or jump to his feet. He just said, sounding surprised, "Oh, I didn't think I was dreaming just now."

She didn't know how to respond, so said, "I'm Katherine from the newspaper. In New York."

"I thought you were that Katherine, but this is the first time you've said your name." He set the basket aside. "I expected to get some real work done in the garden today, but that's OK. Dreaming with you is always better. And I do like this part the best, when you're walking toward me, not away."

Katherine stepped closer and said, "We're not dreaming. I'm really here." Then lamely, "I drove here in a Honda."

Louie seemed unconvinced by this lifelike detail. "I dreamed about you just last night, and you said you'd come. But it will be days before you get here."

Our dreams are *shared.* "Time is funny in dreams," Katherine said. "I was only a few miles away last night. I'm here now, I promise, and you're definitely not dreaming. Can't you tell this is different? Can't you hear?"

He shook his head, hearing only the distant hum of the generator.

"There's no baby crying," she pointed out.

Louie listened. "I guess there's not. But I don't hear it every time."

"So, you're Louie?" she asked, though she knew the answer. She'd known when she first saw the garden, before he even looked up from his basket. She would have known it even if she hadn't just come to the address he'd given her.

He stood. "I'm Louie." Taking her hand, he shook it slowly, and she saw that he felt the realness of her flesh against his and knew she wasn't a dream. "But maybe you should call me Adam."

CHAPTER SIXTEEN

I T FELT LIKE THEY WERE Adam and Eve standing in the Garden of Eden, he'd meant to say, but as usual, Louie's mouth got in the way of his brain. Instead of giving him a look that made him feel like a moron, the look he'd been getting since he was old enough to talk, Katherine just smiled like she understood and turned toward the house, hips swaying, looking for all the world like she belonged there in his garden.

He followed her long dark hair toward the house like it was a leash tugging him home, noting as many things as possible while her back was turned. How, as she strode with purpose, the wrists and hands swinging at her sides looked so dang small. How her shiny ponytail glowed in the sunlight, making it look less brown than red. Her long dress looked like a country bride's wedding gown after lying in a field of wildflowers.

As Louie poured lemonade for them, Katherine mentioned something about people she'd stayed with, and Louie was starting to tell her about his own houseguests (intending to leave out the parts about power struggles and night burials for now), when they heard tires crunch gravel. "Speak of the devil," Louie said when Grider and Devlin approached, having returned from gathering supplies. It was a turn of phrase most people could pull off, but not Louie. He never seemed to be able to muster the levity necessary to make it tease instead of taunt.

"And who's this?" Grider asked. He approached with a wide smile and popped out his hand as if meeting a new survivor were an everyday occurrence. "Saw your little Honda around front. Couldn't believe our eyes! I'm Grider."

Katherine clenched the sweaty glass of lemonade, sitting primly on the edge of Louie's mother's bark chair, and Louie supposed she must be nervous considering how she was cradling her drink between her thighs like it might leap from her hands. The dreams made her familiar to him, but there was so much of her mind he didn't know yet. What was making her nervous? Was it meeting him, or being surrounded by men when maybe she'd expected to find him alone?

She was a career woman, probably used to being the only woman in a crowd of suits, but the world was different now, and this was no fancy boardroom. She wouldn't know that Devlin and Grider were harmless. They were strangers on a farm in the middle of nowhere.

Katherine's hesitation to take his hand caused Grider to exchange a quick look with Devlin. Louie noticed it, and Katherine seemed to as well. After a pause, she stood, wiped the condensation from her glass on her hip, and accepted the handshake, pumping once, fast and firm.

"Katherine," she said. "Sorry, I'm a little out of practice on shaking hands. We haven't done that in the city in a long time, since before Covid."

Devlin gave his name, and she took his hand more easily, while he said something charming about giving her more practice. Louie noticed how Grider had shaken like a buddy and how Devlin hadn't. Katherine, he was pleased to see, released Devlin's hand as quickly as she did Grider's. Then Louie remembered that he'd taken her hand in the garden, and she hadn't hesitated or pulled away at all.

He noted again how pretty she was in her sundress, the faint blush on her cheeks as the men made her the center of attention. He felt strangely proud that she had come. *Look at this beautiful creature I brought here,* he wanted to brag. *She came all the way from the East Coast to find me. Who's a loser now?*

"Introductions out of the way, how about you tell us where you appeared from?" Grider said, lowering his bulk to sit on a step as Devlin leaned—he was always leaning—against the porch rail. Louie despaired as they settled in, thinking how close he'd been to being alone with Katherine for good, if only the men had left for Ohio sooner. He and Grider had wasted too much of the morning at the ranch.

"I'm here from New York," Katherine murmured, taking a sip of her lemonade and casting a look over her glass at Louie. He wondered if she would say anything about the dreams. Devlin had a cop's brain and a minister's mistrust, and he didn't want to give the man any reason to stick around asking questions. They hadn't talked about it them-selves yet, and Louie hoped she felt, like he did, that the secret should remain theirs.

"Long way," Devlin commented. *Please don't like cow-boys,* Louie thought when Devlin and Katherine exchanged smiles.

"Louie and I talked on the phone a while back, so I knew he would still be here. When my friend was gone, I decided to come."

Devlin hadn't looked at Louie much, focused entirely on Katherine, but Louie drew his attention, saying, "She interviewed me for the newspaper after everyone here was gone."

Devlin made a noncommittal sound, and Grider took over. "I'm a truck driver, that rig over there is mine, and Devlin here is a cop."

Was, Louie thought. *Just like I was a mechanic. None of us is anything anymore.*

"Well, this is awkward," Katherine said after a beat. "That car in the drive has expired tags, Officer." She said this in just the way to dispel the tension, and just like that, Louie knew her superpower.

Grider and Devlin both relaxed and started asking one question after another about the state of things in New York and what Katherine had seen on her drive to Michigan. She volunteered stories about Sharon, and how they'd met Mack, Ricky, and Lee at the IGA. She told them about the empty office buildings and closed restaurants in New York, her New Jersey apartment building, baby Ana, and the awful smell in the suburbs. She even told them, sheepishly, about the car buffet and the Jaguar. She was so forthcoming that they would have been surprised to learn she was holding back. She didn't tell them the most important thing—she and Louie weren't strangers.

Louie, now at ease because he could see that Katherine wasn't charmed by Devlin and didn't intend to discuss their dreams, eventually stood and murmured, "I'll just put some lunch together. PB&J is good for the road, I think."

Louie was surprised when Katherine followed him into the kitchen. She spread peanut butter on bread halves and handed them to him for jelly.

"Had enough of the third degree?" he asked. He had sweated circles into his T-shirt, and she could see he was trying to hide them, standing stiffly with his arms at his sides as they worked shoulder to shoulder. She didn't mind. It was a reassuring, healthy sweat from a hot day of working in the garden, not the sick sweat of fever.

Moving closer, Katherine said sotto voce, "I get the feeling if I wasn't here, they'd be leaving already."

"There's a lot to tell you," Louie said. "They weren't going to stick around this morning. Now I'm not so sure."

"Looks like they're packing up tents out there now," she said. "Were they staying outside?"

"No, that was someone else. Like I said, a lot to tell you."

"You're not making me sleep outside, are you?" Katherine asked. She poked her knife in the jar but was focused on his answer.

"No, not you."

Katherine set down the jar. "We haven't really talked about what you said before, when you first saw me. I gather that you've had dreams about me too. That we've shared them."

"Later," he said as the screen door opened.

"We thought we might stay for lunch, Louie," Grider said, Devlin behind him. "Take sandwiches for our dinner, if that's good?"

Louie sighed. "Sure."

Devlin poured water into a dish and took it out to the porch. Katherine saw that there was another dog now. He snuffled Clark, who seemed to be playing possum. "You have running water?" she asked, thinking about the many cold utility baths she'd suffered through recently using jugs of filtered water.

"We do," Louie said. As if to impress her, he continued, "I've got a good deep well and a generator for the well pump and hot water heater. You can take a shower if you want. I've got a couple gennies going actually, and I have a few freezers with beef and other stuff in the basement. We can have steaks on the grill if you want. And air conditioning too, though it's not on now."

Devlin came back inside, and hearing this said, "He's pretty stingy on the air conditioning though. Gotta save fuel."

"I'll put the air on for you, though," Louie was quick to interject. "It's really hot today." She noted Devlin's irritated look and Louie's half smile, sensing there were politics at play when it came to household matters.

"It's been hot every day," Grider grumbled as he helped himself to a sandwich. He flapped it at Louie. "Just one to tide me over. Let's see what's for lunch then." Biting into the sandwich, he opened the fridge and began to poke around.

"There's a ham in there," Devlin said. "Pulled it out of the ice chest last night."

Katherine felt Louie tense next to her, and little wonder. These guys behaved like they owned the place. She smiled mischievously at Louie and said, "Grilling tonight sounds amazing. Fresh asparagus. You grow that in your garden, don't you?" She knew he did.

"And watermelon for dessert, if you like," he said. They had eaten watermelon in one of their dreams together, sitting on the stone bench in the moonlight. The sticky flesh still warm from the day's sun, they had dug it out with their fingers and spit the seeds into the lettuces. This shared secret made them smile goofily at each other.

Katherine capped the peanut butter and jelly jars, feeling intensely happy for the first time in months. After weeks of PB&J and tuna, the thought of fresh food from the garden was heavenly. She would sprinkle the watermelon with fresh basil.

"Steaks and grilled veggies. Keep it up and I'll be staying for dinner," Grider said. He dropped the ham on the kitchen table. "We just sawing chunks off this, or making sandwiches or what?"

"There's not much bread left." Louie frowned at the stack of peanut butter and jelly sandwiches. "I've been thinking I might start making my own. There's only a few loaves in the freezer."

"How about with some crackers then?" Devlin said, exchanging a look with Grider.

"Crackers sound good!" Grider said, as if it was the best idea he'd ever heard. "Louie, you know where the crackers are?"

"In the pantry downstairs," he said without looking up. He was stuffing sandwiches in plastic bags.

"I didn't see any down there yesterday," Grider said.

"Don't know what to tell you. There's two big boxes of Ritz."

Grider headed down the stairs off the kitchen, arching a brow at Devlin as he did so. Louie didn't catch the sly look, but Katherine did, so she wasn't surprised when a few minutes later the man called, "Hey Louie? Help me find the goddamn crackers, would you?"

Louie dropped a sandwich with a long-suffering sigh. His expression said, *You see what I have to put up with?* He was halfway down the stairs when Devlin moved to Katherine's side.

"You can come with us, you know," he said.

"Why would I do that?" she returned lightly. "We're grilling for dinner."

Devlin put a hand on her arm, and that stopped her. "Look, I know you just got here, but this isn't any place you want to be."

Katherine withdrew her arm and narrowed her eyes. "It was fine for you, wasn't it?"

"I don't know what Louie has told you..."

"He hasn't told me anything. But I can see you guys made yourselves at home here. I don't see why I shouldn't stay too if he's offering."

Devlin's attention shifted to the stairs, listening, and Katherine wondered just where Grider had stashed the crackers to keep Louie distracted.

"Listen," Devlin said urgently. "Some stuff went down, and that's why we're going. There were others, and Louie wasn't too happy about having guests. He's possessive of his things, and there was some..." He paused to weigh his words. "There was some violence."

"What kind of violence?"

They heard Grider and Louie on the linoleum stairs. "Behind the powdered milk of all places..." Grider was saying loudly.

"When it's time to go, just say you're coming too."

How do I know you're not the violent one? Katherine thought. *How do I know it's any safer to come with you?* There was no time to ask.

Louie set a box on the table. "Here's your crackers."

"Thanks, Louie," Devlin said easily. "Let's eat."

Katherine wiped the sweat and fog from the bathroom mirror, having just enjoyed the longest, most decadent shower of her life. She'd relished the feeling of hot water running over her skin, and in a lighted bathroom. Naked, she stood there and enjoyed the humid air (with this heat wave, it was like the sauna at the gym) and slid a brush through her hair. She relished every sensation, from the feel of the stiff bristles on her scalp to the scent of the shampoo, as though she'd never washed her hair before. The soap smelled like man, and the dandruff shampoo did too. The masculine scents smelled like a new beginning on her skin.

Had it really been that long since she'd lost power, lost light and clean water? It had only been a few weeks, but it felt much longer. There were people who camped in the wilderness a whole season for fun, longer than she'd been living through the flu pandemic. Still, it felt she had *been through something* and come out the other side. How long was it since she'd last felt clean and safe?

Katherine stopped the brush in her hair and stared into the mirror. She couldn't remember feeling like this ever— not before the flu, not before the depression that came when she lost her pregnancy, not even in childhood. Despite not having much family anymore, she'd had a safe childhood, surrounded by adults who paid attention. But this was different, this feeling of rightness and belonging. She felt at home.

Louie had provided clean clothes that smelled like a dryer sheet. They awaited, folded neatly on the toilet, but she was in no hurry to put them on. She liked being here in this moment, when she felt like she was dreaming—one of the good dreams, a garden dream. She never liked waking from those, because being in them felt more real than the waking world.

As she stood in the hot steam, she thought, *If this is a dream, please don't make me wake up this time.* She heard Devlin and Grider carry their things down the narrow hallway, brushing the bathroom door as they passed, bringing her back to reality. "Just come with us," Devlin had said, and continued to say with his eyes all through their lunch. How could she, though? When he passed the bag of chips, she wondered how she could leave when she'd only just gotten here, when the pandemic seemed almost *forgivable* because it had brought her here. When he passed her a cold can of Coke, she considered that if it hadn't been for the flu, for losing Sharon and Ana, she'd never have driven alone to Michigan and never have had a cold can of anything again. And when she looked over at Louie, hopeful and nervous, she thought how if it weren't for everything bad in the world, she would never have come to him.

Katherine heard the screen door bang when one of the men went outside and realized she should probably see them off. She pulled on a pair of denim shorts that had belonged to someone named Adra. She had thought of slipping back into her sundress, but Louie was going to take her for a drive around town to show her his routine after the other men left, and she didn't want to get it dirty. She used Louie's deodorant, which smelled like bug spray, and put on the old concert T-shirt he'd given her to wear. Though she had her bag of clothes out in the car, she'd accepted it anyway. Maybe it would please him, like they were in high school and she was wearing his football jersey.

Observing that, despite the pandemic, this was the most dressed-down she'd been in ages, Katherine emerged from the bathroom, her hair piled in a wet bun on her head. She tucked the T-shirt front into her shorts as she walked. It came to the edge of the short denim fringe, and if she let it hang, it looked as though she was wearing just the shirt.

Louie met her in the kitchen. His eyes popped a bit at all the leg she was showing, but she thought he played it cool when he eyed her shirt and said only, "Rock on."

"That was the best shower of my life," Katherine replied.

He smiled, which was good, because it made him look less anxious.

"The boys are about to leave," he said.

"I suppose we should go out and wish them well."

They didn't move. Katherine sensed Louie wasn't ready to go outside, perhaps trying to avoid an awkward goodbye. "So what's this thing?" She pointed to a folding table in the corner with equipment on it—a wood box with a metal face, dials and switches, and a long cord curling to a microphone that looked straight off the stage at an Elvis concert. "A CB radio?"

"It's a ham radio, actually."

"Is there a difference?"

"Well, yeah. But not to people who don't care about radios."

Katherine drifted over to it and touched the headset. "What's the main difference?"

"To start with, anybody can use a CB. If you want to talk on a HAM, you need a license."

"And you have one?"

"No, I never did get one." Louie flicked a switch, and the radio began to glow from inside. Katherine expected a crackle of activity, but it was silent. "It was my grandpa's, his hobby after the war. I guess he never really liked me to bother it, so when my mom moved it here, I just left it alone. Besides, it's for talking to people nearby. I didn't care much for my neighbors, but if I had to, I'd pick up a phone."

"Are there people to talk to now?"

"I haven't tried it. Devlin hauled it up from the basement a while ago. He fiddles with it at night when it's hot and he can't sleep."

Katherine picked up on what he wasn't saying. Devlin hadn't asked to bring up the radio. He'd just done it. "They took advantage, did they? Of your hospitality?"

"Can't say I'm sorry to see them go."

They heard Grider's truck start. Louie gave Katherine a small smile and motioned for her to precede him. She knew he wasn't smiling because the men were leaving. It was because he felt it too. How the conversation came easy for them, like old friends.

Katherine couldn't know that Louie was smiling because, for the first time since his mom was alive, he felt like there was someone on his side. He followed her out to the porch.

Devlin and his packed rooftop dimmed Louie's smile, not because they had pilfered supplies he might need later, but because he wasn't stupid. The crackers ruse hadn't fooled him for a minute. No doubt he'd wanted Katherine alone to either tell her Louie was crazy or to urge her to go with them. Neither reason put him at ease.

The diesel truck's loud idle competed with the drone of the many gennies to which Louie had grown accustomed. Grider came over to shake his hand. "Take care of each other," he said to them. Louie looked for hidden meaning and found none. He did see Katherine's surprise when Grider patted her shoulder. Louie didn't mind the contact much. Sometimes all there is when the world is ending are rituals, and Grider wasn't all bad.

Louie shook Devlin's hand too. He wouldn't miss the man, not a bit, but he didn't lie to himself. He would miss the extra pair of strong hands for chores, especially for dragging around gas jugs and propane tanks.

Watching Devlin say goodbye to Katherine, he tried hard not to panic. He did feel like she was on his side and knew they had a connection, but was that a meaningful look that Marlboro Man had just given her? Was Devlin trying to communicate something? If she was going to leave now, he couldn't stop her. A lifetime of insecurity rushed back as Louie waited to see if Katherine would stay.

"Be safe, and I hope you find your family, Devlin," Katherine said. It wasn't a chilly goodbye, but cooler than the one she'd given Grider. Louie liked how quick she'd been to pick up on his feelings about the men. His tension eased. The relief felt like staring into sink bubbles in the morning.

"Mind if I talk to Louie for a moment?" Devlin asked, and Katherine gave him a last wave before meandering toward the dog corral. Devlin beckoned Louie to follow him, dragging his finger through the air. Louie trailed after it, docile now that he was getting what he wanted. He knew he had started to grin but was unable to stop.

Devlin reached the driver's door and turned to him. "Stop smiling, you jackass." He said it like he was ribbing a buddy, but Louie was no stranger to a bully's teasing tone just before getting smashed into a school locker.

"I think Katherine should come with us, Louie," Devlin continued, and Louie stopped smiling.

"She doesn't want to," he said. He threw a quick look toward the corral where Katherine was meeting the dogs. Assured she was neither a figment of his imagination nor climbing into Grider's semi behind his back, he turned his attention to Devlin.

"She may not want to, but she should," Devlin said. "I know you think you can take care of her, Louie, but these last few days have shown me otherwise. I don't know what the hell happened with Adra and that whole mess, I really don't, but I do know that just yesterday you were screaming about being stabbed in your sleep. Katherine should know about your…" Here at last, he seemed to hesitate. "Instability," he finished.

"She knows I'm not unstable," Louie said. "We're getting along fine."

"After an hour drinking lemonade?" Both men gazed at Katherine, who had begun to fill the trough with warm hose water. This was a drain on the generator, and the dogs were used to cool water Louie pumped himself, but he could change his routines for her.

"As you can see, she doesn't need my help," Louie said. "I think she'll be a fine *partner*. She's already chipping in."

"You're missing my point. She might be a good partner to you, but what will you be to her?"

Louie shrugged. Feeling the weight of Devlin's cop stare, his eyes drifted to his feet, where he toed dry dirt into a small pile with his shoe. All he'd ever wanted was to be the hero, but Devlin would never see him as one. Could Katherine?

"Have it your way, Louie. But listen to me now…" He waited for Louie to look him in the eye. "Don't make me regret leaving this woman to go off and find another. I have no idea what I'll find when I get to Ohio, but I know what I'm leaving here, and I'm not feeling good about it. She's a nice, innocent lady, Louie. She's not here to be your girl-friend, she's here to survive."

Louie couldn't explain to Devlin that harming Katherine in any way was the last thing he wanted. The man couldn't possibly understand the connection he felt to her, the part-nership he knew they could have. Besides, Devlin needed to mind his own business. They were adults, and Katherine an intelligent, rational woman capable of making her own choices. *And who says she's only here to survive? She could choose to be my girlfriend, buddy. It's not impossible!*

Louie wanted to tell the man he'd had quite enough of being patronized. Enough of Devlin, with his self-righteous judgment and "level-headed" opinions and goddamn psycho dog. But an argument would just delay his departure further. Louie said only, "I won't keep her here if she wants to go."

Devlin climbed into the Tahoe. Keno began to yip energetically in the seat next to him.

"Hasta luego," Louie said, thinking that's what they say in movies when someone leaves on a very long journey that you hope they won't come back from.

"Take care, Louie," Devlin said. It sounded more like a warning than farewell.

Louie stepped back, and as Devlin rolled away, Louie flipped him the bird. Devlin didn't notice. With one wrist steering the vehicle and his other arm hanging out the window, he caught Katherine's gaze across the yard and slapped his palm on the outside of the door, a macho "See ya," which would have annoyed Louie if he hadn't been so happy to see the man go.

Devlin turned the corner, and the Tahoe crunched over the driveway alongside the house. Moments later, Grider's truck shuddered to life and followed. Louie braced himself for a loud honk, another goodbye, and was thankful when the blast didn't come.

He went to greet Katherine as she stepped out of the corral and fastened the latch behind her. Dust filled the air like smoke. He almost said, "Alone at last," and then realized that might sound like something a creep would say, so he held his tongue.

"Alone at last," Katherine said. When Louie blinked with surprise, she added, "You must be relieved to have your house back again!"

He was more than relieved. It felt like life was starting.

CHAPTER SEVENTEEN

A MONTH AGO, KATHERINE HAD BEEN a New Yorker (by day), wearing shoes that cost as much as a car payment and skirts that hit the perfect spot on her legs. Others might have envied her as the kind of woman who wore things just right and who always had lunch plans. Now, as she sat next to Louie in his old truck, her stomach full of peanut butter and lemonade, windows open and her arm burning in the sun, Katherine looked down at her cutoff shorts and Crocs and thought about how life had changed.

Louie noted her self-observation and said, "Do you miss your old life?"

"It's funny you should ask that," Katherine replied, looking out the window at the rundown houses and dusty air. "I was just thinking about it."

"And?"

"No one's asked me that. In fact, I only just asked myself that same question, which is weird, don't you think? I haven't taken much time to mourn my last life."

"The word 'mourn' says a lot," Louie remarked. He turned the truck at the only four-way stop in town. This route took them away from the few downtown homes and storefronts to a one-lane road that bisected a corn field. She hadn't been expecting the sudden corn rows flying past, so close to town.

"I don't mean it like that. When I really think about it, I don't miss any of it. Is it strange to say that life was more stressful then, considering we're trying to survive a pandemic now? The end of the world, even?"

"Not to me," Louie said. "I'm much happier now." Before Katherine could respond, he continued, "This here is our first stop." They had pulled into a long driveway at an abandoned farm, its red grain silo painted with moss and the barn roof roughly tiled with shingles the colors of an American flag. From the truck, Katherine could already hear the chickens.

They climbed out of the truck, and Louie grabbed a bag from the bed as she approached the barn.

"I thought you had chickens back at the house."

Louie nodded and swung open the door. "I do, but I keep those for eggs."

Katherine's stomach bounced. "Oh."

Louie laughed. "You're not a vegetarian, are you?"

"Plant-based is healthier," Katherine said.

"You sound like a city girl. Besides, who needs diets anymore when there's no doctors telling us we have high cholesterol?"

"Stop," she said, giving him a nudge. "Eating healthy isn't a big city trend. Besides, we have plenty of reason to eat clean now. No doctors to help us when we have a heart attack."

"Well, I've always liked meat," Louie said as they crossed the yard. "But if you want to eat out of the garden and ignore my grilled chicken, that's fine with me. Eventually I won't have much meat around to eat either, though, once the chickens are gone. Unless I hunt for it, which I've never done."

Katherine was thinking about food again, and her stomach rumbled. It stopped when Louie opened the barn door and the odor hit her. She'd expected feathers and earthy smells, but instead, the scent of ammonia burned through her sinuses and eyes. She put her hand over her nose and mouth and said delicately, "Why so many of them? Is this a commercial farm?"

"Oh, no, an actual chicken farm would have thousands of chickens. There's only fifty or so, enough for the family that lived here and to sell to some neighbors, but I haven't really counted." She could see why. The chickens were not in coops. Instead, they were free-ranging all over the barn, stepping in and out of beams of sun coming through missing slats in the roof. Louie shifted the sack in his arms, and the birds began to float toward them.

"What's in there?"

"Oatmeal," he said, and offered it to her. "Want to feed them?"

"I sort of thought they'd eat corn." She took the heavy sack and cradled it into the crook of her arm. "Isn't this a corn farm?"

"Corn's OK for chickens, and they do eat some of that, but it's good to give them variety. Oatmeal is good. They like it, and I remember hearing it makes them less aggressive to eat things they like."

Katherine thought about her bare legs and noted all the sharp-toed birds flocking toward her. "Aggressive?"

"Toward each other," Louie said. "You don't want them pecking and cannibalizing."

"Oh." She'd begun tossing handfuls of oatmeal from the bag, and they bobbed in their funny way toward the food source. "They sure do like it."

One chicken sidled up next to her and pecked at her sandal. "They're kind of cute." She remembered feeding the ducks at the Bronx Zoo as a kid.

"Don't get attached," Louie warned. "I try to think of this as a chore, not feeding the chickens. Otherwise, you can't kill them later."

Katherine continued to dig into the sack of oats. "I'm not going to kill them anyway."

"I figured that. You feed and I kill, sound fair?"

"Only one of those sounds fair to the chickens," she said and turned away so she wouldn't see what he did next. The chickens at her feet trilled and peeped, until they heard a single high-pitched sound call to them like an awful dinner bell.

Back in the truck, Louie said, "I haven't quite gotten the hang of keeping them calm beforehand. I wish I had paid more attention to processing when I was little."

"Who killed the chickens when you were a kid?" Katherine asked. It had been hot and itchy in the barn, and the breeze from the open window felt good as they drove.

"My mom."

"Not your dad?"

"Nope, didn't have one of those. Just me and her."

Katherine glanced over at him. She hadn't heard sadness, only fact. She tried to match his tone. "I was raised by aunts and uncles. No siblings, either, though I had a few cousins."

Most people would have asked probing questions, like what had happened to her parents? Why hadn't she lived in one place? How had this shaped her life? But Louie made a comforting, noninquisitive noise that made her feel relieved. She detested conversations about her family, especially ones that started with a "Sorry about your parents" platitude that required her to make the other person feel better by saying "It's OK, I was young," even though it had never felt OK.

"My mom died of Covid," he said without prompting. "It's very annoying having your mom die in a small town, by the way. Everyone knows about it and asks about it. It's like they have a free pass to say whatever they want, because they knew her for her whole life. Like they own you because you were born here."

Katherine mulled this over. Having lost her parents in a car accident at a very young age and having lived with various Coburn relatives over the years, she could relate. They'd had a certain kind of ownership over her too, and where other young girls wanted to be princesses or doctors, her only ambition had been to be grown, to have her own little apartment with all of her own things arranged just so.

She pushed aside thoughts of her own childhood and focused on what Louie had said, or hadn't said. "Is that why you're happier now?" she asked him. "Because you like to be alone?"

"Happier?"

"Isn't that what you said earlier? That you're much happier now?"

For the first time, he seemed hesitant to share his mind. Finally, he said, "I like routine. With all the people gone, routine is more important than ever."

Katherine thought maybe it was more than that, but said, "I like routine too. I like things to be orderly, clean. People at work used to tease me about my organized desk, my little rituals. That I tidied up after the cleaning staff. You know, I was actually dusting in my apartment the same day I realized there was no one left in the building…"

"Won't find much cleanliness around here," Louie noted, motioning to the windshield, its dusty film hazy in the sunlight. "Up north living is dirty living." He'd used wet wipes on his hands after the chickens, but if he chewed a nail now, he'd probably taste the iron of blood under it.

"It's a different kind of dirt here," Katherine said, still eyeing his nails. "It's not germs, just nature. I'm better with that."

Louie looked at her with approval. "I think it's exactly that. I hate germs, but I don't mind getting dirty."

The next day, it was more of the same. Louie was determined to prove Devlin wrong. He could be a good partner to Katherine, and to him that meant sharing his routine and showing her where to find what they needed. They were up at dawn to avoid the hottest part of the day, and he had already shown her where and how to gather gas and propane and taken her to where he had hidden toilet paper and bottled water.

Now she was in the seat next to him, looking contentedly out her window into the pink sun starting to shine from behind city hall, and he realized he hadn't thought about suiciding in almost two days, the longest stretch in many months. Thinking about it now, he knew he would have to tell her. She should know all of his secrets before she decided to stay for good.

They arrived at Elk Ridge, and Louie parked where he had with Grider the day before.

"This is part of your daily routine?" Katherine looked skeptical.

The place looked deserted of anything needful. The cows in the yard were gone, Louie noted. "Not every day, but I'm curious today to take a look around and see what Devlin and Grider might have taken. Besides that, I thought you might like to see it. It's a pretty impressive place, what with all the barns and everything. There might be stuff you want from the big house."

Katherine glanced around. "It's not as nice as your place."

Louie didn't realize until that moment that he'd brought Katherine here to test her. She'd passed easily, as he should have known she would. She was much classier than he was, but he sensed they were still alike. She knew his place was special to him, and therefore, it was special to her.

"Grider seemed to think I should've moved in here."

Katherine waved airily. "I don't see a garden."

Their eyes met. He knew she still wanted to talk about the dreams.

"Come on, let me show you around."

Katherine followed Louie, murmuring questions at times but mostly staying silent as he gave her the tour. He opened another pole barn, the one he'd come to think of as the toy barn. Inside were all of Murchison's playthings, from hunting blinds and fishing shanties to motorcycles, golf carts and ATVs. Stepping back, he let Katherine move in front of him. He was curious which ride she'd gravitate toward.

"Yikes," she said, strolling in. "Looks like a guy who had a lot of money and didn't know how to spend it."

Louie agreed. Murchison was always buying something new, though a rich man he was not. "He did like to spend, but Fred wasn't much more than a farmer."

"And he bought all this?" Katherine paused to observe a pair of kayaks on the wall.

"Yeah, although I never thought he had this much. I saw him drive a lawn tractor to the bar once because the sheriff didn't count it as drinking and driving. Funny he did that when he had all these to choose from." He pointed at a canoe. "I plan to come back for that one for fishing."

"How does a farmer afford all this? This must be thousands of dollars of stuff here."

Just one of the ATVs costs that, Louie thought. He said, "No vacations, no vices. I think anything Fred ever bought is in his house or these barns. He was all about survival. Thought he'd need these things for the end of the world. To him it was worth saving for."

Katherine glanced back at him. "Guess his idea of the end of the world was a little different than reality. I mean, this stuff is useful to us, but maybe air filters and face masks might have been better for him."

"I'm sure Fred's death came as a shock to him," Louie agreed. "He would have expected the Russians to attack or civil war. Not a cold."

Katherine peered into a golf cart. "There's like four of these," she remarked.

"I'd like to show you some of the trails here, especially those where I hid some stuff. Which do you want to take?"

He knew Katherine had taken a few treats from the car buffet, so this wasn't new to her. She turned full circle now, and he could see her calculating which might be the equivalent of her beautiful Jaguar.

"That looks fancy," she said. She pointed to a black side-by-side. "Razr," she read on the side. "Looks like a Mars rover."

"Yeah, that's about twenty grand there," Louie said. "Good choice. Let's see if it still has a charge."

They bounced over a two-track dirt path, trees close enough that they had to dodge the occasional pine branch.

"What you said back there about this looking like a Mars rover gave me a weird kind of jolt," Louie said.

"How's that?"

"I don't know. I just realized that there're still rovers on another planet, roaming around up there, collecting data. But there's no one to receive it. It's weird to think of all the stuff that's still working on autopilot around the world."

"It's weird to think about it stopping at some point too. Which reminds me of the drive here," Katherine said. "You know, windmills are still turning. Which felt kind of nice and normal to me, driving past them. I could pretend I was on a road trip and picture there being other people out there, using the electricity."

Louie slowed down for a tree limb that had fallen across the path. He rolled over it and then surged ahead. "How many people do you think are really out there, based on what you saw on your way? I asked Devlin, but he didn't come as far."

Katherine grabbed the bar above her door as Louie picked up speed and the buggy jounced over ruts. "Based on the smell alone, I'm going to say not many."

Louie knew what she meant. The summer heat had not helped the matter of decaying bodies. Even a slight breeze brought the smell of decomposition. At first it had made him gag. It didn't anymore, but that didn't mean he was accustomed to it.

"There were a few places," Katherine continued, "where I literally had to plug my nose. You'd think you couldn't smell people shut up in their houses, but boy, can you. When it's a lot of people."

Louie followed the path around a bend. Katherine leaned into the turn, and he pointed out water through the trees on her right.

"Almost there," Louie said.

"Would I be able to find this place without you?" Katherine asked.

"Sure. Notice I only took a few turns. Just keep the water to your right on the way there and on the left coming back."

They drove in silence a few moments longer before Louie rolled to a stop. The electric side-by-side was quiet. Katherine fumbled for the door latch, but Louie placed his hand on her arm.

"I just want to say something."

Katherine waited.

"I think you're very brave."

He could see by her swift blush that she was unused to praise. "Oh?"

"I can't imagine what that must have been like, driving all by yourself across half the country. It had to be scary, knowing a lot of people are dead, maybe all of them. And not knowing what you'd find when you got here."

"It wasn't that bad," she said. "I just kind of put my head down and drove. Well, not down, you know, kept my eyes on the road," she stammered. "Figuratively, head down. But, well, that's very sweet, coming from you, Louie. I mean, you're obviously very capable. Not afraid of driving through town, scavenging in people's homes. You're not just surviving, you're thriving."

"Still. You don't see me going any farther than my hometown, where I've lived all my life. You're something, Katherine. I just wanted to say that." Compliment shared, Louie climbed out of the all-terrain buggy. He stepped off the main path and ducked under a tree, finding the foot trail he'd cleared.

"Wow," Katherine said behind him. "I didn't expect the woods to be so noisy." The air was alive with the sounds of birds and buzzing.

"I know, it's unreal." Louie heard her follow him, picking her way through the trees. They emerged in a clearing. He pointed up at a bundle fastened to a high tree limb, swinging lazily from a bungee rope in the slight breeze. "My stuff," he said.

She shaded her eyes with a cupped hand, following his finger as he pointed at other treetops—all of them holding bundles like giant camo Christmas ornaments—describing each as he went. "Ammunition, medicines, canned goods and jerky. Some other things in that one, like mac and cheese and ramen noodles."

"The good stuff," Katherine said.

"Exactly." Louie beamed, seeing her approval. He was glad he'd shown her these. It would help her trust him.

On the ride back, Louie was explaining how to get the satchels down and about bears—"Bears!" Katherine had exclaimed, though why else would he have bothered to put the stuff in trees?—when they hit a rock in the road. Katherine flounced in her seat, saying "Whoa!" as if he were a horse she meant to slow, and Louie stopped.

He started to apologize for driving too fast when they heard the moaning.

"Oh, my God," Katherine said. "Please tell me that's not bears."

Louie was already climbing out of the buggy. "I don't know what that is," he murmured.

"If you don't know what it is, you should be staying inside, not going toward it!"

Louie brushed a branch from his path and ducked out of sight.

"Seriously?" Katherine hissed. There was the moaning again. "Louie!"

She could hear him pick through the woods, but the sounds of his departure were fading. *Please don't leave me here by myself*, she thought. Then she remembered his calling her brave and felt like a coward.

The moaning grew louder. *What the hell* is *that?*

She got out and walked to where Louie had entered the woods. The underbrush was dense here. "Louie?" she called.

She waited a beat until he finally called back, "Hey, bring that toolbox from the back, would you?"

The toolbox was metal and heavy. Katherine cursed as it knocked against her bare shin. When she found Louie, she saw a wire fence that hemmed a ravine, the water she had glimpsed before a wide creek at the bottom. A giant milk cow had gotten entangled in the wire. As Katherine approached, she saw blood ooze around the wire that dug into its front leg. It pulled tighter when the animal tried to struggle free.

"Oh, no, baby," she said, and the cow moaned low and deep.

Louie came to her and took the toolbox. He made it look light as he swung it back toward the fence, dropping it nearby. He flipped the hatch and said, "Let's see what we got here."

Katherine peered over his shoulder. "Can you free her?" she asked. Of the many tools in the box, she could only identify a hammer and saw.

"I think so," Louie said, rummaging. "I figure this toolbox was in the buggy so Murchison could stop and fix the fence line as he moved around the property. There should be something useful in here, wire cutters or whatnot."

The cow shifted, her hooves dancing in the dirt. The wires dug deeper.

"Hurry," Katherine urged, noting that the cow had backed closer to the edge.

Louie swore under his breath. "No wire cutters, no bolt cutters?" he muttered. "Jesus fuck, Fred."

Finally, Louie stood. "I don't know. He should have something to cut with, if he's out fixing goddamn fences, but I can't find anything like that in here. Maybe he's got wire cutters back in the buggy somewhere. Christ, maybe he carried a pair in his overalls." He wiped his sweaty palms on his pants and approached the cow with a small hacksaw. "Sorry, girl. This is the best I've got."

"Careful," Katherine warned.

"This is going to take more than a snip in one spot." He gestured to where the cow's back leg was wrapped in the bottom wire and her foreleg was trapped in the middle wire.

He eased through the fence and edged toward the cow, nothing but air behind him.

"She's going to die soon anyway," he said to Katherine. "You can smell it."

She came to the cow and laid a gentle hand on her head. The animal's eyes rolled back. Katherine did smell it—sour milk seeping from the bag between her legs. "You still have to save her!"

"I know," Louie said, inching closer. "I'm just saying don't expect to name her Bessie and take her home with us. I can smell her milk's infected. She'll be in pain, even after I get her out of this."

"It's OK," Katherine said, talking to both Louie and the cow.

She saw Louie hesitate, calculating the best way to start. The only thing to hold onto was the cow. The closest post was on the other side of her. "Try to keep her still," Louie said, bending toward her back leg.

"Yeah, I don't know how to do that." Katherine patted the cow and murmured soothing words into her ear.

"What'd you tell her?"

"I asked her to please stop moving."

"I suppose that's one way to do it," she heard Louie say, followed by, "Come on, Bessie. We're just trying to help you."

Louie held the cow's leg for balance and began to saw. It caught on the line, and he lifted, set and started again. While Louie worked, Katherine looked at the valley below. The drop was steep, maybe thirty feet. Looking down at the creek made her breathless. *Be calm, girl*, she thought, and it could have been either her or the cow she meant to soothe.

"Nothing but trouble, using the wrong tool for a job," Louie was muttering just as the wire finally broke. He was covered in sweat but rose triumphant. "Got it!" he said, and before he could say more, the cow shook and reared. The wires, the posts, and the cow suddenly pulled free all at once.

"Aw, shit," Louie managed, and then he was sliding.

The cow bellowed.

Louie fell fast, grabbing but finding nothing to slow his fall.

Louie heard Katherine scream. It happened in slow motion in his mind. He even had time to think, *Please don't let a goddamn cow fall on me.* When he hit the bottom, he heard a crack and thought it was the cow breaking the fence as she took it down with her, but it was his back that had made the sound. He knew it a split second later when he tried to move, anxious to get out of the way, still thinking a cow was about to crash onto him. This time Louie screamed.

He blinked up at the trees moments later, certain he'd just passed out. Through the thudding in his ears came a sound he'd never heard before. The cow was squealing. Louie turned his head and looked up. She was dangling halfway down the side of the ravine, wrapped in the fence she had brought with her. Her useless hooves pawed at the earth.

He couldn't see anything else, but he heard Katherine calling to him.

"I'm here," he heard himself say.

"I'm coming, Louie. I'm going to try to get down there, don't move!" she yelled.

"No," he tried to say. *Don't bother*, he wanted to say. If only he could die, instead of lying there wanting to die, he could just wake up at the sink in the morning. But if Katherine hurt herself trying to get down to him…

"Stop," he said, louder. The cow shuddered in the wire.

Katherine's voice drifted down to him as if a thousand feet away instead of thirty. "What do you want me to do? I can't leave you down there!"

But you can, Louie thought. *You should.* And then he closed his eyes.

When he came to again, it was nearly dark. His head pulsed. The cow's legs weren't moving anymore, but her moos told him she was still alive. He sensed a movement that wasn't hers.

"Katherine?" he managed.

She responded immediately. "Louie! You didn't answer me. I thought…"

"Not dead," he said. *Unfortunately.*

She sounded closer than before.

"Where're you?"

"Almost to Bessie," Katherine said.

"Wha?"

"I went back and got a rope. I tied it around my waist and the other end to a tree. I'm trying to lower myself down, but I'm swinging all over the place. Whew, this is a much better workout than the climbing wall in the gym!"

When he didn't answer, she called, "Louie?"

"I'm here." He sighed.

"I don't think this rope is long enough to reach you."

What are you doing then? he wanted to ask, but he was so tired.

Katherine reached the cow. "Oh, Bessie. Oh man," he heard her say. "She's rolling these big, sweet eyes at me, Louie. She's in such pain."

"What are you doing?" Louie asked. His voice was weak, and he thought she hadn't heard him when she replied. "I just swung around, and now I'm nudged up against her. I brought a box cutter. We probably should have just done this from the start."

"I can't cut you down, sweetheart. I would if I could," she cried.

When Louie surfaced next, it was completely dark. He looked up and knew the cow was still there but sensed no movement. Higher up, a small light danced across the trees.

"Katherine," he called.

"I'm here!" she shouted. "I couldn't get down to you. But I threw some things down. There's a water bottle. It's wrapped in an emergency blanket. It should be by your feet?"

Louie lifted his head a few inches and saw a silver shimmer in the moonlight. Feeling more alert now, he looked to his right this time. The creek was a foot away.

"I see it," he said. His voice sounded faint to his ears, making him hope she'd heard him.

"Try to reach it if you can, Louie. I've got one too. I went back to the ranch. We're going to have to wait until light and then I'll try again, figure something out."

Louie wanted again to tell her not to try, but he had few words left. His head still buzzed and his mouth was dry. Could he die from exposure quickly enough to stop her from risking herself?

"It killed me to do it, but I put poor Bessie out of her misery," she said now. "I'm a fucking vegetarian, and I murdered a cow. I cried the entire time, but I had to, you know? I couldn't listen to her like that. She was in such pain."

Louie thought about Katherine rappelling down a mountain to stop a cow from suffering. And he had thought her brave before.

"Are you in pain?" she asked. "Can you move? I can't even see you, there's so much stuff down there."

Louie figured his back was broken, and surely a few ribs. Not to mention he'd hit his head and, now that he was taking inventory, his ankle throbbed. Scratches burned everywhere. He said only, "Think I'm OK. Listen…"

She waited.

"When it's light out, go home."

"I can get to you, Louie," she argued.

"The radio," he said. "In the kitchen."

"The HAM radio?"

"Call for help."

The sound of crickets and frogs consumed him for a time. When she finally spoke again, she asked, "But how far does it reach? Can I get Devlin and Grider to come back, maybe?"

The HAM radio's range was fifteen, twenty miles at most without an antenna, but Louie said, "Probably."

"Shouldn't I go now?"

"When it's light," he repeated. She was safer here, he reasoned. Otherwise she'd have to drive in the dark through the woods, then truck through town. Though why he should worry about that when the woman had proven her resourcefulness more than once today…

"OK, Louie. I'll get help in the morning. Just try to get some rest."

He thought she might curl up in the side-by-side, instead of sitting on the cold ground. But she stayed, flashlight lit in her hands. He waited until the moon set, then turned his head to the water again. The pain in his back and legs would be unbearable, but it would only hurt for a minute.

Katherine was asleep when Louie rolled into the creek. He lay face down and choked water into his lungs. His injured back made it impossible to change his mind, fortuitous, as his greater instincts for survival tried to take over. The cold water was also a blessing because it prevented him from crying out, even as it felt like it would tear his burning lungs apart.

It will be over soon, he thought. *I'll be OK soon. Just a new one for my list.* Except this time, he counted on being alive in the morning.

He concentrated on the soothing image of a different kind of water—warm and bubbling with soap in the kitchen sink.

CHAPTER EIGHTEEN

ATHERINE DROVE FAST. CORNSTALKS BLURRED on both sides. She'd called down to Louie this morning, still unable to see him in the greenery, but this time he hadn't responded. It had been warm overnight, so he hadn't frozen to death, but what about shock? What if he had a concussion? People weren't supposed to sleep after a concussion! Could he have died from internal bleeding? His silence worried her more than his faint voice had the night before.

Katherine tried not to think about what could be wrong, to concentrate on what she could do now. She would get to Louie's house, try the radio, then look for a longer rope or maybe some bungie cords. Perhaps there were pulleys or something else in his shed that would be helpful for hauling him up. She thought about looking at a map. Could there be a hospital nearby where she could locate an ambulance, get a backboard? Or could she access him another way? She knew the creek wasn't buried in a ravine for its whole length. She'd glimpsed it through the trees at times. Could she get the ATV down at an elevated spot and drive along the water's edge to him? Drag him back through the water in a kayak?

The truck tires skidded when she turned toward town. Katherine eased off the gas. She would be no help to Louie in a ditch. As she drove through the tiny business district, she scratched at the bites on her legs—the mosquitoes were horrific in the woods without bug spray—and read each storefront she passed. None of the signs would advertise an "Emergency Supply Depot," but maybe something else would give her an idea.

When she got to the house, Clark was in the yard. He ran up to the truck, tail whipping. She thought they'd left him inside in the air conditioning. Poor boy! He'd been alone outside all night with no food or water. All of that was inside the corral with the other dogs.

She gave him a thump. "Come on, Clark," she said. "We've got to help Louie. And then we'll get you some food, OK?" Her own stomach cramped. She hadn't thought about food until now, but the last thing she'd eaten was a peanut butter sandwich and chips for yesterday's lunch.

When she reached the porch, she smelled bacon and stopped short. It smelled amazing; even being a vegetarian, she recognized that, but *why* did it smell like bacon? She flung open the door, and there stood Louie, making breakfast.

Katherine thought she was dreaming again. It wasn't a garden setting, but a dream made more sense than this domestic scene.

Louie turned, and his look was that of a man caught masturbating. "I can explain!"

Katherine wasn't a fainter. She wasn't prone to hysterics. Her reaction was completely normal for her, which was to simply stand there trying to process. Frozen in place, she searched Louie's face for clues, though she couldn't seem to get her mouth or thoughts to work.

Louie promptly dropped his bowl on the table, egg splashing over the rim, and reached for her. "I knew I'd freak you out, but woah. I didn't expect you to go catatonic. You still in there?"

She felt his warm hands on her shoulders. They felt real enough, but then, he was always real in the dreams too. She knew she must look dazzled, like he'd knocked her in the chin, but she couldn't seem to move her arms or legs.

"Katherine, you with me?" he asked, squeezing her shoulders again. "Come on now. You're starting to scare me."

She blinked. "I don't eat bacon," she said.

"I'm making you eggs." He pointed to the bowl on the table. "Scrambled."

"I'm a vegetarian. I wouldn't normally dream about eating bacon for breakfast." She was trying to work it out.

"You're not dreaming, Katherine." Louie sat her at the kitchen table. "I know this is a shock, and I need to explain, but this isn't a dream. I was in the creek, and now I'm here. You don't have to worry about getting me out now. I'm fine."

"No, I'm probably not dreaming," she murmured. "I'm pretty sure about that now. I definitely don't dream about bacon."

"OK, don't go cuckoo on me, Kate. Just hold on. I've got some veggies grilled for you, and I'm going to serve them with the eggs," Louie said. "Have to say, the last thing I expected this morning was to talk about breakfast, but whatever you need, Katherine. So, uh, there's orange juice too. It's from concentrate, but better than nothing. It's cold. I used water from the pitcher."

He turned to his preparations and switched off the skillet. The bacon continued to sizzle as Katherine began to breathe heavily. Everything in her body felt numb, except for her chest, which seemed to be unfreezing, breaking through with rapid bursts like oil in a pan. Louie came back to her. "Whoa, now, you OK?"

But she wasn't. She was hyperventilating. Breaking down. She felt Louie push her head between her legs. "Don't pass out now," he warned as she shuddered under his hand. "It's OK, Katherine. Just breathe."

When she could finally speak, she whispered into her lap, "I was so scared, Louie. I thought you were crippled, or worse. I thought, *How will I ever do this alone?*"

He crouched next to her chair and took her hands. "I've got some things to tell you. When I'm done, I promise you won't ever have that worry again."

They ate in silence. Each bite took them farther away from the trauma of the day before, and Louie watched the change in Katherine's face as she began to settle. When she'd finally had her fill, her pale face rosy, looking over at Louie with satisfied gratitude, he knew it was time.

"Let's go sit on the porch"—his chair scraped back—"so we can talk about some things."

She took her glass with orange slices etched on it, still halfway filled with juice, and followed him outside. The sun burned across the grass, but it was cooler on the porch. "The dreams and the garden aren't the only magical things here," he began.

"Not hearing the generators right now is pretty magical, if you ask me." Louie was ready for this. Sometimes Katherine joked when she was nervous. It was better than running off screaming, which he supposed someone weaker might do, having discovered him in the kitchen after watching him fall to the bottom of a ravine.

She continued, "My getting down to that cow was pretty magical. You know, I'm good on the climbing wall at the gym, but it was nothing like that."

Louie waited. She got chatty sometimes too.

Katherine stilled in her chair. "So, magical things. Like dreams? I guess now we're getting down to it?"

Louie nodded. "There's something everyone in town knew about me for a while. Rumors mostly, because I don't think anyone actually saw it happen. There was lots of talk about me, though, and that's probably why I'm half glad everyone is gone now."

"OK," she said.

Not knowing any other way to say it, Louie began, "I guess I've tried to kill myself a few times."

Katherine lifted her glass and drank. After a moment, she said, rambling a bit, "I tried to kill myself once too. I suppose we're not the best last people on Earth, are we? Two people who haven't always wanted to live… One might call that magical…"

Louie looked away uncomfortably. "I guess I said that wrong. I mean to say that I've actually killed myself a few times."

He gave her a minute, waiting for the penny to drop, and when it didn't, because what he was saying wasn't something anyone could comprehend without explanation, even after what she'd witnessed this morning, he tried again. "I've died more than a few times. I've tried a lot of different ways but none of them have gotten it done, I guess you'd say. Not permanently, anyway."

"You mean you've tried to kill yourself unsuccessfully a few times?"

Louie dragged his fingers through his hair, frustrating it into a peak. "I know I'm bungling this, but no, that's not what I'm saying. I'm saying I *can't* die, and I've killed myself plenty of different ways. A lot. Not tried, did it."

When she started to speak, he added, "And before you think I'm crazy, I'm telling you it was no secret. Plenty of people in town saw things, circumstances not unlike those last night, that convinced them. I'm pretty sure there was a betting pool on what method would actually get it done. So it's not all in my head. You can't think it's in my head, not after what you've seen. It's the reason I'm sitting here now."

"So what, you're like, immortal?"

"I'm telling you this because I think you'll believe me without me proving it."

Katherine stood and paced the length of the porch. It made Louie sad, because he knew she was trying to put distance between them. "Because you were almost killed last night, and then were somehow standing here today?"

"Because of the dreams," he said simply. "And I wasn't killed last night. When I realized you wouldn't be able to get me out, I worried you'd hurt yourself trying. I took my life so that I could be here in the morning."

She shook her head and looked away, but not before Louie saw her disappointment. She'd driven such a long way, even left others behind to be with him, and now here he was talking crazy. She didn't seem scared or worried. She seemed sad.

"The dreams," he said again. "Katherine, please look at me."

When she did, he continued, "What would it sound like if you tried to explain aloud how you'd been dreaming about this place? Not even just dreaming about it, but that you'd been here before, with me, in my garden, having conversations that we both remember? Those dreams are *real*, and it's why we're not like strangers. Can you imagine it, Katherine, how it would sound to tell someone about it?"

"No one would believe it," she whispered.

"Of course not. Because it's not *normal*. It's like magic. And that's why you'll believe me about the other thing too. It's not normal for someone to kill himself over and over and come back to life the next day like nothing happened. But it's real too. You *know* there's no way I could have gotten out of there last night and got here before you." He showed her both sides of his arms. "Without a scratch on me."

Katherine returned to her seat. "Assuming I believe all of it, do you think this makes me feel safe with you?"

"Well," he said, "shouldn't you feel safer knowing that the person you've partnered up with can't, you know, leave you?"

"Did you tell Devlin this?" she asked.

Louie rolled his eyes. "Hell, no. He'd have thought I was a nutjob. Like I said, I only told you because I knew you'd believe it, knowing everything else."

"He knew something was wrong," Katherine replied. "He wanted me to leave with him."

"I knew it," Louie hissed. This time he stood and paced away, not so much for distance but because it distracted him from the burning sensation growing in his stomach.

"He said something about violence."

Louie looked back at her, mid-pace. "And you didn't leave?"

"He didn't have time to divulge details…"

Her choice of words reminded him that she'd worked at a newspaper. With a slight smile, he asked, "And if he had divulged?"

She shrugged. "I already knew you, Louie. It was like he was telling me something about someone else, about a stranger. Not telling me about you."

"How many times do you think we dreamed together?" he asked.

"I don't know, at least twenty, maybe? Most nights, for a few weeks anyway."

"In all that time, did you ever feel scared with me? Did any of them feel like a nightmare?"

"No, I hated waking up. Every dream made me feel calm and made everything else matter less. Like floating in the water on your back, when all the sounds from the shore disappear."

"Then you know I'm not violent."

"You're not. But then why did Devlin say—"

"I'll give you the short of it. They came, they took over, one of them got sick, and when I said they should go, I got stabbed in my sleep."

"Devlin?"

"No, some of the others. You can imagine their surprise when I was alive the next morning, after they'd sliced me open the night before. Devlin and Grider didn't know about me, still don't really, though I'm sure they recognized something weird at play. They were pretty fucking confused when

Adra and the boys peeled out of here like their asses were on fire."

"You said something before about my believing you without your proving it. Is that something you want to do?"

Louie came back and dropped down in the chair opposite hers. "Not really."

"Why not?"

"You're more morbid than I would have thought, Kate."

"You called me Kate," she said, distracted.

"I call you that sometimes in my mind," he said.

"I didn't mean to change the subject," she said. "I don't exactly want to see you kill yourself."

"But it would help you to believe."

"I suppose," she shrugged. "Maybe."

Louie sighed. "The damn thing about it is that as much as I know I can't die, as much experience as I have doing it, now that you're here, I'm scared of it. I was afraid to do it last night. There was a moment I thought I shouldn't do it."

Katherine glanced away and looked at the dogs in the corral. "Because you're afraid now it will work, and you'll leave us?"

"It would be my luck, and I'm generally an unlucky person."

"Not being able to die seems like a decidedly lucky thing to me."

Louie grunted. "Not when you want to. You said earlier you tried to die once. Did you feel lucky when you woke up and realized you were…unsuccessful?" he asked, using her earlier word.

Katherine frowned at the dogs, seeming deep in thought. Some of them were eating while others were dozing in the dirt.

"I think I felt very lucky, actually. It wasn't something I'd planned. I'd been feeling very depressed, but the actual urge to kill myself was rather sudden. So you could say I was relieved to come to and realize it hadn't worked."

"How did you do it?" Louie asked clinically. He was thinking about all the times he'd done it and what would work best.

"Louie!"

"Just curious. I know a bit about it these days. But if you feel like it's private…"

"Maybe it is. But really, I don't remember much. I know it was pills, but I think I changed my mind."

"You don't know?" Louie asked.

"I remember walking around my apartment the next day, wondering what to do next."

Louie leaned forward in his chair, intent now. "You didn't wake up in the hospital? They didn't keep you for a few days?"

Katherine shook her head, trying to remember. "No, it's a bit of a blur. I mostly remember feelings, not facts. I remember relief and calm, mixed with a lot of feeling stupid. I'm not sure if I felt stupid for trying it or stupid because I did it wrong. Both, I guess. And I felt worried too, because I'd never have thought I was capable of giving up, but I had given up, obviously. I suppose I was worried I might try it again, in a moment of weakness, and that would be against my own will, if that makes sense, now that I was thinking clearly."

Louie nodded, but he was hardly listening now.

Katherine had tried to commit suicide and lived. She was hazy on the details, but was it possible that she had simply awakened the next day? Was she like him? "I know I was, and still am, glad that I didn't succeed, which probably sounds weird since I only managed to stay alive in time to watch a bunch of other people die. Being a survivor of a deadly pandemic must renew your interest in life."

Louie thought how that hadn't exactly been his own experience. Throughout the pandemic, his suicides had escalated.

"I'm going to clean up the dishes," Katherine said.

Louie rose to turn the generator back on.

Katherine went through the motions of cleaning the dishes. She tried to savor the feeling of water running over the plates despite the loud hum of the generator and well pump, but mostly her mind raced. Could she believe him? He'd said he could show her, but when she responded with interest, he'd backpedaled. He was suddenly afraid to do it, when according to him, he'd done it many times before. When he'd done it just last night. Was there another explanation for his survival? *Could* he have been less hurt than she believed and climbed out of the ravine while she slept? And did she really have to believe him about the dying just because she believed in the dreams?

Louie came into the kitchen, and when he offered to talk about it more, Katherine refused him. "I need to lie down," she said. "I didn't sleep much last night." And she did, curled on the bed in his mother's room, until it started to get dark and Louie woke her. Her mind still felt drowsy, but she could already hear crickets outside the open window. Night fell fast in the country.

"Can you eat?" he asked.

"Yes, I'll help."

She cleaned the asparagus and scrubbed potatoes, cutting them with onions and wrapping them in foil with butter. He grilled his steak, delicious smoke drifting through the window as she set the table. They ate in the kitchen by the glow of candles and hissing lanternlight, the generator off now to conserve fuel. Louie's steak had perfect sear marks and glistened on his plate, and she thought she'd never smelled anything in her life as divine as cooked beef. She should feel justified in eating a cow after what Bessie had put them through at the ranch, but she couldn't bring herself to ask for a bite. She liked that Louie didn't cajole her to try his food or make fun of her, like meat eaters often did. Like Lee had scoffed at her peanut butter and cans of vegetarian baked beans.

After dinner, Katherine dried her hands on the dish towel and threaded it over the stove handle to dry. She stood looking around the kitchen, at a loss for what to do next. Clark lay on the living room couch, watching her with big eyes. When she made eye contact, his tail began to thump against the cushion. Knowing he might be hungry (Louie had given the dog eggs and bacon for breakfast but she wasn't sure about since then), Katherine went to the narrow closet behind the kitchen door. She knew she was on track when the cupboard itself smelled of dog food.

An apron with a faded flower pattern hung from a metal hook on the inside of the door, its ties dangling. She touched it lightly, as if in a dream, knowing without looking that the large gaping pockets held grains of dark soil in the corners and smelled of rosemary. She'd worn this apron before. She recalled its gentle weight as she'd collected herbs in the garden, tucking them into the pockets in tiny bunches.

Louie came in, bumping the kitchen door into the open cupboard, startling her back to life. "Whoops!" he said, and she closed it to make room for him.

"OK, so I believe you," she said. "The dreams are real. So your immortality must be too."

Louie stopped short. "Uh, OK, then."

"But I still think I need to see it."

Louie sighed. "I figured."

"Journalist and all," she said.

"Right. I thought you were in finance, though?"

Katherine squeezed by him and walked to the sink, pulling a wide butcher knife from the block next to it.

"There are no reporters left, so you know, I'm fulfilling a need. Besides, I think you owe me one."

"How so?"

"You could've told me all this earlier and saved me a billion mosquito bites."

Louie stepped over to her and eyed the knife in her hand, watching the glint of the blade with a look akin to love. "One of my favorites," he said.

When she cringed, he said only, "Don't be afraid. I'll see you in the morning. Right here."

"Promise that you'll come back? No bullshit. This is real?"

She let him take the knife from her. "You don't have to watch this part if you don't want to," he said.

Katherine's eyes filled, but she refused to blink. He was doing this for her, and she'd be damned if she'd let him do it alone ever again. She took his empty hand in hers and watched him press the tip of the blade to where his pulse was throbbing in his neck. She shut her eyes when the blood sprayed.

CHAPTER NINETEEN

THE NEXT MORNING, LOUIE WATCHED sink bubbles fizzle over pink water, the curved edges of the casserole dish peeking through the surface. Pieces of coffee cup were lying broken on the counter next to him, dark with sticky blood and smudged with fingerprints.

Behind him, Katherine said, "We might need to try this again sometime."

Louie turned, startled, feeling caught in the act even though he'd been wanting someone to do just that for a while now. "Why?"

She was sitting at the kitchen table, creases on one side of her face like she'd slept on a waffled pillow. "Because I fell asleep sitting here, and I didn't get to see you come back."

The bubble of elation Louie always felt after a suicide fizzled like the soap in the sink. "Damn. I was hoping you could tell me if I just reappeared out of nowhere."

"I'm sorry," Katherine said. "I really tried. If it means anything, the sun was coming up the last I remember, and you were still on the floor."

Louie sat at the table. "So I didn't just disappear?"

Katherine laughed. "Is that what you thought happens?"

Louie, abashed, got up in search of cereal. "Well, hell, I don't know. No one had found my body before, so I kind of thought after I was dead, I disappeared. And then later I reappeared at the sink."

Katherine looked puzzled. "Well, I suppose you might have disappeared after I fell asleep. How often did you do it when your body could have been found?"

"I haven't been very scientific about it, Kate. During the summer, I tried a whole bunch of ways, and no one in town ever told me they'd stumbled across my body. The last few weeks, I suicided every night. Devlin and Grider were staying in the house. Either one could have found me the times I did it in the kitchen or living room."

Katherine picked up on the word. "You call it suiciding, like a verb."

He nodded, moving around the kitchen to gather his breakfast.

"But it's not always been suicide, has it?"

"Well, when they got me in my bed, no, that wasn't."

"Mind if I ask you a question?"

Louie dug into his Frosted Flakes and made an affirmative sound around his spoon.

"Why do you keep doing it?"

He continued to eat for a moment before replying. "Well, it's like a mystery, isn't it? Every time I wake up, there's another piece of the puzzle. The first few months, I was just standing at the sink after. Then it started to change, and I would notice new things."

"Like?"

Louie pointed at the broken coffee cup with his spoon. "Like that coffee cup over there, for instance. I didn't have one at first, then I started holding it the next day. Lately it's sitting broken next to me instead. Today it has blood all over it. Each time, the water is getting darker too. It used to be soapy water. A week ago, I saw blood curling in it for the first time, but the water itself was clear. Now it's pink."

Katherine rose and went to the sink. Louie hadn't pulled the drain plug yet. "Are these dishes always here?" She put her hands on the counter and peered into the water, as if the secrets there would reveal themselves to her.

"Yep," Louie responded. "Same ones every time, no matter what I ate the night before."

"You could have told me that." Trying for a joke, she said, "I wouldn't have cleaned a bunch of dishes if I knew all that stuff would disappear in place of a single casserole dish."

"There's a few forks and butter knives in the bottom, and a drinking glass. Can I ask you something now?"

She turned to him and leaned against the counter, reminding him briefly of Devlin.

"Are you done freaking out?" he said.

"Oh, I was freaking out last night, trust me," she replied, turning back to the sink. She dipped her hand in the water and pulled the plug. "Hmmm, the water is warm, by the way."

Louie hadn't taken note of the water temperature before. "Warm like I'd just been doing the dishes?"

"Exactly," she confirmed. "I half expected it to be freezing cold, but it's like you just filled the sink with hot water, maybe twenty minutes ago. It's cooling, but still warm."

Louie joined her at the sink. "Neat."

She slid a glance at him. "Neat?"

"It's nice to get more clues. Especially when I have someone to mull them over with."

"You've been alone with this a long time, haven't you?" she murmured. She leaned in to give him a kiss.

He was startled by the contact, but not displeased. A moment ago he'd felt sad, thinking he had indeed been alone too long with this burden. Now he felt happy. "You're a pretty special lady, Kate, you know that?"

"How's that?" she asked. She looked like she was considering kissing him again.

"Not easy to make a romantic moment standing next to bloody kitchenware."

She laughed and looked away, the moment broken, but she didn't seem regretful. "How about I wash these and you go clean up?"

Without thinking, Louie stepped back and raised his arm to sniff underneath it.

"It's not that," she said. "You have blood on you."

He reached up to feel his neck, surprised to find it slick. He brought his fingers up to inspect them, expecting blood now, but still mystified by it.

"Now that's different," he said.

"You haven't bled before?"

He wiped his fingers on his jeans. "No, I'm usually clean the next day. I mean, I sometimes still need a shower—it's been hot all summer, you know—but there haven't been any outward signs of how I'd suicided before."

Katherine took the towel from the stove and dabbed at his neck. They both looked at it when she finished. The checked cotton fabric was smeared with red. Katherine inspected his neck, saying, "It's not actually cut where you, uh, pierced the skin last night. But the spot with the most blood is where the knife went in."

Louie took the cloth. "This is what I was afraid of."

"What's that?"

"Every time, it's getting worse. That's why I was reluctant."

"To suicide again last night? And at the ranch?"

He met her gaze. "I want to understand all this. It's like a compulsion. But what if I have to really die to get an answer?"

Katherine smiled, understanding now. "And you've decided you don't want to die after all, is that it?"

Louie had never initiated a kiss in his life, but now it seemed the most natural thing in the world to take Katherine's cheeks in his hands and press his lips to hers. Hoping he'd kissed her the right amount of time, he was getting ready to pull away when he felt her arms come up around his neck to draw him close.

They decided to spend the day together in the garden. After all, Katherine had been anticipating doing just that for weeks now. They both knew it was their favorite thing, and it was on their list of chores anyway if they wanted to continue to eat.

Louie worked down at the end of the row from where Katherine knelt. He dragged dirt with a metal rake, filling the hole that had been his shallow grave a few days ago. It gave her a chill to think of it, despite the hot sun warming her hat. She watched the muscles in his back flex, reaching and pulling the rake, and tried to decide if she found him handsome. Maybe it didn't matter. Earlier, he'd handed her a broad-rimmed sunhat, and she'd recognized it just like she had the apron, meeting his knowing look in a way that she also recognized. That, too, had given her chills, though these were the good kind.

She turned back to pinching delicate leaves of spinach from the low row of plants and set them in her basket. It was already heavy with green peppers and pickling cucumbers, more than they could eat this week, but Louie insisted she gather them anyway or they'd just die on the vine. It had been too hot the last few days to keep everything from shriveling.

"This heat is brutal," Louie said. He dropped a garden pad near her and sat on it, elbows on his knees so that his filthy hands didn't touch his jeans.

Katherine tucked strands of freed hair under her hat, hating the way the brim of it made her skin itch. "It is. I don't remember it being this way, so hot."

"Difference between dreams and reality," Louie said, looking past her into the depths of the garden.

"Speaking of reality"—Katherine rolled to her side to sit—"I was thinking about the only other time we really met, the first time we talked. Do you remember?"

"On the phone, you mean?"

She nodded.

"I do. It was the first time I was lonely."

"Hadn't everyone been dead for like a week at that point?"

"Yeah, but I don't mean it like that. I could have gone forever with everyone gone and not been lonely a bit. I guess you could say I'm pretty much a loner, and I've been training for this my whole life. No, what I meant was that when I talked to you, that's when I really felt it. You know how they say you don't know what you've got till it's gone?"

"Yeah?"

"Well, I didn't realize what I had, or didn't have, until I found you. I guess I mean to say that I didn't realize I was missing you until I met you."

"That's awfully romantic, Louie," Katherine said, pleased despite herself. She thought about past boyfriends who had said they'd loved her or desired her, thinking how none of their platitudes had seemed as honest as the things Louie said offhandedly, how none had struck her so easily.

"What were you thinking, the first time we talked?" he asked.

She grinned. "I thought you were kind of a goof, eating a bag of chips, complaining about almond milk."

Louie's expression grew serious. "But aside from that, did you feel a connection? Like we were going to start dreaming together? That you would come here?"

"Not at all," Katherine said, hoping her honesty would be refreshing to him too.

Louie shrugged. "That's OK. Me neither."

"That's a relief. I would have felt bad if you did." She began to comb through the dirt, sifting for any green coins of spinach she might have missed.

"You know, about the dreams. I was thinking that we're probably going to have a baby," Louie told her. "Remember how there was a baby crying a lot of the time?"

Katherine's hand stilled. "Yes, but I think that was Ana. The baby I told you about, who died."

"You think you were supposed to bring her here, and we dreamed about it, but then she died, so…"

"So no baby," she said firmly. She began to dig again, scraping. She tried to ignore the disturbing feeling of dirt under her nails. She should have worn gloves.

"Here's the thing though," Louie said, "I think our dreams were of the future."

Digging. Searching. "Why would you think that?"

"For one thing, you were tanner. Your hair was a little lighter, maybe from the sun. Do you remember?"

Katherine paused and then rolled back onto her knees. She shifted down to the next plant and began to pick. "Not really," she said after a while.

"Sometimes I struggle with reading people unless they're obvious about their feelings," Louie told her. "It's why I've never been very popular around here. But with you, it's different. I can sense you're upset, but I'm just not sure why. Is it thinking about Ana? I didn't mean to bring her up."

"I'm not upset," Katherine said, and that was true. She wasn't upset. But she *was* unsettled. One kiss and the guy was already talking babies? Sure, they had a connection—a very weird, mystical, connection—and sure, less natural things than childbirth were going on around here, like Louie's inability to die, but none of that meant they were destined to have babies.

Louie tucked his knees to his chest, looking awkward now. "Is it that I said I think we're going to have a baby?"

Katherine frowned at him. "I've never wanted babies. The end of the world doesn't change that."

She felt Louie watching her paw at the plants. At last, he replied, "I didn't want to live, and the end of the world hadn't changed that for me either. But meeting you has made my outlook different."

Katherine stopped and turned back to him. "Do you really think we're supposed to be some kind of Adam and Eve, Louie? We're literally the two worst people on the planet for that."

"How do you figure?"

She rolled her eyes at him. "Let's see, a career-focused woman who doesn't want kids. In fact…" His raised eyebrows egged her on. "In fact, I was pregnant once before, and I didn't want it. Definitely disqualifies me for restarting the human race, doesn't it?"

Louie only looked at her, so she continued. "And you, well, you've tried to kill yourself how many times now?"

He shrugged.

"A few dozen times or more?"

Louie was grinning now, like he was rather enjoying seeing her riled up. He pumped his thumb in the air, telling her the number was a bit higher.

Staggering to her feet, Katherine clapped her hands against her apron. She stepped over the row of spinach to the heirloom tomatoes. The tall plants in their cages came to her chest. She slipped between two of them, putting a little distance between herself and Louie. Over the top of a plant, she said to him, "OK, so you're not exactly a stable parent either, are you?"

"I suppose not," he answered.

"Well then? What makes you think we're supposed to have a baby?"

He thought for a moment. "Well, it kind of seems right that the last two people maybe can't die, or at least, can't die until they've fulfilled whatever their destiny is."

Katherine was angrily tucking tomatoes into her apron, but this gave her pause. A fat one dropped in the cage, and its weight loosened another. They bounced through the plant and landed on the ground next to a few more, their skins slipping off and rotting into the earth. Louie was correct. Everything in this garden was too ripe.

"Is that possible, maybe?" Louie pressed.

"What do you mean *two* people?"

"I have a theory."

"Oh, I bet you do," Katherine said. "You know, the end of the world would have been a lot simpler if I could have just gotten the flu like everyone else. And by the way, we're not the last people. It just feels that way."

Louie chuckled and rolled to his feet. He brought the basket to her and began to pluck tomatoes from her apron pockets. "Not yet, we're not. But I think, and just hear me out here," he said before she could interrupt, "maybe when you tried to kill yourself, the time wasn't right for you either. Maybe, if you'd tried it more than once, you would have found out what I found out."

Katherine put her dirty hands on her hips, trying to steady herself. "And just how do you expect to test that theory, Louie?"

He pinched a smaller tomato from the vine and put it to his mouth and chewed it for a while. When he started to answer, she stopped him with a flat hand. "We're not doing that."

"I wasn't going to suggest…"

"The hell you weren't."

"Katherine, honestly. I wasn't. I wouldn't take that chance!"

She backed away, brushing at her empty pockets. "You better not think that again, Louie."

"I wasn't!"

"Ever, Louie. You've told me how obsessed you've been, trying to understand it all, suiciding every night just to see an extra damn bubble in the sink. So you better get it out of your head that I'm another puzzle for you to solve."

Louie raised his hands like he was surrendering. "You're safe here, Katherine. I promise. I couldn't take the chance of being wrong. I mean, I don't even want to do it to myself anymore. There's more blood every time. And whether I'm getting closer to death, or just getting closer to whatever destiny I'm supposed to have, I prefer to think I haven't died for a reason."

Katherine eyed him carefully. He seemed sincere, but knowing he thought her immortal still made her worry. She was less certain about her life here than she'd been an hour ago. "Fine."

"You're safe here," he repeated.

"Yes. Of course."

"OK, then."

"No more baby talk either."

"No more baby talk, I promise," Louie said, but that twinkle in his eye had returned, and it made her uneasy.

CHAPTER TWENTY

"WHAT DO YOU MISS MOST?" Katherine asked. They were eating salad greens from the garden with oil and vinegar, snapped green beans (also from the garden), Louie a hotdog crisped over the fire, and watermelon for dessert. Though the fare was light, it was not from a can and tasted good after a hard day's work.

"My mom," Louie said promptly. He regretted saying this almost instantly, because now Katherine would think he was a mama's boy. She would probably ask him about her now, and he'd have to think about it again.

"You said it was Covid?"

Louie sighed and stabbed a stack of veggies with his fork. "Yeah."

"I'm sorry."

"She was the first person in the area to die from it, early on, you know. I mean, it was downstate and pretty much everyone knew all about it by then, but folks up here weren't taking it very seriously."

"There were a lot of reports about people not really believing it was real, you know, in rural areas, because of the president," Katherine said. "Most of our content was about the Trump administration, how they were making a bad situation worse. We're pretty left-leaning, obviously."

Louie looked at her, calculating the odds of her still liking him if she knew he'd voted for Trump. He regretted the decision, but still. There were some things a city girl just might not understand. "My mom and I didn't care much for politics," he said, which was true even though they voted in every election. "We never saw anyone do much for us, on either side." (Also true.) "But with Covid, it wasn't so much that people didn't believe in science. It's just that they thought it was overblown on the news and everything. We didn't understand why we had the same restrictions here that they had in Detroit when we had fewer people, when we're so spread out."

"Did attitudes change when your mom died?" Katherine picked at her beans, eating them one by one. Louie was charmed by this, even as the topic depressed him. He didn't miss politics one bit, or all the divisive drama in his state during Covid, but he'd go back there if it meant he could listen to his mother muttering at the news again. How she'd sit in her threadbare dresses and fluffy slippers, rocking her recliner in the glow of the TV, asking him how the world had gone so wrong.

Thinking about his mom's attitude reminded him that Katherine had asked a question. "At first attitudes did change some. It was kind of like a celebrity sighting. Like, you see all the movie stars on TV, but you never think they'll show up around here. It was like that to start with, people wanting to hear all the details about her symptoms, compare her medical history to their own, to make themselves feel better, get some reassurance. It was like her being sick, one of their own, made it real. They actually did a parade in their cars past the house."

"You said at first. So it changed, then?"

"After a while, when no one else had gotten sick, some people were just over it. There were others who seemed actually mad at us. She wasn't getting well fast enough to suit the story they were telling themselves about how it was no big deal. After a week or two, no one was calling anymore. All they wanted to do was bitch about the governor to each other and stretch every rule as far as they could. I'd hear they were still meeting at the bar, and I could just picture them saying how sad it was that Jean didn't seem to be getting over her 'illness,' but they were still sitting at the fucking bar, you know?"

"Did you take her to the hospital around here? Or did you have to go to a metro area?"

Louie finished his hotdog, bunless because he hadn't had the foresight to freeze any packages of those, and reached for the watermelon. "We got her diagnosed up at the Rite Aid. And at first, it wasn't too bad, no worse than a bad case of the regular flu. So we stayed home. Mom waved at the car parade through the window when they did that. When it got worse later, I wanted to take her to the hospital, any hospital, but she didn't want it. She wanted to be at home. We'd seen the stuff on TV, and she knew once she was in the hospital, I wouldn't be able to be with her. She didn't want to be on a ventilator."

He ate his watermelon in three large bites, seeds and all.

"And when it got bad?" Katherine asked. "I would have taken Sharon to a hospital if there'd been any doctors or nurses left. Her dying at home was hard."

Louie stood to gather their empty plates. He took his time with an answer, thinking as he scraped rinds into the trash and put the dishes into the sink with a quiet clink. Suddenly all he could hear was the sound of his mom trying to breathe those last few days, like her lungs were stuck in a mud puddle.

"When it got really bad, Mom couldn't breathe," he said at last. "I could hear the effort it took. I knew I should call for an ambulance, but she begged me not to, and I already knew by then that she wasn't going to make it. She had scarlet fever when she was a kid and lived on a farm. My grandparents weren't much for doctors, except for the animals, and they waited a long time before they got her treated. She always said she'd had a weak heart after that. I was pretty sure they couldn't have helped her at the hospital anyway. So we stayed."

"That must have been really hard," Katherine said and moved beside him to dry the dishes he washed and placed in the rack. She rubbed them in slow circles, the kitchen towel becoming damp in her hand, and Louie thought about what she'd said. Yes, it *had* been really hard. But hadn't it been really hard for a lot of people during Covid? Millions of people had died. Billions dead now from the flu. He felt foolish accepting her sympathy.

"So many people have died… I get she was just one person," he said.

"No, I wasn't thinking that. I was thinking how lucky she was to be loved like that."

Louie nodded, unable to speak around the strange tightness in his throat.

"I was also thinking that your cleaning dishes is a good sign that you don't intend to suicide tonight," she continued. "Otherwise, you'd have saved us the trouble."

They watched the sun dip behind the trees while Louie told Katherine more about Adra and the others. Rocking into the night was their new evening routine, and Katherine would have been comfortable, if not for the information Louie was imparting.

"So, there's something I don't really understand," she interrupted.

Louie raised an eyebrow.

"Why did you care about the boys being sick? I could see how the others might worry, but you already know you can't get sick. They were no danger to you."

Louie rocked his chair. "Told you, I hate germs. It's like PTSD from Covid or something. After my mom died, I just couldn't stand the thought of being around anyone sick."

"Really? You are *so* offended by germs that you suggested euthanasia?"

"Well, I didn't exactly say it like that," he insisted. "I suggested they move somewhere else, and we'd drop off supplies to them."

She made a face at him, thinking he must have said more and much worse if they'd been mad enough to kill him. He took in her expression and said, "OK, thinking back to the conversation, the looks on everyone's faces, maybe I did say it like that. Maybe just like that. Or that's how they heard it, anyway."

Katherine looked away, troubled. She appreciated Louie and all he'd done, all he was doing to help them survive. But she had to admit, he was one weird guy. Would she have come here if she'd known about the suiciding and about how things had gone down with the others?

"You want ice cream?" Louie asked suddenly.

How could he seem so regretful one moment and so impulsive, almost childlike, the next? "OK," she said, and watched him go.

Louie was very good at compartmentalizing his feelings, and that made her worry. When he'd said that thing before, about her being like him, what if he really got it in his mind to test it? Could she stop him from hurting her?

Clark lumbered onto the porch, drawing her attention. It was a warm evening, and the long hot day had sapped his energy. Nevertheless, when he flopped on the porch and sprawled in the shade, he put his nose by her feet.

"Hey there, boy," she said, and he nudged her. She bent to scratch his ears, reminding herself that Clark was only here because of Louie's compassion. The same was true for all of the dogs, and some chickens and other strays. He couldn't drive through town without seeing an animal he wanted to help. That should tell her everything she needed to know about him. Louie returned with scoops of mint chocolate chip piled high on sugar cones. The bowl of vanilla he set in front of Clark reinforced her opinion that, when it came down to it, Louie was as gentle as they came.

Clark chased the scoop around the bowl with his tongue while Katherine and Louie ate in silence. The frogs croaked and the sun had set when Louie said, "I was thinking about a day trip tomorrow. Have you ever been fishing?"

"I haven't. We could eat the fish?" she asked.

"Do you eat fish?"

"I did sometimes before. Now, yes, I think definitely." Actually, the thought of fresh fish made her as giddy as the burst of sweet ice cream on her tongue.

"We'll need to find some of those ice packs that you freeze for the cooler. I don't have any. But we could also cook some up on the shore if you like. On the boat even. I snagged Murchison's keys to his Crestliner. He keeps it in a slip up in Cheboygan. I'll bet he's got one of those grills for it. Or we could find an even nicer boat in the marina if I can get keys."

Katherine glanced around the darkening yard, noticing for the first time that Louie didn't have the outbuildings and toys she'd observed at the ranch and other homes. It seemed like everyone had an ATV in a shed, snowmobiles leaning in the grass, a pair of wave runners on a trailer. And everyone had a boat, either one they wanted or one they were selling in front of their house. As she caught the smell of gas from under the porch where the generator hummed, she thought about how expensive it all must have been to run.

"Sounds like a good plan," Katherine said. "Maybe we could bring back a nice boat and fish on one of the lakes around here too. I passed a lot of water on my way here. Seems like there should be plenty of places."

"Oh, there are. This is Michigan!" Louie said. Katherine noticed he was smiling the goofy smile again, the one that made it seem like he was out of practice or just learning to show his pleasure. "We can do whatever we like."

"You're pretty excited about stealing, aren't you?" she remarked, licking ice cream from her thumb.

"I like the idea of stealing a new boat, sure," he said. "But it's more than that."

"Oh?"

"It's been a long time since I've made plans."

"What do you mean? You plan stuff all the time! Your day is more organized than mine, and that's saying something."

Louie rocked, savoring the last bites of his ice cream cone, or maybe just savoring his thoughts. Katherine had almost forgotten her question when he said, "I mean plans to look forward to. What I mean is that you give me hope, Kate."

She gave him hope. And wasn't that just about the sweetest compliment she'd ever received?

That night, Katherine rolled onto her side in the spare room's twin bed. She kicked at the quilt, which seemed necessary to qualify what she was doing as sleeping but was completely unnecessary for warmth, even with the air conditioning.

It wasn't the heat, or the drone of the generators running that air conditioning, that kept her awake, however. It was confusion. How could she feel so flattered when Louie said things like that she gave him hope, but at the same time feel so apprehensive about being his sole source of happiness?

Katherine thought about Brad, the last person she could reasonably have called a boyfriend. The stripper who'd gotten her pregnant was a one-off and definitely didn't count. She'd met him standing at a bar while waiting for her drink order, enjoying a rare after-work hangout with the girls from the office and the start of a solid buzz. Brad was young, cute, cocky, the type she usually hated because his clothes and attitude made him so obviously one of *those* guys. The kind who'd gone to prep school and summered with family on Nantucket. He'd given her his business card right away (of course he had), and she'd known before looking at it that his name wouldn't have roman numerals after it because he'd be the spoiled youngest son, and that he'd have an unlikely title for his age, bestowed on him by whoever owned the family business. She had been right on both counts. He was a VP at a company bearing his last name.

Brad had offered to buy her a drink, and he didn't blink when the one drink he'd meant to buy turned out to be a round of drinks for friends back at her table. His easy laugh about it was enough to score him the first date, and the fact that he opened doors and didn't like sports got him the second and third. That he was less selfish in bed than Katherine had expected got him a dozen more.

They'd dated for about five months, and though it was sort of flattering that Brad had started to include her when talking about his eventual life plans, she felt like he was talking about a life he'd planned when he was twelve and was just filling in her name. *Mad Libs: The Life Edition.* Katherine wanted to be more than the write-in, but since she wasn't really committed to the idea of a long-term relationship anyway, she slept with him three months longer than intended. In the end, she broke it off in a text after he suggested a trip upstate to meet his parents. (His mom was called Tippy—she'd really dodged a bullet there.)

Louie was so different from Brad, from any other guy she'd met in the city. He was quiet, awkward, blunt. He lacked their confidence, and yet, didn't he have more to be confident about? He could actually *do* things like fix cars and grow food. He knew how stuff worked. He could kill a chicken! He didn't just move numbers or have lunch meetings. She thought again about Brad and how he wouldn't survive the apocalypse without his smart phone and a search engine. She wondered whether he would have saved a corral full of orphaned dogs.

OK, so even though they were an unlikely match, Katherine cared for Louie. Dreams and possible destiny aside, she actually liked him, rough edges and all. But there it was again, that nervousness in her stomach when she thought about being responsible for his feelings. What if she weren't enough, and he became suicidal again? What if she didn't always make him want to keep going? Would she have to be perfect all the time to live up to his expectations?

Katherine flopped onto her back and kicked the quilt to the foot of the bed. Sleep was impossible. Her brain was in overdrive.

She heard a creak outside her door and turned to see light under it. "Louie?" she called softly.

The door pushed open. "Are you still up, Kate?"

He called her Kate sometimes, and she kind of liked that too.

"That makes two of us," she said.

He came into the room and sat on the edge of the bed, handing her a glass with cartoon characters on it. "I thought this might help."

She scooted into a sitting position and took the milk. She sniffed it. Did almond milk help you sleep? She sipped it. "How did you know I was up?" she asked.

"I waited for you in my dream, but you weren't there," he said simply.

She looked down at her hands and thought how much better this glass of milk was than Brad's whole round of chocolate martinis. "Will you stay with me?" she asked.

"It's awfully warm in here…"

Katherine sighed. "Then take me to your bed, Louie," she said, looking him straight in the eye.

"Oh."

Louie expected to wake up with Katherine curled up at his side, her head on his shoulder, her long hair pinned under his arm or draped across his throat, like something sexy in a movie. Maybe there'd be something extra you couldn't see on TV, like the smell of a good time cooling on them both. He expected to wake up and watch the sunrise with her from the bed, the two of them looking out his window at the light coming up to warm the garden. Last night had been magical, and he expected the morning to be *sublime*.

But Louie woke standing at the kitchen sink, the broken coffee cup covered in blood on the counter, a shard of it wet in his hand. Louie's first thought was how unexpectedly the morning had turned out, and the second was that his first orgasm with another person must have surely killed him.

Le petit mort. The little death, the French called it, except this little death had been a real death, and it made the sink water red.

Louie looked down and saw that he was naked but for his underpants. *Well, this is new.* On his belly, just below his nipple, there was a dark, round burn. A bullet, he thought automatically. Someone put a bullet in there.

He staggered back from the counter, shock making his legs go rubbery. *Katherine*, he thought next. *Where is Kate?*

As if he had summoned her in his mind, Louie heard a scream outside and knew it was her. Clark was whining out there too. Without thinking, Louie banged out the kitchen door onto the porch, artless and panicked.

"Clark!" he cried, and the dog came running back around the house.

"Where is she?" he asked, and right then he almost thought the dog would answer. Crazier things had happened this week.

In his own way, Clark did, because he ran to Louie before turning back to disappear around the corner of the house again. This was the most energy Louie had ever seen him expend. Instinct had Louie grabbing a shovel leaning against the side of the house, and he followed where the dog had gone.

The Tahoe.

Engine running and driver's door open, it was idling near the house, half parked on the gravel drive and half in the grass, as though it had come to a stop in a hurry. Inside the cabin, a man Louie knew must be Devlin was struggling to keep his grip on Katherine, who was fighting like a rabid animal.

As Louie ran to her, she twisted away and half fell from the vehicle, landing awkwardly on her hip, one leg still in the footwell. Devlin scrambled to follow her down, and that's when he saw Louie. He paused, mouth sagging, surely not expecting to see Louie ever again, and certainly not in his underwear yielding a shovel.

Louie didn't hesitate and brought the shovel down on the man. If he'd hit where he'd aimed, he probably would have cleaved Devlin's head in two, what with the adrenalin pounding through him. As it was, the shovel sliced down to his shoulder, taking the cop's ear with it and bringing him to his knees. He fell over Katherine as she attempted to rise.

The blow shook the shovel from Louie's hands. He hauled Katherine to her feet and dragged her away from Devlin, who would have used her to stand. "Get back!" he shouted, a command that could be meant for either of them. He pulled her farther out of reach.

Devlin had one hand pressed where his ear used to live while the other reached toward where Louie had dropped the shovel. Before he could get to his feet, Louie and Katherine began to run to the house, followed by Clark. The dogs in the corral came running alongside them, divided by the paddock fence but excited by the action.

"Inside!" Louie shouted over the baying dogs to Katherine, pushing her up the porch steps, and when she was in, to Clark: "Go! Get!" The dog stopped in confusion, shied away, then came back. Louie waved him toward the yard. "Go!"

Clark whined, dropping to his belly, but Louie didn't have time for him. He stepped over Clark and reached under the porch. There were two fresh cans of gasoline next to the generator.

Katherine was inside the kitchen and turned to see Louie come in behind her, a can of gas in each hand. Her eyes widened as he set them down and closed and locked the door. They heard a new eruption of sound coming from the yard. The dogs were going nuts again, and that's when they heard Keno barking on the other side of the house. Devlin had freed him from the Tahoe.

"What are you doing?!" Katherine jumped out of the way when Louie began to splash gas through the kitchen. One can emptied, he raised the other and loosed it over the counter, across the broken mug, over the casserole dish in the sink. Katherine was screaming, but Louie couldn't hear her words through the chanting in his head. *You can do this. You can do this*, he told himself. *Be the hero. Be her hero.*

Fire. He had never written it on his list. He couldn't bear it. But next to losing Katherine to Devlin, he could do it. *You can do this.*

"Louie!" Not Katherine this time, but Devlin on the porch.

The door was closed, but Louie could see through the curtains. Keno was at the cop's feet, trembling on his haunches, ready to go like a runner on the block. Devlin clutched a bloodied hand to his wounded ear. Clark was long gone.

"You need to let Katherine come out," the man shouted at the house.

Louie set the can on the table and turned to Katherine. She went to him immediately, and he noticed for the first time that she was dressed, not in her underwear like him. That meant Devlin had forced her to put clothes on after he'd shot Louie in bed in the early morning hours.

"He's lost it, Louie," Katherine said now. The words fell out as she gripped his arms. "His sister was dead. Everyone was dead. And he just fucking lost it. He drove straight back here. He thinks he's *saving* me!"

As if to prove this conclusion, Devlin's voice rose again. "Louie, let her go! No one needs to get hurt."

The fumes from the gas made Louie cough. He hustled her toward the back of the kitchen, away from the door. "I'm sorry, Katherine," he gasped as he moved her. "I'm so sorry that we have to do this."

He saw her eyes change the moment she understood that she was standing in a room of gasoline, fumes building. As if she finally got that he was going to burn the house.

He turned to rummage through a junk drawer, searching for his mom's cigarette lighter.

"No," Katherine moaned behind him when his hand found it. "Louie, no."

He turned and saw her eyes were lit like they were already aflame, full of panic. "Please don't, Louie. You don't want to do this."

"I promise you'll survive, Katherine. I *know* it. There's no way there'd be a me without a you. Tomorrow we'll be standing at the sink."

Now Katherine was struggling with Louie like she had with Devlin. She pushed and pulled but Louie felt unshakable, knowing what needed to be done.

"Let go of me!" she cried. "Burn yourself up if that's what you want, but not me!"

"I have to. He needs to think you're dead or he'll never leave us alone!" Louie insisted, even as Devlin began to kick at the door.

"I will be dead! I'm not like you!"

He took Katherine's face in his hands, their eyes streaming from gas fumes and fear, lighter pressed to her cheek like a final kiss. "I love you. We'll be OK."

Katherine grabbed Louie by the shoulders and tried to reason with him. "Go fight him. Or kill him if you have to. Don't kill me."

The pounding continued. With each kick, the glass window in the door shook and Keno's keening rose.

"And if he shoots me again? What then? He'll take you and I'll never find you! He'll have you out of the state before I'm standing at the sink again. Just trust me. If there's an Adam, there's an Eve. Remember me, remember the garden, and come back to me."

The door swung open, and when Devlin burst inside, Louie stood his ground, a partial can of gas in one hand and the lighter in the other.

Devlin stopped short. "Louie," he said simply.

It was too late for family meetings, the time for talking done. Louie dropped the can and raised the lighter. Devlin forgot his gun, seemed to forget everything, dazed by the lighter in Louie's hand. When Louie expected him to lunge, Devlin instead stumbled backward, falling out the door and onto the porch. He dropped to his knees where Louie could see him through the rusted screen.

When Devlin finally thought to scramble for his weapon, Louie's thumb went to the striker, and in the split second before the single flame flicked to life, he thought about what his last line should be. If he had been the hero he'd always wanted to be, he would have said something catchy or clever to his nemesis, like, "Smoke it, Marlboro Man!" But what he said was "Forgive me, Kate."

CHAPTER TWENTY-ONE

HAD LOUIE REALLY THOUGHT ABOUT those daisy dishes or the crack in that Pyrex dish the morning after his tantrum in the kitchen, he might have concluded that the more times he suicided, the more damage remained afterward. Like a bruise or stain, there were remnants left of the day before, ones not completely erased as if it all had been a bad dream.

He thought about this as he stood in front of the sink in his family kitchen, which was now burned beyond recognition. His hands were bright red, the hair on his arms and chest missing. The house still stood, but it was destroyed. His *gift* had saved him from the explosion, but it could not spare his home. Fire was more powerful magic.

Lowering his head to his chest, he cried. He cried for Katherine, because she wasn't standing there with him, and that was his fault. (He couldn't even blame Devlin. In his panic, he'd been unable to think of another way.) He cried for his mother's home, and for how the curtains she'd sewn were burned to ash, how the linoleum tiles they'd pressed down together were gone, the kitchen floor nothing but stickiness under his bare feet. He cried because the dark smudge where he'd been shot still hurt his stomach. Mostly, he cried for how he'd wasted the last year of his life killing himself over and over to solve a damn mystery, and now that he knew the answer, it still wasn't enough to give him peace.

He had a new wound this morning, but this one was a memory that hadn't been there before—the memory of the night he killed his mother. She'd wanted him to do it, so maybe *killed* was wrong. She asked with words at first, and later, her eyes begged him when she couldn't breathe enough to speak. She trusted Louie to do it and do it well. Her trust was a gift. The woman who had raised him on her own, so tough, so stoic at times because she didn't have the time for too much feeling, had trusted her son to do this last chore for her.

He'd crossed off the last item on her to-do list, and he'd done it swiftly, compassionately, with little fuss just as she would have wanted, and that was his gift to her in return. After he took the pillow from her face, he sat with her for a long while, holding her hand, wishing he could take it back. But he also knew if he had to do it again, he would. Her pain left him without choices. Each breath she took hurt his own chest as much as if he had been the sick one.

When he roused himself from her bedside, he wandered to the kitchen and wondered what he would do next. He thought about Jean's few friends, the nosy people in town, and the questions that would follow from the sheriff and coroner. He wondered if he could tell anyone about her last moments, and if it would be over tea and coffee in a Styrofoam cup, stirring with one of those tiny straws to dissolve the powdered creamer, standing in his best shoes on that awful floral carpet at the funeral home. He'd stood on that carpet before, but never for someone close to him.

Louie had slept in the living room that night and made the necessary calls the next morning. People came and went after that, and the first of the casserole dishes began to arrive. The morning after he got her ashes and dug a spot for her in the garden, he sat at the kitchen table alone and ate cold macaroni and cheese baked from his mother's own recipe straight out of Judith Narkey's Pyrex dish. He'd drunk milk from the cartoon character glass his mom had bought him at the gas station when he was ten. When he was done, he'd walked the dishes to the sink and dumped them in, put in the drain plug, squeezed cleaner across everything, and started to fill the sink with water. He began to clean.

There wasn't much thought to it, certainly less than he'd given to fulfilling his mother's last wish. One minute he was cleaning the coffee mug the sheriff had used, and the next he had struck it on the countertop. He took a smooth piece of broken cup and carefully drew it over each wrist, then carved deep lines the length of both arms, barely feeling the pain because inside it was so much worse. He dropped the glass and bent over the sink to let his arms fall into the suds, letting them drift over the glass shipwreck, and felt relief crawl into the slices, up his arms and into his chest. He would never wash dishes again. He would never have to do or be anything again. His mother was gone, and now there was nothing to care about anymore. He could be gone too.

It was a blessing that Louie hadn't remembered his first suicide. The real one. The one he meant. When he did it, he thought he was at his lowest. The loss of his job during Covid, when he couldn't bear the germs on people's cars coming into the gas station, the loneliness of being the town loser, what he'd done for his mom. Nothing could feel as bad as all that. But now Louie knew that there were lower places, and thought again of Katherine. As he stood there at the sink and remembered the truth, he at last understood that the penance he would pay for the weakness of his first suicide would be to relive it piece by piece for eternity.

Eventually he straightened up. If killing himself a hundred times had taught him anything, it was that he had no choice but to live. He looked around the kitchen, a warm black shell, one last time, and then shuffled to the doorway. His key ring usually hung from a hook next to the door, but there was no door anymore, and part of the wall was also gone. Picking around on the floor, he found his truck keys still intact.

Louie stepped outside, not caring that he still only had on the underwear he'd been wearing when the house exploded. He'd had little use for decency yesterday and none today. Most of the porch was ruined, so he navigated over the gaps and hopped down to the ground, avoiding what was left of the stairs. They weren't ash, but they weren't sound enough to take his weight either.

He saw now that the fire had spread across the backyard, fueled by the dry grass. There were no dogs left in the corral, but then there hadn't been a corral anymore once the wood fence and gate had burned. He saw no corpses, so at least there was that. The dogs would have stayed in the center, freed when the gate went down.

Movement caught his eye, and Louie turned to see Clark. He almost cried again, because his big goofy dog was wagging his tail as if nothing had happened. He bounded up and licked Louie's thigh, reminding him that he was half naked. OK, maybe there was room for a little decency, and he did need protection from the sun. The life Louie had known might be over, but he wasn't a freaking animal. He'd have to locate some clothes in his size.

He went to the shed and grabbed an open bag of dog food from a large storage container meant to keep out the rats and squirrels. The bag would go in his truck. There wasn't much else to salvage. He wasn't sure yet exactly where he intended to go, but he couldn't stay here.

"Come on, Clark," he said, and the dog trailed after him. They passed the garden, and Louie tried not to look. From the corner of his eye, he saw blackened remains as well as spots of green that had survived the small wildfire caused by the explosion. Much of it was gone, but some of the lusher plants that had borne overripe fruits and veggies were wilting but alive. His mother was in there, her ashes among the asparagus, and Katherine's spirit and the best memories of her too. He couldn't bear to see how he had let both of them down.

He walked on, knowing if he stopped to wallow, he would be overcome by what he'd done. He'd probably suicide again, maybe more than once, if he could. If he wasn't careful, he could put himself into another loop of self-destruction and never leave it, the garden his personal purgatory where he could never get clean.

The day was already hot, and the seats in his truck were almost too much for the backs of Louie's bare thighs. He shifted uneasily from cheek to cheek. Clark leaned out the passenger window to taste the air as Louie drove them from the only home he knew.

He went to Murchison's ranch, even though he knew he wouldn't stay there either. The entire house smelled like Fred and his wife. He held his breath as he passed their recliners. After that, he tried to breathe through his mouth as he stole through the bedrooms, putting whatever looked good into a laundry basket.

Fred had been a massive guy, so Louie didn't consider taking his clothes, but one of these rooms had been his son's, and they'd hopefully still kept it for him when he visited. The last room he entered had wrestling posters on the wood-paneled wall, and he knew he'd hit the jackpot. Louie took in the trophies on the dresser and photos on the bulletin board and wondered how it would have felt to return to a room that was a shrine to your high school popularity. Had Joey Murchison been proud to see the reminders of the stud he had once been, or did it feel sad considering he went on to be an ordinary guy who sold appliances at Witbeck's in Petoskey after graduation and never stopped?

Louie flipped through drawers, ignoring sports jerseys and muscle shirts with big wide arm holes that would show his ribcage. He took worn jeans, cargo shorts, plain T-shirts, and underwear, even though it galled him to wear Murchison's drawers when the guy had been the ringleader for the group that had ruined Louie's social life in school. It did give him a small ping of pleasure to take shoes and boots from his closet, though, thinking back to the time Joey had stolen his.

The guy wasn't selling washers and dryers anymore, was most certainly dead now, and that gave Louie a moment's peace, until thinking about Joey being dead made him start to think about other people being dead, and his thoughts came back to Katherine. All thoughts would come back to Katherine, until she found her way back to him. Why had he thought she'd be at the sink with him in the morning? It wasn't until he was in the truck, driving through town, that reason returned, and he realized the obvious—she would have returned to the place of her first suicide, just like he did. She'd be back in New York. Her body wasn't in the kitchen, evidence he might have noticed if he hadn't been overcome by other realizations.

If he'd been thinking straight at the time, would he still have done it? Would he have taken Katherine with him, knowing that to keep her safe he would have to send her a thousand miles away from him? Louie wasn't so sure now, but he did know that if he was right and she was immortal, wherever she was, she was pissed. When she came back to him, he'd be ready with a new home for her, and maybe that would help her to forgive him.

Louie moved to the bathroom that would have been Joey's and dug through the vanity drawers. The bottom one was full of faded Hustler magazines, and Louie paused to consider Joey's poor mom, who must have cleaned in here when her son came home. This made Louie marvel at the depravity of an adult Joey spanking it in his childhood home, and he decided it was officially time to leave. He'd gotten much too intimate with the Murchison family today.

Outside, Louie dragged generators and old fuel cans to the truck, and then, when the sweat was rolling off him, waded into the pond behind the barn to rinse off. He left his underwear floating in the water and pulled on fresh clothes over his wet skin.

Now that he was cleaner, his mind felt better. But a big worry had come to him as he splashed in the water and kicked at the curious fish stalking his feet. He had driven past the Tahoe when he left his property earlier. Occupied with thoughts of Katherine, the vehicle had only registered in his brain enough for him to drive around it, but now he considered the implications. If he thought Louie and Katherine had died in the explosion, then wouldn't Devlin have driven off in his Tahoe? He wouldn't have wandered away on foot, bleeding out of the hole in his head. Maybe the explosion had killed Devlin too. And since he hadn't seen Devlin's body anywhere as he'd gone about his chores…

Louie wanted to think that he was special, that there was no way a Devlin could be an Adam, but if his logic said Katherine was alive, he had to consider Devlin might be too. Where would the man have regenerated? Had he ever died before? And if he indeed came back to life somewhere, would he deduce that Louie and Katherine might also still be alive? In his haste to burn down the house, Louie hadn't considered Devlin could die, come back to life, and seek them out again. They might even be in more danger than before. With the ghost of a bullet burning in his belly even now, Louie felt weakened. He wondered if he'd survive another death.

Assuming Devlin was alive, he knew about this place, which meant Louie had already been here too long. Feeling vulnerable, as he wasn't on his home turf anymore, he spared time to search for any remaining weapons. There was nothing in any of the barns. Grider and Devlin, those bastards, had stripped the ranch of everything worthwhile but the dry goods and batteries he'd already stashed away. Louie went back into the big house, knowing that at least Grider wouldn't have stepped foot past the smell in the living room, and retraced his steps, checking closets and shelves for anything he might have missed.

He eventually found a .38 special revolver and a box of bullets in Barbara Murchison's nightstand. It was nickel-plated with an ivory grip, a feminine gun that felt small in his hand, but at ten feet it might still give Devlin pause.

He considered sticking it in his waistband like they did on TV, but Louie wasn't the most experienced gun guy, and he decided this might be a good way to accidentally shoot himself. He dug around more and found an ankle holster in the back of the drawer. As he strapped it on, he remembered bumping into Barb and Fred at the Ponderosa in Gaylord. He'd seen them there many times before, and maybe that had been when he'd last seen them alive. Fred halfway through a steak with a stack of dirty dishes from the buffet next to him to be cleared, Barb eating chicken wings, drinking iced tea with Sweet and Low, probably planning on soft serve with caramel for dessert, the gun on her ankle concealed under one of her long prairie dresses. It all fit except for the weapon. Even in death, people still surprised him.

In the kitchen there was a big map of Michigan on the wall. Little red pins dotted it, and at a quick glance, Louie saw the pattern. The Murchisons had marked all the lighthouses they'd visited together. He peeled it from the wall, brushed off the pins, rolled it up, and then took a pad of scratch paper and pencil from the counter. He had begun to formulate a plan.

Louie hadn't expected to return home, but Clark didn't seem surprised. He jumped out of the car and bounded into the backyard, happily back and oblivious that the house was a disaster. Louie wasn't here to stay, though. Despite the sad pang he felt at the sight of a couple of his rescue dogs milling around now, returned after the blast in search of food, he had to carry out his mission.

First, he inspected the Tahoe. What he hadn't registered earlier was that it was parked close enough to the side of the house that it had been wounded in the explosion. The tires were partially melted, and though he didn't look under the vehicle or its hood, the wiring was also probably shot. One door still ajar from when Katherine had fallen out, he could see damage inside too. Whether Devlin had walked away last night or possibly awoken this morning in the debris, newly alive, he wouldn't have driven out of there in this car.

Louie walked the property, kicking through still warm heaps of debris, checking behind bushes and outbuildings, just to make sure the man hadn't staggered off somewhere to die. He found no trace of him, though there were still plenty of places for a body to hide.

He'd wasted enough time wandering and wondering, determined to get his work done and get the hell out of there. The burning smell had crept into his sinuses, and Louie felt like it might never leave him. Assured it was just him and the dogs, at least for now, Louie opened his tailgate and pulled out the plastic buckets and pots he'd found at the ranch, the hand trowel, the garden gloves, and paper and pencil. He went straight to the garden and began.

An hour later, sweaty again, Louie and Clark set out to explore new territories. At dusk, Louie parked the truck on the side of a dirt road and curled up on the bench. Clark stretched out in the truck bed with two other mutts, plus three cages of chickens and several generators, all hidden in a jungle of full pots and buckets. Louie closed his eyes and tried to dream, hoping the garden still had enough magic to bring him Katherine.

CHAPTER TWENTY-TWO

THE PHONE IN HER HAND was silent, the pools of vomit around her dry. Weak morning sun came through the eastern facing window of her apartment. Funny how last time Katherine had awoken this way, she'd thought it was Ana's mother's vomit around her, and maybe some of it had been, though it had only served to disguise her own. It hid what her mind hadn't wanted to remember.

Her first thought when she woke after the explosion was that Louie had been right about her after all. But the relief she should have felt at being alive was overwhelmed by memories, not just of the fire but of her two other deaths.

The first time Katherine had died (the time she meant to but didn't know she'd accomplished it), she'd taken pills out of her medicine cabinet. Like she told Sharon, she'd done it without much forethought. If she had planned, she wouldn't have just paid her rent. If she had planned, she would have recently filled a prescription, and had a nice full bottle of pills to use. Instead, she had to scrounge—a few tablets of Xanax from a bad patch of anxiety a few years ago, expired Vicodin from when she'd pulled her back at the gym, antihistamines with yellowed labels, and whatever else she could find.

What she didn't tell Sharon was how she'd taken a few pills, then proceeded to clean her bathroom sink with a toothbrush before taking more. How it seemed to take forever, hours of taking them, one and two at a time, thinking that would be the best way to avoid simply throwing up and passing out. Hours, pill after pill. It wasn't until she finally started to feel drowsy and sick that she panicked.

It was like the one and only time she'd smoked pot, when she felt the change start and would have given anything in that moment to stop it. Feeling like that train was going to keep on rolling no matter what she did. Self-preservation, the simple impulse to live, outweighed any previous desire to die, and she couldn't even remember why she'd taken pills now, only knew that she wanted them out of her.

Katherine staggered to the phone but couldn't seem to concentrate long enough to punch in the three numbers. She went to her door, and her fingers wouldn't touch the locks. She fell to her knees and, in desperation, stuck her fingers in her throat, vomiting copiously around her. But the dizziness kept coming in waves, the high bubbling up from the top of her head like someone was pulling strings out of her scalp. She lay back on the floor, holding the phone in one hand. With the other on her head, she tried to steady her mind, until there weren't thoughts, only feelings, and then there weren't any more of those either.

As much as this memory pained Katherine, who up until now had only recalled taking the first pills and the next day when she'd walked around in a fog thinking she'd escaped death, there was another one. Now she understood why Ana had been so dehydrated, why Katherine had lost time before she answered Sharon's phone call.

After Ana's mother had collapsed in the hall, Katherine fell herself, slipping in the vomit all the way down to her elbows. She turned to watch as the woman seized and died. Katherine lay there for a long time, paralyzed with disbelief at how fast her situation had changed. She'd just been making calls from the phone that was now bleeping on the floor. She started to rise, to reach for the baby, when she heard a man's voice call from the stairs.

"Marta!" he called, "Marta, did you find someone?"

But Marta couldn't answer, and Katherine froze. She tracked the sound of running footsteps below.

"Marta?" The voice was closer now. The man had reached her floor.

Katherine lay there, still stunned, as the man approached and stumbled over to the dead woman. Ana was howling, but he ignored her. "Don't leave me," he said, and laid his palm against the woman's cheek. In a detached sort of way, Katherine watched him cry and thought about how sad it was that she wouldn't ever find a man now who would mourn her this way.

"What happened to my wife? Why didn't you help her?" he asked, but Katherine didn't know how to answer, and the baby's crying grew louder. Her eyes traveled to his face, and she noticed the familiar red around his nose and mouth, the beads of fever on his brow. He was sick too. Both parents were sick, and they'd only been trying to find help before they died.

The man lurched from the woman's body into the apartment. His eyes took in his daughter where she'd been dropped, the vomit on the floor and on her clothes, the baby bag cast aside, sweeping the room like it was a crime scene. "Why didn't you help, you bitch?" he demanded.

"I don't know," Katherine said, and she didn't. Why couldn't she have opened her door and invited the woman inside? Why wasn't she the kind of person who could have just taken the baby and promised her mother everything would be OK?

Katherine started to rise again when suddenly the man was on her. Even with his hands wrapped around her throat, even as her feet kicked out beneath him, she wondered if it was a joke. A cosmic joke. She would die in the pandemic after all, but her sickness was apathy. Even in her last moments, she couldn't bring herself to care that she was about to die. Unlike the pills, there was no hope that she could stop what had been started, and Katherine wasn't sure she even wanted to. What was the point anymore?

She relaxed into the man's grip and watched his expression turn from rage to disbelief to horror until her vision faded.

The rest of what the man did she could only imagine, but what she did imagine was worse than unknowing. She pictured the man, still knowing he was dying, sitting next to her body for a long time, unsure what to do next. She heard Ana cry for her daddy, but he only stared, no will to take her since he was sentenced to death and a murderer, in that order. He didn't deserve the comfort of his daughter's little body next to him when he died, so eventually he staggered to his feet and walked right past Ana, closing the door behind him.

When Katherine next knew anything that was real, she was alive the next morning, the phone in her hand ringing with Sharon's call. Ana had lain on the floor all night while Katherine's life reset, until the sun rose on a new day. Already dehydrated, the baby had rejected the spoiled bottle though Katherine made her drink it anyway. Sharon had known it all along.

It was the same when she awoke this time, dried vomit, phone in hand though service had since ceased. No Ana on the floor now, of course, though very likely Marta was still outside the apartment door. Still stunned and grieving for herself, Katherine was in no hurry to check.

She got to her feet, and like the first time, she felt compelled to walk around her apartment, this time digesting the facts of her deaths. She also thought of Louie, that fool, and how cavalier he had been with her life. That fact that she was alive didn't mean he wasn't wrong to do what he'd done. She could just as easily have been toast in his kitchen. His panicked decision had been no more than a guess.

"No Adam without an Eve," she snorted. Before she knew it, she was dusting her apartment, muttering about Louie and all the things wrong with him. "He's mental if he thinks I'm going to drive another 800 miles to him after this…"

When she was done, the warm room smelled like vomit and lemon furniture polish, and she wondered what was so wrong with her that cleaning was her default for expressing emotion. It made her mind cleaner, though. Her frustration vented through a dust rag, it seemed clear to her now that her best move was indeed to return to Louie. Her circumstances were no different than before. She was alone, he was alive, and they were connected. Even now she blushed to think about their night together before Devlin had burst into the room at sunrise, how careful Louie had been with her, asking over and over "Is this OK?" If she were meant to spend eternity roaming the Earth, she should do it with Louie. That homicidal idiot.

The silver lining to her reset to New Jersey was that she could check on Mack and Ricky. She wondered if the teenagers had made it back to the brownstone, if Lee had ever bothered to return. Katherine prepared for another road trip. She browsed her own closet, putting clothes into a trash bag because her suitcase was in the basement storage. Now that she knew her final destination was rural Michigan, she had a better idea of what to pack—her casual dresses, the chino shorts and polo shirts from her one and only weekend camping trip with Brad, the flipflops she wore on laundry day.

In the bathroom, she took all of her makeup. Did Michigan have a Sephora? She tossed in her favorite facewash, hand cream, and other beauty supplies. If she was roughing it on a farm for the rest of her life, she might as well take a few things that made her feel like herself.

When she was done, clothes changed and bag packed, she looked around her apartment and wondered if she would ever be back. Would she die over and over like Louie, finding herself here again on this floor? If she cleaned up the vomit, would it be there if she returned?

She stepped over Marta in the hallway, eyes averted but seeing the dead woman with her nose. She hurried down the hall as if ghosts followed, quickly down the stairs and out to the street. This time when Katherine emerged from her apartment building, carrying a full garbage bag, she wasn't surprised by the quiet street or the smell of dead flesh permeating the air. When she walked a block and turned at Main Street, she saw that the rocking chair moved slowly with the breeze, but the nice man was gone. She set her bag on the corner and walked down the street, helping herself again to the car buffet. She was a bit more selective this time around because she needed good mileage and a full tank of gas, but finally settled on a reliable-looking Subaru Forrester. *Get me halfway to Louie*, she thought. *But first, a house call.*

The brownstone looked deserted, an assumption which seemed confirmed when no one answered the door, but Katherine continued to stand in the heat, knocking, calling out. She could hear a generator churning somewhere. It wasn't safe to invite yourself in these days. She was about to leave when she finally sensed movement. The door cracked open.

"Katherine?"

It was Mack.

"It's me," Katherine said, relief flowing through her, now assured that the kids had gotten back to New Jersey from Ohio. "Let me in?"

Mack seemed to hesitate before stepping back, allowing Katherine into the cooler sanctum of the old house. She turned to look at Mack. "Oh, hey, no question now," she said, pointing to the girl's belly bulging under a tight tank top. She certainly looked pregnant. Very pregnant.

"Yeah, I know," Mack murmured and slid past Katherine.

"You're feeling well?" Katherine asked, following her. It had only been a week since she'd seen her last, but Mack seemed more pregnant and distant. "Still throwing up?"

"Sometimes." Mack lowered herself on the couch, picking at her nails.

"Is that normal? Doesn't that usually go away?" Katherine, a grown woman, felt a bit strange asking a fifteen-year-old that question. Based on her friends and coworkers, who'd often shared every minute detail of their pregnancies with her, she'd thought that only lasted through the first trimester.

Mack shrugged. "My mom used to say she was sick all the way through with me. That's how she knew I'd be a healthy baby."

Her low energy felt off. Was this pregnancy blues, or was Mack feeling embarrassed about how they'd left things on the road?

"Where's Ricky?" Katherine suddenly realized she didn't hear him anywhere.

Mack looked away. "Why are you here?" she asked instead.

"I was worried."

"Wasn't your friend there in Michigan?"

"He was," Katherine said slowly. "But I thought it was important to check on you."

"So you like, what, turned around and drove all the way back?"

Katherine did the math. She basically would have had to do just that to be sitting here. She wouldn't have had time to spend several days with Louie and make the drive. "I was really worried."

When Mack said nothing, Katherine added, "I'm *still* worried. What's going on, Mack? Where's Ricky?"

Mack said nothing but glanced over Katherine's shoulder. She turned, but no one was there.

"Is Lee here?"

Mack nodded.

"Are you OK here, Mackenzie?"

Mack hesitated and then nodded again.

Katherine heard a creak outside in the hall. "Lee?"

He emerged a moment later, looking like he hadn't cleaned himself since the last time she'd seen him. That would have been on moving day, with Sharon's body.

Katherine tried to act normal. "Geez, you look like shit, Lee," she said.

"What are you doing here?" he asked, ignoring the jibe. This was unlike Lee, who loved a sarcastic retort.

"I came to check on you guys," she said. She noticed Mack seemed more uncomfortable with Lee in the room, her gaze now trained on her lap. "Do you have a bottle of water, Lee?" The polite question was meant to assure him that she knew whose house this was now and get him to leave her alone with Mack.

Lee said nothing but left the room. Katherine turned swiftly to the girl.

"What is going on here?" she demanded. "You're not acting like yourself."

"Nothing's wrong," Mack said. She continued to pick at her nails, and Katherine studied her more closely, noticing now the bruises on her arms.

"Is he hurting you, kid?"

Poor choice of words. "Not a kid, Katherine." There was a glimmer of that teenager sass she remembered.

"Answer the question."

Mack shook her head as Lee returned. He handed a warm bottle of water to Katherine. "Sorry you came all this way," he said. "But you should be going now. As you can see, everything is fine."

Katherine stared at him for a long moment. "Where's Ricky?" she asked bluntly.

"Ricky's gone."

"Gone where?"

"Where everyone else goes," Lee said, and this time there was a hint of a smirk Katherine didn't like. In fact, it made her stomach turn over. She'd disliked Lee before, a danger to her sanity and, as it turned out, to Mack's innocence, but she hadn't thought him physically dangerous until now.

Her mind flashed to the man's hands choking her in the apartment, how his weight had felt pressing her into the floor. She never wanted to feel that again.

"You should go," Lee repeated.

Katherine stood up and considered this. Could she take Lee by surprise? What was the worst that could happen? She'd have to find another car, drive back here and try again. And again. She wasn't leaving Mack with this man.

"Lee…" Mack began, and the man turned on her in an instant.

"Shut it," he snapped. Mack shrank from him, and it was the girl's fear that flipped a switch in Katherine. She reached for the impotent lamp on the end table, heavy brass like the rest of Sharon's outdated décor. Bless Aunt Patty and her awful taste, Katherine thought, ripping its cord from the outlet and wielding it above her head.

"I think *you* should go," Katherine said to Lee. "I don't know what's going on here, but I think we have a problem."

Lee stalked toward her. "It's you, Katherine. You're the problem."

She began backing toward the fireplace, leading Lee away from Mack. "Mack, is he hurting you?" she asked, not taking her eyes off Lee. "Did he do something to Ricky?"

Mack began to cry. "He said Ricky was sick."

"What did you do?" Katherine asked Lee. He followed her around the couch.

"He made him leave, that's it," Mack answered for him.

Lee was shaking his head. "But he didn't want to go," he said. It was a taunt. Katherine knew he wanted her to swing the lamp. He would dodge it easily, and she'd be left empty handed. "No one seems to want to leave us alone. We just want to be left alone, Katherine."

She edged toward the fireplace and felt the stand of fire tools at her back. Her hand fumbled onto one of the handles. "You know why I really came here, Lee?" she asked, hoping to distract him. "I came here because I'm a fucking superhero."

"Oh, is that right?"

"That's right. I'm here to save the day. Rescue the girl. You're the one who doesn't belong here."

"See, this is exactly why I wanted you to go. You're a crazy bitch, you know that?"

Please let it be the fire poker. Katherine frantically tried to get a grip on the tool behind her. *I've got to stab him.*

"Mack, if he kills me, I want you to know something. You shouldn't be afraid, OK? I will come back. I can come back, and I'll keep coming back. I know you don't understand what that means, and it sounds crazy, but I will. I've done it."

Mack shrank back into the couch, half turning to watch them, her hands protectively on her belly. "Katherine," she moaned. Lee glanced at her, and Katherine saw her chance. She swung the lamp.

As she'd expected, Lee bobbed and then slapped it away. But he wasn't prepared for the weapon in her other hand. *Please let it be the poker*, Katherine prayed again. She swung it around.

It was the shovel. *Oh shit*, she thought, but she let it fly anyway, pretending she was following through on a tennis swing. She'd played with Brad a few times, and it felt just like that, only higher. It hit Lee on the side of the head, and she almost heard the sound of a perfectly placed ball hitting the sweet spot of a racket's strings, though the real sound was more of a clang of metal meeting skull.

She expected Lee to flinch the blow off and then come at her like the bad guy in a film, but he dropped instantly. It was almost anticlimactic.

Mack jumped to her feet. "Katherine!"

"I had to," Katherine insisted.

"I know, it's just—hit him again!"

Katherine looked up and saw tears streaming from Mack's eyes. "Please, hit him again. Don't let him get back up."

Katherine hesitated. Lee didn't look like he was going anywhere. Besides, the first strike was self-defense. The second... could she actually kill this guy?

She decided she could. She brought the flat of the shovel down again, and again, and then a third time in the same spot of his head, like she was John McEnroe after a bad call. A tennis racket would have been trashed, but the fire shovel had held up fine.

She dropped it, panting. "He was hurting you, wasn't he? And he did something to Ricky? Please tell me I didn't just kill an innocent man. He was an asshole. But, you know, tell me he wasn't an innocent asshole, Mack." She was babbling.

Mackenzie came around the couch and reached down to check Lee's pulse. Like Katherine had done to Sharon, she placed her two shaky fingers at his neck and waited. He didn't move. "He's not breathing, and I don't feel anything," she confirmed. "And yes, I think he killed my brother. If he didn't, he sure wanted me to think he did."

She wiped at the tears on her face, squared her shoulders, and then ruined the brave effect when she doubled over, cradling her belly.

<hr/>

"Tell me again exactly what we're doing, Katherine?" Mack asked.

It was late, the kind of late that was almost morning.

"We're making sure he doesn't come back."

Katherine glanced at Mack and sighed. She knew the girl was questioning whether she'd replaced one crazy for another. "I'm not crazy," she added. "I know you don't know all the facts, but let's just say if Lee is still lying here by noon, I'm good."

Mack started to object when she groaned and curled in on herself.

"Another one?"

Mack nodded. "Yes, but it's mostly just uncomfortable. It's not really pain. I'm not sure how to describe it."

"You need to try to stay calm, OK? I'm hoping this is false labor, because I don't know what we'd do with a preemie."

They'd counted back, calculating that she was around thirty weeks, which was much too early to deliver without the benefit of a hospital. If Mack could last another month at least, Katherine would feel much better about their chances.

She could see when the tightening stopped, because Mack eased back into the couch. "Have you ever heard of Braxton Hicks?"

Mack shook her head.

"Well, it's like a warm-up. Sometimes moms think they are having the baby, but it's not real labor yet."

"Does it mean something is wrong?" Mack asked anxiously.

"No, I don't think so. It's really common."

"How do you know? You don't have any kids."

Katherine smiled. She could see a little spark returning to Mack. "I have friends, and I've seen *Grey's Anatomy*."

"Yeah, I don't know what that is. What if it's real labor?"

Katherine realized Mack wouldn't have been born yet when McDreamy was the hottest thing on ABC. That was sad, but she tried to focus on the girl's question. She wasn't sure how they'd tell false labor from real labor but tried to sound confident. "I think labor will be more intense, and the contractions will come regularly. There should be time to get to my friend in Michigan."

"Is he a doctor?"

"Well, no. He's a mechanic."

Mack rolled her eyes. "That hardly counts for anything."

If Mack had ever seen *Grey's Anatomy*, she'd know that being a surgeon was just like being a mechanic. It was all about fuel, spark, and working parts.

"He's not a doctor, but he's very smart. He knows stuff about animals."

Mack huffed. "My brother knew stuff about animals when he was two. You know, a cow goes moo. A cat goes meow…"

Mack's sarcasm was refreshing. Maybe she was strong enough now to really talk. Katherine looked over her shoulder at Lee. Yep, still there. Mack followed her gaze.

"So, you want to tell me about what happened with him?" Katherine asked.

Mack shrugged and resumed watching her hands rub small circles over her belly. "He was here when we came back, had set up a generator for the refrigerator, pretending like he'd been here all along when we all knew he'd taken off. I'm not sure how far he got before he decided to turn back, but he did." The girl seemed self-satisfied at this—she'd called it.

"Ricky and Lee never did get along. How was it when he came back?"

"Ricky was pissier than ever," Mack admitted. "Lee said it was time to move on, find a place that we could set up better. Ricky told him we'd already been on our way to do that in Michigan."

"What did he do?" Katherine prodded. "What did Lee do to Ricky?"

Mack plucked at her belly button, now a large nub beneath her tight shirt.

Katherine waited, sensing that Mack's interest in her pregnant belly was a stalling tactic.

Finally, Mack said, "They had an argument the first night. It was terrible. Ricky made a comment about Lee knocking me up, about my mom, and Lee lost it. He hit him. Like a slap, but hard."

Katherine waited for her to continue. Catching her gaze, she encouraged her with a nod. "Keep going."

"Well, I tried to get in the way, and Lee knocked me down. I mean, I only fell back on the couch. But Ricky was *shook*. Nobody had ever hit us before. My mom wasn't like that. So anyway, he told me we needed to leave, and then when I told him I wasn't going anywhere without Lee, he wanted to know how long we'd been smashing. Lee got mad about that because he said it wasn't like that."

"Smashing?"

"Doing it like, casual. Not a serious couple."

"OK, so Ricky wanted to leave?"

"He wanted to leave for sure, but more than that. He wanted us to leave together, and he wanted me to break up with Lee or whatever. I'm pretty sure that's the only reason he came back with me. If Lee was here when we got back, he wanted to make sure that I cut it off. He didn't want there to be any relationship."

"And Lee didn't like that," Katherine surmised, remembering the times Lee had asserted himself as their leader. He wanted to be listened to, and he expected to be in charge. He wouldn't accept a teenager telling him what to do about anything, especially not something like this.

"No, he really didn't. But Ricky wasn't backing down either. He didn't like how Lee was being with me. Already, he had been kind of rough about things. He was kind of different. There wasn't anything sweet about him anymore. He came back, but he was like barely hanging on."

"Rough how?"

"He wanted me in whatever room he was in. He kept hauling me up, dragging me around. Like I was the one who took off and left, not him. I mean, I only left because *he* left first! He was pretending like he didn't even disappear on us. And he was still totally paranoid. Looking at Ricky like he was going to get us sick."

"What happened after he hit Ricky?"

Mack shrugged. "I convinced Lee to leave him alone, got him to go upstairs with me. But he didn't want to let it go. Later I heard them talking downstairs again."

"What were they saying?"

"I couldn't tell. They were arguing, but I couldn't catch anything. My stomach was hurting, and I was just so tired. I should have gone down…" Mack's eyes began to fill. "The next morning, Ricky was gone. Lee wouldn't say where."

"So you don't know for sure that Ricky is…"

Mack shot her a look. "I know."

"You suspect."

"I could just tell by Lee's body language. I kept asking when Ricky was coming back. At first he tried to say that

Ricky took off for Michigan, to find you. And when I said that was impossible because Ricky could have just stayed with you in the first place, that he wouldn't even know where to find you, then Lee told me to *stop asking fucking questions.* He warned me not to ask about things I didn't want to know the answer to. He's dead, I just know it."

Katherine watched Mackenzie palm tears from her cheeks. It was probably true. Ricky must be with Sharon and the others next door. Damn, Lee. She looked over again. Still there.

"Do you want me to look for him?" she asked Mack.

"I don't think so. It would hurt more to know for sure."

"We can leave a note for him, just in case."

Mack frowned. "You're not thinking we're going to go now, are you?"

That's exactly what Katherine had planned. Louie would be waiting for her. "Well, yeah."

"I'm not getting in a car in this heat. I feel sick all the time. I might be in labor!"

"I don't think you're in labor."

"Says you," Mack said. "I think I know my own body."

Spoken just like a teenager, a teenager with an adult problem. Still, she wasn't wrong. Katherine couldn't know what was going on inside Mack or how she felt.

"I need to get back," she said.

"You should leave then," Mack replied. "Everyone else does." At Katherine's look, she added, "I don't mean that like it sounds. I just mean that I'll be fine on my own. God will watch over me."

Katherine rolled her eyes and stood. She strolled over to Lee and kicked him lightly. He was still dead. "I can't leave you here alone. You can't have a baby all by yourself."

"I won't be alone."

"God's going to come down to Earth and deliver your baby for you?"

It was Mack's turn to pull a face. "God's *watching*. It's Jesus who is coming back."

Good Lord, Katherine thought. When she wasn't behaving like a teenager, Mack was an evangelist. Hormonal mood swings were real.

"Jesus isn't going to deliver your baby either," Katherine said. Not for the first time when talking to Mack, she reminded herself to sympathize even if she couldn't understand her reasoning. The girl was scared, and of course, God, Jesus, and all the rest would be a comfort now more than ever. "You need a real flesh-and-blood person to catch it, wipe it off, cut the cord, feed you both. I'll be your person, sweetie, but we can't stay here waiting for it to happen. It's going to be weeks yet."

"Can't we just wait until I'm feeling better?"

Waiting was the last thing Katherine wanted to do. This was why she'd never had children—no patience. None at all.

"You'll feel better tomorrow," she assured Mack. "And then we'll go."

CHAPTER TWENTY-THREE

MACK DIDN'T FEEL BETTER THE next day, or the day after. Katherine schooled herself on patience, and in the meantime, confident Lee was dead for good, she dragged him out to the backyard. His final resting place was on some rain-starved dirt and flagstones. He didn't deserve to have flowers placed on his hands or lie next door on a bed with good people. Besides, Katherine couldn't bring herself to go over there. Mack was right. It was better not knowing about Ricky.

Every night, while the brownstone and Mack slept, Katherine dreamed. She walked through the burned garden, and it was like walking inside a grave. Life was gone. Dirt remained, but Louie did not.

She searched for him every night. She called to him. She waited on the stone bench, undamaged and sticking out of the char like a piece of bone. Louie never returned. Had he finally done it with that last death? Was he dead for real this time? With unease, Katherine remembered how he told her that with each new puzzle piece, there was more blood. It had made him afraid to suicide again, and yet he had done it for her twice more. Maybe the last time had been one time too many.

If he wasn't dead, by now he surely must think she was. It had been two months of reasoning, hoping, cajoling, pleading, and still Mack wasn't ready to leave the brownstone. Summer had broken, giving way to the first chilly evenings of autumn, and she was still in Jersey.

Every day Katherine thought today might be when Mack turned a corner, waking up feeling well enough to leave so that Katherine could go to Louie, but Mack always made an excuse. She'd been up all night trying to get comfortable, everything was swollen, she was cramping, her skin itched, the labor pains were back. If not for the huge belly and circles under her eyes, Katherine might have thought the girl was faking the entire thing. She'd never known anyone to feel so rotten every moment of her pregnancy. There had never been a burst of energy, a nesting period, a glow. Mack waddled outside to urinate a dozen times a day, but otherwise, she'd banished herself to the bedroom, only summoning herself to speak when she had a complaint.

Katherine couldn't say anything right, especially when it came to her desire to leave or her irritation with the justifications Mack made to stay. One word or skeptical look and Mack threw Katherine's childlessness in her face. *How would you know?* Mack's favorite retort always struck a chord with her because it was true. She didn't know what it felt like to be young, pregnant, without the comfort of her mom or family, about to give birth to a baby that hadn't benefited from prenatal care and wouldn't be delivered in a hospital with the help of modern medicine.

Katherine did her best to be supportive, to ignore the mood swings and make Mack comfortable. She kept herself busy preparing for the birth. After a few weeks, she ventured to the library, finding her way through a window because the doors were locked. It felt like she was breaking a law, though no laws existed anymore but her own. The building had been quiet as usual, and Katherine found the sign by the front desk that read "Silence Is Golden" ironic. Whoever coined that phrase had no idea how silent a sullen, pregnant teenager in a pandemic could be. What she wouldn't give for some library-level whispers now.

There was no librarian to stop her, so she took every book that had been published on pregnancy and delivery since 2000, hoping she'd know enough to help when the baby was ready to come out. She gathered supplies, went back to the store for over-the-counter folic acid and iron gummies, and picked out the right-sized diapers, clothes, and car seat. Ana had prepared her more than she expected, and she found herself nesting on Mack's behalf.

In her dreams, Katherine sometimes sat on the bench and told Louie these things. He wasn't there, but maybe he could still hear her. All of her dreams were still lucid, always in the garden. It wasn't unimaginable that she could communicate with him somehow. She told him how guilty she felt about killing Lee even though he'd deserved it. She complained about Mack and how helpless she felt waiting for something to happen. She told him how afraid she was of the birth, that she wouldn't know what to do when the time came, despite what she'd read. She worried that the delivery would be complicated or that the baby would come too soon.

As time passed, the last worry began to fade. Mack must be in the safe zone by now. And then one morning, as Katherine was rousing from another empty dream, she heard a small cry. She leapt from the bed like an expectant father, but she didn't need to grab car keys and an overnight bag. She was the doctor, the nurse, the priest.

When she entered the room, Mack was so quiet and still, Katherine worried that something had broken inside her and the baby wouldn't come at all. Shouldn't she be writhing in pain or panting? For the hundredth time since the flu, she reminded herself that not everything in life happened like on television. "Mack, are you OK?"

The girl shook her head. "There's water between my legs," she whispered. "You said when that happened, it would be starting. I thought it wasn't so bad at first, that I could handle it, but it's hurting worse. I don't think I can do it."

Katherine shared the same worry, though she didn't say so. Mack didn't have a choice about what to do or not do, but she was so young. Maybe she *couldn't* do it. She looked tiny in the bed, even with her pregnant belly.

Meticulous preparation had gotten Katherine through her toughest projects before, and she prayed it wouldn't let her down now. "You can do it, just not all alone, hon. Don't worry. I have a checklist. Everything is ready, and we're just going to go step by step."

Hours passed, and when night came, Katherine began to worry. What if the baby hadn't turned like it should? The contractions had continued, and they came more often, but at a certain point, things just seemed to stop down there. Mack continued to moan when the pain came, but according to Katherine's research, she ought to be more dilated by now. She kept asking Mack to describe the pain, flipping through her books, and this irritated Mack. The sweet, God-fearing fifteen-year-old was barking at her to stop reading, to pay attention, to get the baby out.

The longer it went on, the weaker the girl seemed to get. There was blood on the sheets, and Katherine wasn't sure if that was right or not. Most of the early motherhood books didn't get into the level of detail about births she needed. One written by a doula was more helpful, but even that didn't get down to the nitty-gritty on every topic. From what she'd read, it seemed like some blood was OK but heavy bleeding was not.

"What the hell is considered heavy?" Katherine asked aloud. Had Mack lost more than a pint? "What exactly does a pint look like when it's soaked into cloth?"

"What?" Mack asked worriedly. She tried to sit up farther and peer down between her legs.

"Stop, Mack. Just relax."

"Something is wrong," Mack said again. She'd been saying it all afternoon.

"I don't think so. I think this is just how it goes."

Mack seemed to sense Katherine's uncertainty. "Are you sure? I don't feel right."

"Like how, besides the contractions?"

"My head is pounding."

That wasn't good. Katherine had read that teenagers were at higher risk for high blood pressure, preeclampsia, and hemorrhage in the third trimester and during delivery. First-time mothers were also more likely to need a caesarean.

"Here's what we're going to do. You're going to stand up."

"I can't," Mack said immediately. "I'm too tired."

"Look, you know I'm not a doctor, and all the reading in the world isn't making me the best person to do this. But I think you're not dilated enough yet. We want you at baby-head size, and you're still at mayonnaise jar. You're probably swelling and you're getting more and more tired, which is going to make it even harder when you have to push. So, I'm going to walk you around the room."

She helped Mack from the bed and forced her to walk. "Can't we do something else?" the girl begged. She was sweating and exhausted.

"No, this is what we have to do. And then you're going to, um, stimulate your nipples."

"Huh?"

Katherine blushed. Talking about these things with a teenager was embarrassing. "I read that walking and stimulating the nipples might help to get you to dilate. I don't know if that should have been done sooner, but it can't hurt. We need you to do that so that you can get ready to push."

They walked and sat, walked and sat, until dawn broke. Mack had now been in active labor a full day. The light seemed to energize her, though, and she grew stronger even as the contractions began to come faster and longer. "My head feels better at least," she said when a contraction had passed. "But I feel like I'm burning up. I just want to take my nightgown off."

Katherine helped her sit on the edge of the bed. In one swift move, she yanked the garment over the girl's head. Mackenzie's hands flew to her bare breasts. They looked like they were filled with lead. "Just us girls here," Katherine said, annoyed. Now the girl was shy? Where had that modesty been nine months ago? "I'm going to go get some more wet towels," she added. "Maybe try the nipple thing when I'm gone."

Mack nodded, grimacing as another contraction gripped her. She'd just had one. Katherine was halfway down the hallway when she cried, "Wait, come back!"

Katherine ran back in time to see Mack fall to a squat alongside the bed, palms on the floor. She was bearing down.

"Wait! It's too soon to push," Katherine warned, but even as she said this, she could see that Mack was fully open and the baby was coming. The last few centimeters had certainly happened fast. "Ignore me," she said now. "You can push. I can see it!" Mack didn't need permission. She couldn't have stopped even if she'd wanted to.

Katherine had expected a break and then more pushing. She'd read that this part could still take a lot of time, especially in a first pregnancy, but Mack didn't stop. She'd expected screaming too, but Mack was almost silent, clutching her knees like she was going to rip them apart, her face red with the effort.

This is how it was done for thousands of years, Katherine thought, her hands splayed, ready to catch. Not lying on a bed screaming at a husband and nurses and begging for the epidural, but hunkered down, concentrating, doing a woman's work. It was how it used to be done and would be from now on.

The baby came faster and was slicker than Katherine anticipated, but she caught him like a champ. A boy—a giant boy with a full head of hair. Wasn't a first-time, malnourished teen mother supposed to have a small baby? This guy was tiny and huge all at once. Katherine reviewed her mental checklist and swiped the baby's mouth, hoping to remove any amniotic fluid. There was no need. The baby coughed and began to cry, doing the job himself. She felt immediate relief. Everything she had prepared for led to the moment when the baby cried for the first time. They'd done it!

When Mack tried to roll to her side on the floor, Katherine pulled her up and helped her to the bed, one arm cradling the baby. "Good job, girl!" she said. "You have a boy."

"A boy." Mackenzie sighed.

"You did so good. He looks perfect. Kind of messy, but perfect." Katherine laughed.

"It still hurts," Mackenzie said. "Why does it still hurt?"

For all Mackenzie now knew firsthand about sex, pregnancy and active labor, she was still uneducated about the process. She'd refused to read any of the books and didn't want to talk about it beforehand.

"You still have to deliver the placenta," Katherine told her. "Does it hurt as much as before?"

Mack was staring at her baby. Katherine repeated the question.

"No, it's like cramps now. But still."

"We're going to finish this and then it will all be over, OK?"

Katherine wrapped a paper towel around the umbilical cord and began to slowly tug as she pushed on Mack's belly. She'd read various things about this final stage of delivery. Some said to cut the cord right away before delivering the placenta, others said cut after a few minutes, and newer information said there were health benefits to waiting to cut until after the placenta was delivered. The baby would get more essential nutrients that way. Knowing the baby hadn't received much nourishment on their reduced diet, Katherine figured he could use all the help he could get in his first few minutes of life.

"Push for me, Mackenzie. Let's get this done."

Mack pushed and Katherine pulled gently, and the placenta came out. She wasn't surprised when there was blood too. Her reading had prepared her. But when the natural compression inside should have slowed the bleeding after delivery of the placenta, it continued. Katherine grabbed the menstrual pads she'd prepared and pressed one between Mack's legs.

"Stop," she said. "Don't push anymore."

"I'm not," Mack murmured. Katherine looked up and saw that Mack was still staring at the baby, as if until just now she hadn't known the thing inside her would come out all put together. The pad was soaked, and Katherine grabbed another, pressing it on top. A minute or two went by before she fumbled for the bag of sanitary napkins and unwrapped another one. She hadn't planned on needing more.

She went through two more pads before she started feeling like something was wrong. Mack had gone quiet, but her eyes were still open, looking at her son. "I think I should name him Richard," she said softly. "It was my dad's name. And Ricky's."

Katherine said nothing and kept working. It had been at least a half hour since the birth, so why was Mack still bleeding? *How heavy is too heavy?* She tried to get a look at the placenta, but it was buried in towels and soiled napkins. Had the whole thing come out?

Katherine waited, pressing a new pad on top of the others until eventually there were none left in the package.

The bleeding was supposed to be like a heavy period, maybe a little worse. This had to be too much.

Mack had fallen asleep. Katherine didn't know whether this was from blood loss or simple fatigue. Her plan had been to cut the cord and get the baby set to breastfeeding as soon as possible, but now he lay at Mack's side, sleeping like his mother.

Something's wrong, Mackenzie had said during her labor. It wasn't true at the time, but maybe it had been a premonition.

Katherine finally threw in the towel—literally—wadding up pads and bedding and throwing them on the floor. This was it. She had to stop, should've stopped an hour ago. All the reading and research hadn't prepared her for the biggest challenge—acceptance that if something *was* wrong, there wasn't a damn thing she could do about it. She wasn't a doctor. This wasn't a hospital.

Katherine cut the cord and swaddled the baby—at least her homework had prepared her to do that successfully—and then crawled onto the bed beside Mack. Everything smelled bad, and this made it difficult for her to relax. This kind of dirty didn't feel like the good garden kind. Eventually, exhaustion won out, and she drifted to sleep. She dreamed of the garden and thought about where Louie had gone. If he wasn't dead, maybe he had given up on her.

Katherine slept until what would have been lunchtime. When she awoke, Mack was dead. She wanted to cry, to rail against someone or something for taking the last people so painfully, one at a time so that she could feel each like a wound. She didn't cry, because the baby was alive, hearing Sharon in her mind reminding her to keep it together for him. She also didn't cry because she needed to wait. Her patience with Mack had worn thin over the last few months, but she could be patient once more. Because maybe the girl could come back.

A day later, Mack was still dead. Katherine drew a sheet over her, having not done so before for fear Mack would come alive and be frightened by the shroud. She recited most of the Lord's Prayer over her, the only one she remembered from childhood. She knew she would want a blessing, and for the first time, she didn't feel annoyed by Mack's faith.

Trying to find a bright side, which wasn't always her strongest suit, Katherine decided that at least with Mack dead, she could finally leave the brownstone. She could be with Louie in two days, sooner if she drove overnight. Having found a fully gassed car the week before, she might only have to swap vehicles once if she could find another one with a full tank somewhere in Pennsylvania. The baby things were mostly packed. She only needed to gather the essentials she'd brought inside.

Mack had named her baby Richard, and because calling him Ricky would be too painful, Katherine decided to call him Richie. She cleaned herself and the infant as best she could with a faded washcloth and bottled water. He did not appreciate this chilly baptism. Then she contemplated Mack. Should she move the body next door or leave her here undisturbed? It was unlikely, but what if Ricky came back and found her dead like this?

Ultimately, Katherine decided to spare the girl the indignity of dragging her to the neighbor's house and herself the horror of possibly finding Ricky there, and left her in peace on the bed. She taped a note on the door, jotting her destination at the bottom.

> Ricky, if you find this, I'm sorry. Don't go in this room. Mack is at rest here. She named the baby after you. Come to this address if you need me and want to meet your nephew. —Katherine.

Katherine strapped Richie into the seat next to her. "I know this is supposed to go in the backseat," she told him. "But I'm guessing a car accident is unlikely at this point. Besides, the back is full of supplies, and also there's a limit on tragedies. I think we've capped out."

The newborn slept, and Katherine thumbed away quiet tears as she drove. She'd been OK until she remembered parting with Mack at the rest stop. She wished she hadn't told her she wasn't a good girl. Maybe she wasn't an angel—sleeping with her mom's boyfriend and all—but who was she to judge? She'd made plenty of her own bad decisions, without the excuse of youth. And could she even call the things Mack had done "decisions"? Mack had been impulsive but innocent, too young to consent. Lee was the one to blame.

"I always say stupid things," Katherine whispered to Richie. "It's like I think everyone deserves to know what's going on in my head all the time. Why do I think that? Why did I have to say that? She was just a kid. A victim. Your daddy is the bad guy in that story."

Katherine realized baby talk was tough but talking to a baby was easy. Richie didn't judge her, and even though he wouldn't remember it later, he might understand her. Maybe he was newly reborn, fresh off a past life, and there was a little bit of lingering wisdom in there. She'd learned weirder things lately.

"He would have gone to jail if this was normal times," Katherine said. "It's called rape. And he did it to Mack, even if she didn't think so."

Richie was silent on that matter, and this was just fine with Katherine. "That's not really nice talk for a baby, but I think we're going to start off being straight with each other, me and you. You should know that I gave Mack justice by doing what I did to Lee. And, so you know, we're on our way to see a better man. A good one. I really hope he's the guy who'll be your daddy. God knows you need one, because I'm not much in the mommy area."

She glanced over at the dozing baby and tried not to be paranoid about the fact that he slept so much. Newborn babies did that. And she tried not to be worried that she would have to stop the car every two hours or so to feed him. Babies ate a lot, and Louie would either be there, or he wouldn't.

"He's going to be thrilled about you, by the way. I know that because he was all twinkly-eyed about the idea of my having a baby. He thinks we're a new Adam and Eve or something. I don't know what that means, Richie, honestly. Like if we're supposed to rebuild the world or something, but that sounds crazy to me, and if you were older, you'd probably think that was crazy too.

"Because we're the last two people who should be running things or bringing things back or whatever. We didn't even want to *be* here for a long time, and I know you don't know what that means, but I'll just say it—since we're being honest here—that we don't deserve to be if we're talking from a moral perspective. We're pretty messed up, as people go."

Katherine knew she was rambling, but one of them had to keep the conversation going. Other than the rare sniffle or head turn, Richie wasn't much of a talker.

"I want to be good though," Katherine said after a moment. "For you, which is kind of hard for me to believe, because I didn't care about anything but myself for a long time. Don't tell anyone I said this, but I don't think I cared enough about Ana. I never really bonded with her. She was too much of Sharon's, and of Marta and her daddy. I know that makes me sound inhumane, that I couldn't care about her because too many people already had a piece of her, because I should have cared or worried more about her just as a person, but I promised I wouldn't lie to you, and it's true. I didn't want a kid, and I kind of still don't, but I also don't have a choice anymore because I'm all you've got. Just knowing that makes it easier."

She glanced at the clock in the dash. It was time to stop for a feeding, and this actually made her happy. She was going to love doing this every two hours, twenty-four hours a day. It was reliable, and she was good with routine. People used to say the only thing certain was death and taxes, but neither of those things existed anymore. Now there was another truism—*the only thing certain is the baby is always hungry.*

Richie *was* always hungry, and Katherine dutifully stopped when he needed to eat. He took to the bottle from the start, the nipple flow seeming just right. He didn't seem to mind that the formula, which she had mixed with distilled water, wasn't warmed. He didn't fuss or spit up. It was as if he knew that Katherine was on tenuous ground as a new mom, and he was telling her she could chill out—they were already a team.

Shortly into the trip, she pulled over to change the diaper from his first movement, and when she found it was odorless, she couldn't resist praising him. *Such a clever boy to do such a good doody,* she'd told him as she pitched the dirty diaper out the window.

Jesus, Katherine. A good doody? she mocked herself. And it wasn't even a *good* doody, at least not for her to experience anyway. As predicted by the books, this good doody was a blackish green tar that seemed impossible to clean from his bottom. (She also knew it wouldn't stay odorless for long.) Katherine reassured herself that the only reason for her profuse praise was simple relief. Richie had a movement—validation that he was full-term and likely healthy.

To make up time for her many stops, Katherine drove through the night. Even when she felt tired, and the yellow lines on the dark blacktop started to float, she pressed on. She switched cars in the early morning hours, finding a dealership with gassed up loaners for the taking, and pulled into Louie's driveway around breakfast time.

The clock read 10:00 a.m., though time was meaningless now, and her stomach was the only true timekeeper these days. She was starving and had been thinking about eggs and pancakes for the last fifty miles of her drive. Hunger forgotten now, she took in the house for the first time. It was practically gone, burned to the studs in most places, the roof collapsed on the backside near the kitchen. Katherine should have expected this, suspected disaster based on her dreams, but she hadn't thought past the worry that the burned garden was a mausoleum where Louie was buried beyond her reach.

"Stay here, Richie," she said, and got out of the car. She walked around the house and peered through the burned bones into the kitchen. He wasn't standing at the sink, that was certain, and though there were no signs of life, she called his name. She couldn't bear to look at the corral or garden but called his name again and then, head down, went back to the car.

She sat next to the baby, staring at nothing for a long time before a flutter caught her eye and she saw the note on the mailbox.

Go where my mom is buried, it read. She did.

Katherine scraped at the soil with her bare hands. Louie had buried his mom's ashes in the asparagus, and even though the garden was now dust and leaves, she knew this place like it was her home. She'd found the spot straight away and the next note easily.

Kate,

Couldn't take the chance that Devlin might be like us and alive, so I thought I'd send you to a place he won't know to look. If you're reading this, I'm not sorry about anything now, because you're alive and you're on your way to me.

I'll pump some gas for you and leave it in cans at the station. Go there and fill up. You must be low by now. I'll get a road map and figure out where to go. Once I pick a place, I'll circle it for you and leave it on the counter.

I didn't think there was a God. But if you're reading this, Brave Kate, someone gave you back to me. I will worship him the rest of my life, however long he gives me.

Louie

Katherine read the note a second time in the car and sniffled. "He could have signed it 'Love, Louie,' or drawn a little heart, or x's or something." She'd tell him that when she found him.

"Sorry, Richie," she said, starting the car. "I know I promised you pancakes, but it looks like we aren't home yet."

CHAPTER TWENTY-FOUR

ATHERINE PULLED INTO THE GAS station, Louie's former place of employment. How happy he must be not to work there anymore. The signage was rusty, the pumps so outdated they didn't have a slot for credit cards, the crumbling pavement choked with weeds—the neglect wasn't recent. Inside, the shelves were empty, like they'd been picked clean by turkey vultures.

The only full rack was a tiny spinning one of road maps. Katherine hadn't seen an actual road map in ages and thought about how retro this seemed. Her car's satellite navigation was still working, probably would for a while, though it would certainly become less accurate over time. Katherine noticed that several maps were missing from the rack, which gave her a small thrill. Louie had probably taken one. The other opened on the counter was for her.

A big red X marked the spot, and though it wasn't the XO closing she would have liked on Louie's letter, it made her heart pound all the same. When he'd laid this out and put a pen to it, he was thinking of her. She could see that he must have chosen his spot and come back to update the map. Next to the mark on Crooked Lake, he'd written an address. How long ago had he been here?

Next to the map was another gift to make her smile—a large bottle of vitamin water and two packages of Hostess pies. A note taped to the bottle read:

You're almost there, Kate. Just a little farther. You're only fifteen minutes away. Louie.

She folded up the map and stuffed it in her back pocket before digging into her meal. She was so hungry she ate the first pie at the counter, shoving gooey cherries and glazed crust into her mouth in five quick bites.

She was picking crumbs off her T-shirt and eating those too when the bell over the door rang. She spun toward the door, but her mental expectation of Louie didn't line up with reality—it was Devlin. He was holding one of the road maps and a pistol.

He seemed paralyzed, and though he must have been expecting her, having obviously been in the station before to take a map and see Louie's note, on some level he must have thought it impossible she would actually appear.

"Put that gun down," Katherine said, and it came out like a scold. She realized she wasn't afraid. He couldn't hurt her, not really.

He lowered the weapon automatically. "I've been hanging around here for weeks, off and on, but I didn't really think you'd come."

"Why? Because like you I'm supposed to be dead?" Katherine turned her back on him and reached for the water, uncapped it and took a long drink. She opened the second pie.

"How is this possible?" he asked, and she heard his disbelief. She realized that, unlike her, he'd had no one to prepare him for the possibly of coming back. He was still stunned that he was alive.

"I'd like to give you answers," she said, taking a bite. Apples and sugar flooded her mouth, and they tasted so good she almost moaned. "Unfortunately, we don't really know how it works. Just that we can't die. So, you might as well put the gun down. You know you can't kill me." Even as she said this, Katherine suddenly remembered Richie in the car. He couldn't kill her, but he could shoot her and take the baby. Maybe she was afraid after all.

"Louie is going to be so disappointed," she said instead. "He was sure we were the only ones with the gift."

"I don't know what you mean. Did Louie give me a gift?" Devlin asked carefully. "One minute I was in the kitchen, and the next I was down in a hole in the porch. You and Louie were gone, everything gone. Not even bodies, which is strange, because I looked."

So the explosion had been Devlin's first death. If he died again, he'd just resurrect a few miles away. Not enough lead time for Katherine to kill him, even if she could manage it, and get a real head start to Louie so they could run away. Devlin knew where to find them. Her only chance was to reason with him.

"Why are you here, Devlin?"

"I'm not sure," he said, his voice full of wonder. "I shouldn't have survived the blast, but I did somehow. Not a scratch on me."

"I hate to break it to you, but you didn't exactly survive," Katherine said bluntly.

Devlin actually looked down at himself, as if to take measure of his body and its relationship to the Earth. "I don't feel like a ghost."

"You're not. You're alive again."

He started to laugh, but she suspected there wasn't enough joy in him to make a sound. "I'm so confused," he said instead.

Katherine finished off her pie and took another drink of water. "Look, I know it's really confusing. But the only way I can explain it is that you died, I died, Louie died, but we're all alive again. So there's no point in you trying to take me again or hurt me or go after Louie. None of us can die. Got it?"

"I have to stop him," Devlin said, looking down at the gun in his hand.

Katherine realized that without anyone to rein him in or distract him, Devlin had wandered for the last two months the way she'd wandered her apartment the day after her suicide. He seemed stuck in a loop, focused on the last thought he'd had before he died. Katherine's only thought had been to live, and so she awoke confused but focused on that. Louie had died sad and alone and awoke with one thought in mind—how sad and lonely he was.

The map crinkled in his hand, drawing her attention. "How long have you been around here, Devlin? You saw the address, you saw Louie's note. Why didn't you go there?" He was still being a cop, she realized, waiting for evidence. He couldn't go to the address without seeing her alive, and since the map and note were still here, he'd concluded she hadn't gotten this far yet. His focus wasn't on Louie. It was on her.

"I had to make sure you were OK," he confirmed. He had such a kind look on his face that her heart turned. Devlin had never wanted to do anything but protect. He wasn't the bad guy. She had just seen him that way through Louie's eyes—Louie's sad, lonely eyes. He had this warped view that everyone wanted to invade his house, like they had invaded it and his privacy when his mother died. He'd been stuck in a loop too. If she, the woman from his dreams, hadn't shown up, he might still be in that loop. *What loop am I in?* she thought.

Katherine wanted to live. She had died fighting every time—the overdose she wanted to take back, the man strangling her in the apartment, even Louie blowing her to bits. She still wanted to live. That was her loop.

"I know you don't really understand what I'm saying, but it's true. Louie and I have died before, and we came back each time. We don't know why, but we do. Louie thinks we're meant to do something, like maybe restore humanity or something. He's killed himself a lot of times, like hundreds. I've died three times, suicide and murder. And you died too, Devlin, in the explosion. And I'm sure you have a purpose to serve too, and that's why you're still here. I just need you to understand that I'm not that purpose. I'm OK. Louie is OK. We'll be OK together."

Devlin looked sad. "I think maybe you're supposed to be with me. Louie's crazy, and he gave you a crazy idea. He's going to end up killing you, Katherine."

She approached him and gently took the gun from his hand. "He did give me the idea, but I promise he's not crazy, and I promise he can't kill me again, even if he wants to. The most he can do is send me back to Jersey where I first died. I can prove it to you. I think I *have* to prove it to you, or you'll never leave us alone."

Katherine looked down at the gun in her hand and sighed. She really didn't have time for this shit.

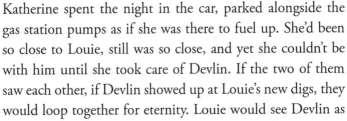

Katherine spent the night in the car, parked alongside the gas station pumps as if she was there to fuel up. She'd been so close to Louie, still was so close, and yet she couldn't be with him until she took care of Devlin. If the two of them saw each other, if Devlin showed up at Louie's new digs, they would loop together for eternity. Louie would see Devlin as competition, the person trying to make him lonely again, and Devlin would see Louie as a criminal, a man bent on harming Katherine. They'd probably take turns killing each other until eventually whoever had come up with this grand plan decided neither of them deserved another revival.

She walked Richie back and forth alongside the car, careful to keep the sunlight out of his face with a visor but craving it herself. It had been cold in the car all night, and she'd been chilly all day, even as her skin got pinker in the sun. At dinnertime, she listened to her stomach grumble and wished for more pies.

Richie had finished taking a few ounces of formula, and she was crooning to him about how sorry she was that his first day of life had been spent in a car, when she saw head-lights. It was near dusk, and Devlin had arrived.

Katherine wondered how this would play out. She set Richie back in his seat and climbed out of the car. Devlin approached, looking sooty and vexed.

"You fucking shot me," he said without preamble.

"Yes, I did," Katherine agreed. "And then I sat here, with a baby mind you, for almost twenty-four hours to make sure you're fine."

"I don't understand what the fuck is going on here!" He said this loud enough that Richie began to cry from the car.

"Dammit, Devlin. Get control of yourself," Katherine admonished him. She reached for the baby and cradled him to her breast before adding, "You're very angry this go around."

"Can you blame me? I just climbed out of a hole in a porch!"

"Hey, when I got reset, I went all the way to New Jersey. Get over yourself."

Her gaze fell to the gun on his hip. So, when she'd left it on the counter in the station, it must have disappeared when Devlin did. (And he had eventually disappeared, right in front of her, though not right away. Not until time synced up, she supposed, so that he could reappear at the proper place and time of his first death. Louie would appreciate that detail.) Interesting, the gun was part of his reset like the vomit was for her and Louie's dishes were for him.

"I'm not saying I believe you, but assuming we can't die…" Devlin began.

"Assuming we can't die? Exactly how many times would you like to wake up in that hole before you get it, Devlin? I don't have all day here."

"You're still going to Louie." He seemed surprised.

"Yes, and before you dare object, consider this. All the things about Louie that you thought made him 'crazy' weren't in his imagination. You and the others *were* invading his house, mooching off him. Those assholes *did* kill him and bury him in his garden. And he knows that he and I are meant to be together."

Devlin leaned against the car and crossed his arms. Louie would have recognized this as his Marlboro Man look, when he was settling himself in for a nice long debate and needed to give his knees a rest. "If none of us can die, who's to say you and I aren't meant to be together? And also, when the hell did you have a baby?"

Katherine began to pat Richie's back, hoping for a nice burp instead of spit up, and took the second question first. "He was a friend's, and she left him with me. She died, but she wasn't like us."

"How many are like us?"

"I don't know," Katherine said. "Probably enough to get us up and running again, population-wise, that is. Enough to keep us from extinction. Maybe like a Noah's ark, minus the boat."

She shifted Richie to her other shoulder. "And about me and Louie, we dreamed about each other for weeks before I came to him. There's no question in my mind I'm meant to be with him."

Devlin's face went slack.

"Wait, have you had dreams about someone?" Katherine asked.

"A few nights ago," he murmured.

"There you go," Katherine said, pleased. "Leave my family alone and go find your own mate."

"It wasn't really like that. I was dreaming of Grider actually. I've had a few about him."

"Well...I'm sure the New World needs all kinds of families," Katherine began.

Devlin shot her a look. "It wasn't like *that* kind of dream. I just thought maybe he needed help."

Katherine considered this. "Maybe the dreams just pull us toward people we have some kind of destiny with. It doesn't necessarily mean it's a romantic one. Do you know where he is?"

Devlin shook his head. "No."

"When you dream about him next time, ask him. Tell him what you know. He's dreaming about you too. Louie and I shared ours." It gave her a pang to use the past tense. She missed dreaming with him.

Devlin stared at the ground, seeming to grapple with his next move.

"I know you'd much rather be a cop saving the damsel in distress. But trust me, Devlin, I'm not in distress. Maybe Grider is. Maybe it's just that he's with someone or will meet up with someone you're supposed to meet. I don't know how this works, but you should go. You have your own puzzle to figure out."

"And you've figured out yours?" he asked.

"I think so."

"You're going to make babies with Louie, huh?" For the first time, Devlin managed a laugh. He still looked like she'd blown his mind—not literally this time—but he was starting to settle. His focus had begun to shift.

"I'm not sure. Our purpose may be to rebuild the world as Adam and Eve, but maybe it's simpler than that. Maybe we're just meant to rebuild each other."

"Sounds oddly hopeful for two people who both tried to kill themselves. Weird kind of love story if you ask me."

CHAPTER TWENTY-FIVE

KATHERINE LOOKED UP AT THE fairy-tale chalet nestled on Crooked Lake and thought about Devlin's words. She hadn't asked his opinion, thank you very much. But she and Louie were a weird kind of love story. How so much death and sadness had amounted to a happy ending, she'd never know.

Louie had outdone himself. The beautiful two-story home he'd claimed was at the end of a small canal, acreage on both sides, wide decks wrapping around both stories. The roof had an impressive array of solar panels along one side. There was a huge pole barn, and as she walked up alongside the house, Richie's car seat bopping against her leg, she saw a whole house generator too. It was humming along, but not so much that you'd hear it inside. It didn't wake the baby.

She came around front and found a long dock, T-shaped with a bench at the end, stretching its arms into the water and cradling a canoe on one side. Lily pads and reeds hemmed the bank. Katherine noted a gazebo with a stone fireplace and wicker furniture off to the left, a tidy greenhouse farther in the distance, and the beginnings of a new garden to her right.

Setting Richie on the porch, she walked toward the rows of plants. Without Louie telling her, she knew he'd taken them from his mother's garden. With plenty of water and sun, they would flourish. He probably already had seeds for next year in his greenhouse. She loved a man with a plan.

Louie wasn't in the garden. She could see this easily over the short plants and through the trellises, which had no vines growing on them yet. She went back to Richie and had just picked him up when Clark came out a doggy door onto the deck. He was mad for her and jumped and licked while she shielded the car carrier from him. He came around and snuffled at the baby. Richie, good boy that he was, slept through it, even when they were joined by two more dogs.

The dogs led her inside, and Katherine stopped to admire the great room, all windows for admiring the lake, and the pine kitchen cabinets and stone countertops in an open kitchen that stretched for days. Skylights let in the light, so even without a generator, they'd be able to see until dark. Louie had thought of everything.

In the living room, the man himself was enjoying an afternoon nap in the sun, curled up on the big leather couch. She approached quietly and sat next to him, stroking the hair off his forehead. It was getting long, and he'd grown a rough beard. She tugged on this gently, and he opened his eyes.

"Am I dreaming?" he mumbled.

She shook her head. "Not this time."

"I'm so glad I didn't kill you," he said artlessly, still half asleep, and propped himself up on his elbow. Richie sniffed, and Louie looked at him.

"Well, you did. Kill me, that is. I haven't quite for-given you," she said, drawing his attention back, "but I came anyway."

He reached for her. "Kate," he said.

She smiled. "Maybe you should call me Eve."

EPILOGUE

L OUIE WAS GOOD WITH HIS hands, in more ways than one, and eventually he did coax a baby out of Kate. And then another, and then one more, until eventually four little people would stand on the lake bank in late afternoons, fishing for their dinner with their father. He taught them all the things he knew about the world before and what to do with the things that remained, so that they would grow up confident and content.

Why are we here? Louie asked Kate once. "Fate and mystery," she said, and thinking of Mack, "Maybe a little bit of God."

When she asked him the same, Louie said, "I think we were in purgatory, one of our own making. But it cleaned us, and we filled the empty places. We're in heaven now."

"I didn't know you were a poet," she replied. But he was, in his way. "How do you know this is heaven?"

He smiled. "Isn't it obvious? I got the girl."

As time passed and the children grew, Kate and Louie stopped questioning what had made them immortal. Whatever the reason, they both sensed that their gifts were gone now. Their brief immortality had fulfilled its purpose and been replaced with the gift of a peaceful life. If they died now, it would be forever.

Kate still sometimes missed people, best friends and busy restaurants, but she liked the idea of their own private heaven more, and because of this, she never told Louie about Devlin. Louie had always wanted to be the hero, and without Devlin living in his world, he could believe he had saved the day.

Kate knew that she was the one who had really saved them. When the men would have looped themselves end-lessly, caught in the ideas that had destroyed them, she gave them purpose. When she saw Louie's happiness, the pride he took in his children, she knew he had healed and would never suicide again.

When they noticed how their youngest daughter looked at young Richie, how she would follow him and try to hold his hand, even when he shook her away, Louie predicted the future to Kate, laying it out as if he was reading from a book. They would be their own Adam and Eve, and what had been the ending was now the beginning.

END

AFTERWORD

There's nothing romantic about suicide. There's no coming back. There's no reset button that puts us at the kitchen sink ready to try again. I don't judge Louie's choices in this piece of fiction; the grief and guilt of his mother's death, the loss of his job during the Covid pandemic, and the realization that things never got better after high school all compel him to *suicide* the first time. I don't judge Katherine's choice either. Her situational depression after miscarriage led her to an impulsive (and instantly regrettable) suicide.

And I don't judge my friend to whom this book is dedicated, who took his own life during Covid not by impulse but by premeditation. My friend who can't come back, even though he was a superhero, our "iron man," in real life. It's not romantic, the choice he made. He got to author his own ending and stop all the pain and questions in his head, but he left the rest of us with the What Ifs.

What if I'd been a better friend? What if I'd called him more, been funnier or kinder? What if he'd waited one more day? What if he'd known that we are not better off without him; we loved him and would have moved mountains for him, if only we'd understood how deeply in their shadows he stood.

Knowing his sense of humor, interest in the crazy, and honesty about depression and suicide, I think he would have liked this story. He would have gotten it, even as he helped me poke holes in the plot. He would have said a book about suicides should be bloodier, he'd have called for more sex scenes. (And he certainly wouldn't have let that part about poking holes go by without a joke.)

I started writing this book long before his death, but it stalled when the last thing I wanted to write about was the world dying in the midst of a real-life pandemic. It threatened to remain unfinished. When he died, I picked it up again. Sometimes writing about something is the best way to process it, and though my goal with this book is not to normalize suicide, meeting it head on in this way, over and over, helped me to understand.

Healing Louie, forcing him to see all the pieces of himself in his most vulnerable moments and put them back together, helped me past the anger. The statement I meant to make with the book softened, became less important. The characters who were meant to be bad guys became flawed but relatable. The ending that would be meaner and darker became more hopeful. The least I could do was give Louie and Katherine a happier ending.

That's all fiction is good for. We write about things that aren't and make them what they could be. We try to answer the What Ifs.

If you are considering suicide, call or text the National Suicide Prevention Lifeline at 9-8-8, or text HOME to 741741 to reach a trained Crisis Counselor through the Crisis Text Line, a global not-for-profit organization. It is free, 24/7, and confidential.

If you've lost a friend or family member to suicide, SAVE (Suicide Awareness Voices of Education) offers free grief support. Visit save.org.

ACKNOWLEDGEMENTS

I'm sure I made mistakes in this book, but it would have been worse if not for many people who gave feedback and advice.

Thank you to Officers Kelly Pate and Devlin Williams for teaching me not only that police officers are real people with the same worries as everyone else, but about gun safety, K-9 dogs, and other things that made Officer Devlin Kelly more believable. He is named for you both, and I hope you like him.

Thank you to Gary Mendyka for sharing his knowledge about gas station operations and accessing fuel the hard way, and to the real-life (James) Grider (rhymes with cider) who told me about long-haul trucking and lent some advice towards CB radio talk. Thank you to my friends with kids, keeping the world populated so that I don't have to, and for answering endless questions about babies and births. Between you and Google, I hope I've portrayed Mack's pregnancy and delivery realistically.

Thank you to the Pavich family for feedback on an early draft. You pointed out flaws that helped me to make the protagonists better and hopefully more relatable.

Thank you to Beth for your perspectives on New York living. I hope all New Yorkers forgive me for any errors I committed while trying to imagine their thinking and geography.

Thank you to my mom and dad, "first readers" always. You always believe that something I've written is going to be "the one" to make it, and your confidence keeps me writing. I'm still trying to hit it big so I can buy you a beautiful retirement home on a golf course. Or put you in a nursing home on a golf course, depending on how long success takes…

Thank you to Katie-Marie who influenced pieces of Katherine. Child-free, vegetarian, but more importantly, someone who doesn't give up and goes all in, full throttle, on the things that matter.

Special thanks to my husband, who has his own interests and hobbies and thus never complains when I disappear into writing mode. Your thoughtful answers at 2:00 a.m. to random questions like "Would an explosion melt truck tires?" and "How long do you think it takes vomit to dry?" when you didn't even know what I was writing about at first, were invaluable. When it came time to read the first draft, you actually read it without falling asleep once. This was a huge compliment that motivated me to keep working. Your help to find inconsistencies in the plot and talk through suicide timelines and revivals while we ate dinner made this a better book. Your being the kind of man who actually knows how to do things, not just Google them, is incredibly attractive and inspired pieces of Louie's character that also made this a better book.

Thank you to anyone else I may have missed. Fifteen years (on and off, mostly off) writing a book is a long time, and I know I received plenty of help along the way. I tried hard to make a fast-acting pandemic as realistic as possible so that the unrealistic, magical parts could feel more believable. You gave great advice to help me establish trust with readers, and all mistakes interpreting your notes are mine.

ABOUT THE AUTHOR

Jo McCarty is a first-time novelist from Michigan. McCarty shares her time between vibrant city life and rural lake living, inspired by the people and landscapes to write about both. She is at work on another novel.